GOODBYE TO THE PRESIDENT

Justin Kerr-Smiley

Merman Books
London, U.K.

Published by Merman Books 2014
Copyright Justin Kerr-Smiley 2014

Merman Books
20 Groom Place
London SW1X 7BA
editorial@mermanbooks.com

For Marc and Oliver

From now on, like a departure seen from a distance,
in funeral positions of smoke or solitary embankments,
from now on I see him hurtling into his death
and behind him I hear the days of time closing.

Pablo Neruda 'Absence of Joaquín'

He who serves a revolution ploughs the sea.

Simón Bolívar

DRAMATIS PERSONAE 1973

LOYALISTS

Salvador Allende - President, Popular Unity government
Hortensia 'Tencha' Allende - his wife
Beatriz 'Tati' Allende - eldest daughter
Carmen Paz Allende - middle daughter
Isabel Allende - youngest daughter
Laura Pascal - Communist Deputy and Allende's sister
Veronica Ahumada - Office of Information and Radio (OIR)
Dr Patricio Arroyo - Palace Medical Team
Dr Danilo Bartulin - Palace Medical Team
Carlos Briones - Minister of the Interior
Miria 'La Payita' Contreras - Presidential Personal Secretary
Edgardo Enríquez - Minister of Education
Fernando Flores - General Government Secretary
Joan Garcés - Academic and presidential adviser
Dr Patricio Guijón - Palace Medical Team
Daniel Gutiérrez aka 'Jano' - GAP
José Huenchullán - GAP
Enrique Huerta - GAP and Palace Intendant
Arturo Jirón - former Minister of Health
Carlos 'Negro' Jorquera - Presidential Press Secretary
Jorge Klein - Socialist and presidential adviser
René Largo Farías - Chief, Office of Information and Radio (OIR)
Orlando Letelier - Minister of Defence
Maria Lizama - Nurse, Central Post Hospital
Augusto 'Perro' Olivares - Director National Television
Enrique Paris - Presidential Adviser Education and Science
Eduardo 'Coco' Paredes - former Director of Investigations
Osvaldo Puccio - Presidential Secretary, Chief of Staff

Osvaldo Puccio Jnr - his son
Dr Alvaro Reyes - Registrar, Central Post Hospital
Dr Oscar Soto - Head of Palace Medical Team
Vicente Sotta - Socialist Deputy
José Tohá - former Minister of Defence
Ariel Ulloa - Socialist paramilitary
Daniel Vergara - Under Secretary for the Interior

General Alberto Bachelet - Chief of National Distributions
General José Sepulveda - Director General Carabineros
General Jorge Urrutia - Carabineros

Detective Carlos Espinoza - Service of Investigations
Detective Quintin Romero - Service of Investigations
Deputy Inspector Juan Seoane - Service of Investigations

REBELS

General Ernesto Baeza - Director General of Investigations
Admiral Patricio Carvajal - Ministry of Defence, Navy
General Nicanor Díaz - Ministry of Defence, Air Force
Admiral Gustavo Leigh - Commander-in-Chief, Air Force
General Augusto Lutz - Chief of Military Intelligence (SIM)
General César Mendoza - Inspector General, Carabineros
Admiral José Merino - Second-in-Command, Navy
General Javier Palacios - Director of Army Instruction
General Augusto Pinochet - Commander-in-Chief, Army
General Gonzalo Prieto - Minister Of Justice, Junta
General Arturo Yovane - Carabineros

General Mario Bórquez - Director of Health, Air Force
General José Rodriquez - Director of Health, Army
Dr Tomás Tobar - Institute of Medical Law
General Luis Veloso - Director of Health, Carabineros
Dr Miguel Versin - Director of Health, Navy

Commander Sergio Badiola - Military Attaché
Captain Jorge Grez - Naval Attaché
Colonel Eduardo Sanchez - Air Force Attaché

Captain Roberto Garrido - Infantry School Regiment
Colonel Rafael González - Air Force Intelligence (SIFA)
Lieutenant Daniel Guimpert - Navy (MOD)
Lieutenant Colonel Luis Ramírez - CO, Tacna Regiment

I
TONIGHT I CAN WRITE THE SADDEST LINES

Tonight I can write the saddest lines.
Write for example, 'The night is shattered
and the blue stars shiver in the distance.'

The poet's house is perched above Chile's Pacific coast, just a few yards from the wave-lashed shore. He is of course Pablo Neruda, the Nobel laureate. I visit his home at Isla Negra on a cloudy, windswept day. It is early summer and although the sun is obscured, the air is warm and swallows flit among the pines which grow upon the escarpment. Below the house the sea booms and crashes upon the rocks and races whitely up the beach, finally dissipating into the sand. I stand in the garden planted with geraniums, agaves and flowering succulents and gaze out towards the distance. Beyond the horizon the next landfall is thousands of miles away. Apart from the occasional ship there is nothing except ocean and sky. A fine place for a poet to live and indeed to die.

Although fatally ill with cancer, Neruda survived long enough to see his beloved country engulfed by the military coup of 11th September 1973. The cataclysm was not only tragic, it was personal. His great friend President Salvador Allende perished in the government palace La Moneda, after it was bombed by air force jets. Rather than surrender he took his own life, it is said, with an AK47 given to him by Fidel Castro: two shots fired in rapid succession to the head. The military, fearful of a public funeral and the anger of the multitude, buried Allende's body in secret at a relative's mausoleum the following day. Among his close family only his wife Hortensia was there, the president's three daughters could not obtain the necessary permission to attend.

I turn away from the sea and enter the poet's house. Neruda's residence is filled with various objects, which he collected through the years. There are carved figureheads from the prows of sailing ships, which plied the oceans before finally being broken up for scrap. As tall as the ceiling these guardian angels kept watch over the poet and his wife and muse Matilde. The names of Neruda's friends who preceded him to the grave are carved into the roof beams, some victims of the Spanish Civil War. One in particular is notable: it is the writer Federico Lorca, murdered by Nationalist soldiers. There is even a bar, where Neruda liked to play barman and make his guests drinks. Every available space seems to be filled with glassware, ceramics or shells. The poet was a magpie and collected anything that took his fancy: from Toby jugs and wooden cowboy stirrups, to rocking horses. He admired the physicality of inanimate objects and said each one had a story. His writing desk is fashioned from a ship's hatch that washed up on the shore one day. I wander through the rooms and think about the two old comrades, the poet and the politician, sitting in solitude and drinking their whiskies as dusk encroaches, the sea a restless presence outside. As the moon and stars appeared they would refill their glasses and continue to discuss politics and their dreams for Chile.

After touring Neruda's house I go back outside. I sit on a bench and write some postcards home, the gulls crying and wheeling above my head. The sun comes out from behind the clouds and the ocean turns aquamarine. I can smell the sea and watch lizards scuttle among the rocks. A group of school children see me and say "*hola gringo*" and laugh. People in Chile are naturally curious and it is hard for the northern European to hide their origins in South America. The postcards written I buy some pretty stamps and send the missives from the nearby post office. I decide to eat before I take the road north to the apartment I have rented in the coastal town of Reñaca and a tour guide tells me there is a restaurant next door.

I walk down the dirt lane and see an old house. It is a traditional single-storey building with a pan-tiled roof and solid adobe walls painted blood red. A sign indicates it is an inn and I am about to enter, when a man sitting at a table hears my footsteps and looks up. He has a mane of silver hair, a thick beard and dark, intelligent eyes. I recognise him. On my shelves at home I have a book about Neruda called 'Absence and Presence', a collection of photographs and reminiscences by those who knew him. Among the contributors are a young couple, Charo Cofre and Hugo Arevalo. She is a folk singer and he a musician. They had known Neruda in Paris when he was Chile's ambassador in the early 1970s and were some of the last people to see him alive.

"*Hola,*" the man says with a smile. "*Estás visitando mi casa?*"

"*Si,*" I reply. "*Pero es un hostelería o no?*"

"*Si, es las dos.*"

And he smiles again.

"Please, take a seat," he says in English, with only a slight accent.

Like the children Arevalo also knows that I am a gringo. We introduce ourselves and I sit down, while he pours some coffee from a pot. It is as if he has been expecting me. Or perhaps he is just a friendly sort who always has a spare cup on the table, in case someone drops by.

"I'm sure I recognise you," I say, taking the cup and sipping its bitter contents. Chileans like their coffee strong and never add milk. "Were you Neruda's friend?"

Arevalo's dark eyes shine and his face creases into a grin.

"Yes. We knew him well. Me and my wife."

"I thought so. I have a biography about him. Both of you are in it."

"*Ausencia y Presencia,*" he affirms. "A lovely book. Is it in English now?"

"Yes," I say and my host beams.

"I am so glad! I hoped that would be the case, but I didn't know."

We sit there drinking coffee and he asks why I am visiting Chile and I explain that I am writing a novel.

"About what?"

"The coup."

"*Ay, el golpe.*"

Arevalo nods slowly as though it is perfectly natural, even right, that a gringo like me should be writing a book about a catastrophe which he has experienced personally.

"That is good. Very good. We don't talk about it in Chile. Not enough anyway. I guess the memories are too painful," and he looks wistful, as if the memory is indeed still raw like a bereavement, or a lover's broken heart.

I speak in Spanish and he replies in English, until it becomes apparent to both of us that his command of my native tongue, is better than mine of his. I want to know what his impressions are of Neruda. I have never met anyone who has known the poet personally.

"He was a great man of course, but also good fun. He had a real sense of mischief. He loved jokes. Any sort, silly jokes, practical jokes. I have a theory that very intelligent men, geniuses, are essentially childish, or maybe child-like is the better word. Apparently Picasso, whom Neruda knew well, was the same. Always making jokes and giggling. I remember his laughter mostly."

"You first met him in Paris?"

"Yes. He was ambassador. I'm sure you know that. Charo and I had been there since August '72. We were penniless students. I mean really poor. We didn't have two francs to rub together. When September came Neruda called together all the Chilean students at the Sorbonne and said 'hey, we're going to have a party on 18th September,' which is our national day. 'Bring branches,' he said. Branches!" and Arevalo starts laughing and gently shakes his head at the memory. "We had no idea what he was going to do, but we came with some branches which I'd stripped off a tree in one of the parks.

"Can you imagine? This palace of an embassy was transformed into a peasant inn. He gathered us in the hall and made us sing and we sang without stopping. All sorts of songs, but mostly folk. As we stood there, a footman wearing a powdered wig and dressed in eighteenth century costume announced the ambassadors as they arrived," and Arevalo laughs again. "They must've thought we were mad...Anyway, Neruda greeted them all formally wearing a humble peasant suit, which had been made from his Nobel tailcoat. We all drank *chicha* and *pisco* and everyone got tight. They were good times..."

Arevalo stirs some sugar into his coffee and takes a sip. He puts the cup down and looks pensive.

"When did you come back to Chile?"

"The following June. It was winter and things were miserable. There was real tension in the air. On the 29th the military staged an uprising...," he looks at me with his dark eyes, to see if I know what he is talking about.

"Yes, the Tancazo."

"That's right. The Tancazo. Well, they failed that time. But we knew they would try again. I think the only person who believed the military would remain loyal was Allende. It's hard, I guess, if you're president. A man like Allende only wished to see the positive. Anyway, Chile was in a bad place. We had strikes and lockouts and everything. Not from the workers mind you, from the *momios*, the rich people. It was just a matter of time..."

There is silence and a wind gets up and whips the myrtle bushes in the garden, making them rattle. A paper napkin flutters off the table like a little bird and I pick it up and place it under my saucer. Arevalo does not notice. He is staring into his coffee cup, deep in his own thoughts.

"So, then the coup happened."

My host looks up from his reverie and remembers.

"Yes…the disaster. A few days afterwards we decided to visit Neruda, to see how he was. He wanted his friends around him. We came here to Isla Negra. By this time he was very sick. He was dying. The transformation was pitiful. It hardly seemed like a year had passed, since we had partied at the embassy in Paris. We went upstairs and saw his bed had been moved to the diagonal, so that he could look out over the sea. 'My children,' he said. 'I'm very ill, as never before; they call me from all over the place and I can hardly move my hands. Stay with me, but bring your car in, otherwise they'll take the number. If you're connected with me, they'll come after you.' He was remembering his own experiences of the Fifties, when he had to flee the country and also his time in Spain during the civil war. It hadn't occurred to us that we might be in danger. I mean we were just musicians. But we were naïve. We had no idea of the brutality that would happen. Neruda did.

"The TV kept showing pictures of tanks and soldiers in the streets and people being arrested. It was very upsetting. We all watched, although Neruda could barely take it in. I think it was a combination of grief at what was happening and his illness. The next day the phone, which had brought calls from well-wishers from Italy, France, Sweden, Mexico, all around the world, was cut off. Even so Neruda insisted we celebrate our national holiday. A friend had sent him some red wine and he said we could get *empanadas* from the inn.

"It was hard to celebrate, it was more like a wake. All the time the same scenes on the TV. We didn't care to watch, but it was impossible not to. Neruda warned everybody about the repression that would follow. He told everyone to be under no illusions. I think he was trying to tell us to get the hell out while we still could."

Arevalo pauses and offers some more coffee from the pot, but there are only dregs. I raise my hands as if to say "it doesn't matter" and ask him to continue. He frowns in concentration as though trying to piece together fragments of memory, which were buried long ago and only now have been unearthed.

"That night we heard him cry out from our room. 'It's so cold in here, can they bring a stove?' We knew it would not be long. Matilde woke us at dawn. 'Pablo has had a terrible night,' she said. 'He's writing at the moment…'"

The sun remains behind the clouds and the air is noticeably colder. A shiver passes through me as I sit there and wonder what it must have been like to witness the great man's final days. Arevalo draws himself up in his chair and sighs.

"We never saw Neruda again. An ambulance came that morning and took him away and we drove after it to the clinic in Santiago, where he died shortly afterwards. And so, that was his last day and his last night at Isla Negra."

The wind rushes madly around the garden and with it comes the sound of the sea. It is time to talk about something else and so I ask my host what Chile is like now and as we are discussing the current climate, an attractive middle-aged woman appears. She smiles broadly, her dark hair is streaked with white and drawn back in a bun and she wears a long, floral patterned dress. I realise this must be Charo.

"*Ay Charita!*" says Arevalo, throwing his arms wide open. "Come and meet my new friend Justin. He's come all the way from London to see us."

I stand and Charo gives me a kiss on the cheek, then we sit down. She immediately asks if I would like to join them for lunch.

"It's just fish," she says. "Please stay."

I can hardly refuse. Not only are they Neruda's friends, but Chile has some of the best fish in the world and we are a hundred metres from the ocean. After a short while a waiter appears and we start with a popular dish called *machas*: a shellfish not unlike a razor clam which is split open, sprinkled with grated cheese and grilled. They look like cats' tongues and sure enough are known as *lenguas del gato*.

This is followed by pan-fried *merluza*, or hake. It comes with boiled rice and a tomato and onion salad dressed with lemon juice and olive oil and lightly seasoned. The meal is washed down with a bottle of chilled Chardonnay from the local vineyard. After the plates are cleared we drink coffee and Charo and her husband smoke cigarettes and we talk some more about Chile and their work. Charo Cofre is a popular folk singer, who is often travelling and performs all over the world. Apart from being a musician, Arevalo is also a documentary film-maker and has made several videos of her concerts. They kindly ask me to stay the night, but I feel that I have impinged on their hospitality enough and tell them I must return to Reñaca. I only have one spare day in Santiago, before my flight back to London. We promise to keep in touch.

As we say our farewells the sun comes out and the air is filled with birdsong. A yellow-billed thrush flits through the trees and alights on a branch near us. We watch as the bird tilts back its head and pours forth a stream of music.

"The poet has come to say goodbye," says Charo and we all laugh.

I walk up the road and turn round one last time. The couple are standing at the gate, smiling and waving in the afternoon light. Arevalo has an arm draped over his wife's shoulder.

I drive away and it is early evening when I reach my apartment. The day began with a visit to Neruda's house and has ended with meeting two of his oldest friends. I can hardly believe my good fortune. I open the glass doors of the sitting-room and step onto the balcony and look out across the water, towards the rocks and its colony of sea lions. They yelp and bark as they dive into the ocean and I realise they must have occupied the same place since the beginning of time. Evening draws in and I go inside and get a pen and a sheet of paper from a drawer. I want to write and wonder if the words will come.

I watch the seals cavort in the surf as an incandescent sun sinks beyond the horizon, the clouds catching fire in its wake. I want to pay homage to Neruda and also have a memory of the day. I look out across the sea, then start to write. After an hour the sun has gone and the poem is finished, or at least I have finished writing it. I read it again and realise the work is no good and put it aside. I am finding it harder to write poetry these days and I wonder if it is because I have become so obsessed with this novel. I used to write a lot of poetry, but not any more. I remember a poet, I cannot recall which one, who said that writing poetry, 'is like trying to catch a black cat in the dark.' It certainly feels that way now. I wish I could write poetry like Neruda's friend Nicanor Parra. The old boy is one our greatest living authors and recently celebrated his 100th birthday. He is very popular in Chile and indeed across the world. Parra also wrote one of my favourite poems 'I Take Back Everything I've Said', which is what he calls an 'anti-poem'. He often recites it at the end of a reading.

> *Before I go*
> *I'm supposed to get a last wish:*
> *generous reader*
> *burn this book.*
> *It's not at all what I wanted to say*
> *even though it's written in blood.*
> *It's not what I wanted to say...*

It is clever and ironic, not unlike Parra himself, who also used to teach physics at the University of Chile. He comes from a talented family. His sister was the folk singer Violeta Parra, who tragically committed suicide; (of course it was tragic, suicide always is, but it looks naked without the adverb, so it stays). People sang Violeta's songs at protests during the Pinochet era. But, enough of poetry and the Parras, it's time to get back to the narrative...

The waves crash and boil upon the shore. The air is cool and the sky a dark cloth rinsed with stars. A full moon rises above the sea and hangs in the heavens like a ship's lantern, its ghostly light reflecting upon the oily water. Apart from the occasional bark by the sea lions, everything is quiet. Night becomes a prayer. I leave the doors of the balcony open and go to my bedroom. I undress and get beneath the covers and watch as moonlight streams silver across the opposite wall. It has been a long day and I fall asleep with the sound of the ocean roaring in my ears.

*

The city of Santiago lies in a rocky bowl ringed by the Andes and is divided by the shallow waters of the Mapocho River. To the west rises Manquehue mountain. It is over four-thousand feet high and while by no means the largest peak in the cordillera, it is certainly the most distinctive. With its sheer sides and flat top, it looks as though a veil has been draped over a chalice. Its name in the Mapuche language means 'eagle's nest'. In summer the skies are boundless and the deep blue of lapis lazuli. In winter the weather is cold and clouds descend for days at a time. When it rains the whole world turns grey. Then, just as suddenly the rain stops and the sun comes out. The smog is cleared and everything appears brand new. On their peaks the mountains wear a dazzling mantua of snow.

The city was founded by Pedro de Valdivia in 1541. It was officially named Santiago de Extremadura, after its patron saint James the Apostle and the region of western Spain, from where the conquistador came. The Spanish presence in Chile was always precarious and there were several uprisings by native Indians, particularly further south. In 1553 Valdivia and a small force were ambushed by the Mapuche at Tucapel. The Spaniards were massacred and only their commander and a priest survived. There are various legends as to how Valdivia died, all of them gruesome. One claims that his heart was torn out by a warrior with a knife and handed still beating to his chief who drank its blood, while another says that Valdivia had molten gold poured down his throat. Yet another legend states that his forearms were hacked off and roasted and eaten in front of him, before he was beheaded. In any event the Spaniard's own death must have come as a relief.

Few conquistador buildings remain in Santiago, as the country is prone to earthquakes. One that has survived is the church of San Francisco, although it has not been unscathed and the bell tower has been rebuilt twice. A Franciscan monastery was founded on the site in 1544 and the first stone of the church was laid in 1572. It also contains the image of the Virgen del Socorro, an icon brought over by Valdivia.

The church lies in the city centre on Avenida Bernardo O'Higgins, marooned by traffic and dwarfed by glass and steel office blocks. Santiago, like most modern cities, is forever evolving, the skyline constantly changing as new tower blocks are built and older buildings torn down. The glories of once grand neighbourhoods have faded like dowager duchesses, shiny new suburbs springing up as society moves ever outwards.

The jewel in Santiago's crown is the government palace La Moneda. It was once the national mint where all the country's coins were made and where the gold was secured, hence its name. It is a handsome neo-classical building shaped in a rectangle. Within its solid walls there are twin courtyards: the Cannons' Patio and the Oranges' Patio. The palm trees which line the main street known as the Alameda are filled with bullet holes, a legacy of the coup. In the Plaza de Armas behind the palace stands a bronze statue of a man in a gown, wearing thick-framed spectacles. The inscription reads: 'Salvador Allende Gossens' and the date 1908-1973. Beneath it is the simple inscription: *Tengo fe en Chile y su destino*. 'I have faith in Chile and her destiny.' Words he uttered on the last day of his life.

It is also my last day in Santiago and I have an important meeting. It is with Miguel Lawner, a Socialist and a former member of the Popular Unity government, which was toppled by the coup. He is one of the few surviving members of Allende's cabinet. Lawner is now in his eighties and lives on the seventeenth floor of an apartment block in Providencia, a pleasant middle class neighbourhood less than a mile from the Moneda. He has a fine view of the Andes from his study, which is lined from floor to ceiling with books. Lawner trained as an architect and was Allende's housing minister, a position that ultimately saved his life. He was responsible for the construction of new quarters for the military and for which they were grateful.

A trim man with white hair, sideburns and a neat moustache, Lawner looks fit for his age. He sports a pale yellow short-sleeved cotton shirt, with a top pocket for his spectacles and beige slacks; summer wear for the senior citizen. On his nose are steel-framed glasses and behind the lenses, his green eyes are limpid and evidence of a sharp mind. He indicates a chair opposite his desk and asks whether I want a drink.

"Coffee, orange juice….tea?" he smiles.

I get the joke and return the smile. I am British and therefore I drink tea. Instead I ask for water. It is hot even though it is mid-morning and the breeze from the open window does not quite reach us. He brings a glass of water and sits as I take up my notebook and pen.

"So, where would you like to begin?"

"Tell me where you were and what you were doing on the day of the coup."

"I was at my ministry. I heard about the coup on the radio and then a couple of comrades called and said that Allende had gone to the Moneda. I got to the ministry at eight o'clock and, I am very proud to say this, everyone turned up for work. Nobody stayed at home. None of us were sure whether this was a real uprising, or just another Tancazo. But we feared the worst and as the morning wore on, we knew it was for real."

"What happened next?"

"I told my comrades that it was safer to stay in the ministry than to try and return home and so that is where we stayed. We saw the jets pass overhead as they went to bomb the Moneda and heard the explosions. At around four o'clock in the afternoon the soldiers came and myself and some others were arrested…"

As Lawner speaks I jot down some notes. He stops talking and allows me to catch up. I look at him and ask him to continue.

"The soldiers were actually quite polite and we were taken to the Chile Stadium, which is not the same as the National Stadium that everyone knows about. They used that later, when the numbers of those they had arrested became too large. We were taken to the stands and told to lie on the ground. Later we were allowed to sit. Various names were called out and the person would get up and be escorted away. Then we would hear gunshots. Another name would be called and the same would happen: the person would be led away and then more shooting. Evening came and it was really cold, we only had the clothes we wore to work. This happened throughout the night. I don't recall how many names were called out, but there were a lot. Certainly thirty or forty. Maybe as many as fifty. I didn't count. Then at dawn my name was announced."

He pauses again as I scribble in my notepad. This time I put pen and paper down. I have a good memory and decide it is better just to listen. I can write it up later, or note any salient point if I have to.

"What did you think when you heard your name?"

He smiles again.

"I thought, 'well that's it.'…Those around me said: '*jefe* take my ID, give me yours. They'll never know and you'll be out of here before they find out.' It was brave of them. But I refused. I couldn't be responsible for someone else's death, because they were carrying the wrong ID. So I stood up and a soldier took me to a room. When we got there he announced who I was and the reaction astonished me.

"They were very friendly. You see I was the housing minister and Allende had been concerned that the military should have decent quarters, particularly the ordinary soldiers. He asked me to design their homes. 'Make them really good,' he told me. And I did. I made sure the houses had a yard at the back and a porch at the front, so they could sit outside and socialise. The soldiers liked them a lot. So, everything was fine and I was relieved. Maybe I wouldn't be executed.

"*Señor* Lawner," a lieutenant said. "You shouldn't be here. There's been a mistake. I'll make sure you get home," and he offered me coffee and a cigarette.

"As I was sitting there thinking this wasn't too bad and at least I wasn't going to be shot, a senior officer arrived and the atmosphere changed instantly. Everyone jumped to their feet and saluted. Except me," and Lawner gives a soft chuckle.

"Who was he?"

"I don't know. I never found out. But he was a colonel, probably in military intelligence and he looked like a real...*hijo de puta*. That's the only way I can describe him. I then realised that I was not going to be so fortunate. After a brief exchange of words with his subordinate he left."

I take a drink of water. The room is still and my glass reflects the morning light. Outside are the sounds of the street: cars passing, drivers honking their horns, children shouting and playing. The world is unconcerned and goes about its daily business unaware of what is happening in this room. In a modest apartment in Santiago, an elderly man is calmly describing how he was condemned to death.

"What did you do?"

Lawner blinks behind the steel frames of his glasses. It is as if he cannot quite believe what he is saying himself.

"I did nothing. What could I do? I sat there and thought 'shit'. Fortunately the colonel had more important things to do, otherwise I'm sure he would have had me shot there and then. When he left the other officer said he was going to make some calls. He spoke to a senior general whom I knew, because this general had been in charge of the housing project and we had had many meetings together. He outranked this bastard *milico* and I'm sure he saved my life. Later that morning I was sent to the Military Academy, where they had detained other members of the government and senior officials. So, in the end I had a very lucky escape."

Lawner tells me about his incarceration at the Military Academy along with other prominenti, some of whom had been with Allende in the Moneda. They were indeed the lucky ones, their government positions and reputations saving their lives. Several of those who had been arrested alongside them after they surrendered at the palace, were taken away to a military barracks and later murdered. Lawner describes how he and his fellow prisoners were flown south to Dawson Island in the Magellan archipelago, where they were made to do hard labour. It was still winter and the conditions were harsh.

As an artist Lawner wanted to record the daily scenes of prison life and managed to scrounge, or barter with the guards, the implements that he needed to draw.

His pictures are some of the few images which record life at the prison camp. They are now on show at the Moneda museum. Lawner gets up and goes to a shelf and takes out a book. It is a collection of drawings about his arrest and incarceration, which were published in a South American edition. He opens the book and shows me his work, turning the pages slowly.

"Some I drew later from memory, others from life which I

had to hide from the guards."

Several are scenes of soldiers at the Chile Stadium who threaten prisoners as they sit cowed in corners, their hands over the heads. There is menace in the air and a look of malice on the soldiers' faces. Others are less brutal and show Lawner's fellow prisoners at Dawson Island chatting, playing cards and smoking pipes. They are much better than any photograph and I tell him this and he smiles modestly.

"They're just sketches," he adds. "But I'm very glad I made them," and he puts the book aside.

After two years at various concentration camps, Lawner and his wife were exiled and granted asylum in Denmark, where he worked for the government on housing projects. He has fond memories of the Danes and jokes that the weather at Dawson Island prepared him for the long Scandinavian winters. He and his wife returned to Chile in 1989, as democracy was restored.

We talk some more about his time at the Chile Stadium and he speaks of the other prisoners who were with him. There is one man in particular, whom he is keen to mention.

"I remember seeing Victor Jara, the singer. He had been arrested at the State Technical University. He wasn't in the stands, but below me in the arena. He and his comrades had resisted the military all day, until they finally ran out of bullets. They came in for special treatment from the soldiers. I have to say they were very brave, particularly Jara who was their leader. I feared for them. There was nothing anybody could do. Later he was transferred to the National Stadium, where he was murdered. Apparently the guards broke his hands before they shot him, even so he was still defiant. They killed him, but they have never been able to shut him up. His spirit lives on in his songs. It lives forever.

"This is why the Moneda museum, a project that I have been working on, is so important. It keeps the memory of the *desaparecidos* alive. They found Jara's body in a mass grave recently, along with a whole bunch of other people they murdered, and he finally got a proper funeral. Thousands of people came and sang his songs. It was wonderful."

Lawner then speaks of his detention at other prison camps further north, which were not as bad as Dawson Island, and how he spent the time improving his English by studying Shakespeare, among other authors.

"Talking of which, I've been reading TS Eliot's 'Murder in the Cathedral', do you know it?"

"Yes, quite well," I say. "We performed it as a play at school."

Lawner nods approvingly and continues.

"I was struck by the similarity of Thomas Becket's murder by the knights and the death of Allende. The president also died in the Moneda, which is the cathedral."

He picks up a well-thumbed copy of the play from his desk and opens it.

"Let me read this to you…you will see what I mean. Thomas is addressing the knights who have broken into the sanctuary and are about to kill him."

> *But for every evil, every sacrilege,*
> *Crime, wrong, oppression and the axe's edge,*
> *Indifference, exploitation, you, and you,*
> *And you, must all be punished. So must you.*
> *I shall no longer act or suffer, to the sword's end.*
> *Now my good Angel, whom God appoints*
> *To be my guardian, hover over the swords' points.*

II
DELUGE

It is midnight in Santiago and the Plaza de Armas is deserted. Nothing moves in the surrounding streets. Tall buildings enclose the square, uneven silhouettes against a cold and starlit sky. Palm trees rise above a large bronze statue, which glistens in the falling rain. It is Chile's founder Pedro de Valdivia. The conquistador is bareheaded and sits astride a horse, facing the baroque edifice of the Metropolitan Cathedral. All around him the gardens seethe and are filled with shadows. Fear permeates everywhere like a dark stain.

In the distance comes a sound of engines. The noise increases with a roar and there is a sudden rush of tyres upon the road as a pair of military vehicles approach. Inside the leading truck seventeen-year-old Rubén Maruri nervously fingers the strap on his FAL machine gun. He is in full combat gear: two grenades, their detonators primed, hang from his webbing. The weight of his tin helmet makes his head pound and his face and neck are streaked with sweat. Maruri is with his platoon. They are all conscripts, except for their sergeant and the thin-faced lieutenant. The officer has told the squad to expect resistance and Maruri does not doubt his word.

Despite his earlier bravado the lieutenant is also nervous and like his men, he has never seen combat before. He stares moodily ahead and avoids eye contact. The soldiers sway with the motion of the vehicle, the metal fastenings of the tarpaulin clinking against the steel carapace. Beneath their boots the floor trembles as the wheels bump along the cobblestones.

The soldiers are on their way to destroy a pro-government radio station as part of Operation Silence. It is the first stage of the coup, which began on the stroke of midnight. The purpose of the operation is to wreck all communication facilities, thereby leaving the Popular Unity government voiceless. President Allende has already provided arms to media installations in the event of an uprising. Sitting next to the lieutenant, Maruri is fearful. Not only has he never been under fire, he has only just completed basic training.

The lorries turn into the plaza and come to a halt opposite the towering art deco building of Radio Nacional. The officer orders his soldiers from the vehicles and they jump down and quickly surround the place. Escorted by several men, the lieutenant marches up to the entrance and bangs on the door with his fist.

"Open up! This is a raid!"

On the other side of the door is a janitor. He had heard the lorries arrive, but was reluctant to get out of his chair. The old man suspected it was a raid. Only the military would be driving about at such an hour and he hoped the soldiers would look elsewhere. Now he has to get up. He sighs as he levers himself out of his armchair and goes to the door. He peers through the judas and sees the bulging fish eye view of the lieutenant's face on the other side.

"What do you want?"

"Open the fucking door or we'll kick it down!"

The janitor knows that if he refuses, the soldiers will carry out their threat. Slowly, he slides the heavy bolts across and opens the door. It is barely ajar before the platoon rushes past, knocking the old man to the ground. He is hauled to his feet and shoved against the wall, a machine gun pointing at his stomach.

"Where are the weapons?"

"What are you talking about?....There aren't any guns here!"

In fact there were, but they are safely locked away in the storeroom, the door of which is hidden behind a bookshelf. The janitor has the key on a chain attached to his belt.

"You'd better be telling the truth," says the lieutenant, his

eyes merciless. "How many people with you?'
"Just those on the night shift and me. Seven in all."
"Where are they?"
"Upstairs."
"OK, lead the way."
"You can go and see for yourself..."
"Don't fuck with me!" and the officer grabs the old man's collar and jams a pistol against his neck.

The janitor tries to speak, but no words come and he can only gasp. The lieutenant releases him and lowers his weapon. He turns the old man around and prods him in the small of his back towards the stairs.

The janitor leads the way, followed by the officer and a group of soldiers, which includes Maruri. The conscript has slipped the safety catch off his weapon, his finger poised on the trigger guard.

The squad ascend the staircase with the lieutenant at the head and the janitor in front. They take the steps two at a time, which is faster than the old man can walk so that he is propelled up the stairs, his feet barely touching the ground. He is sweating and breathless. There is a sharp pain, like a knife in his chest. It seems as if the air is being squeezed out of him. The janitor wants to stop and tell the lieutenant that he does not feel well. He needs to sit down. But the officer's gun is in his back, pushing him along.

The soldiers burst into the newsroom and a group of startled faces turn round.

"This is a raid!" shouts the lieutenant, jabbing the air with his weapon. "All of you put your hands up and go over to that wall," and he points with his gun. "You too grandpa," and he shoves the janitor towards the journalists.

Three men and two women get up from their desks and approach the opposite wall, their hands above their heads. One person remains behind. The journalist is not actually in the newsroom, but in an adjacent studio. His back is turned and he is wearing headphones, so he has neither seen nor heard the soldiers. The man is known simply as 'Domingo' and is handsome, bearded and broad-shouldered, his voice a sonorous baritone. He is one of Chile's most popular broadcasters, with his own late night political show. The journalist has by far the largest postbag in the newsroom and is something of a housewives' favourite, which his colleagues never cease teasing him about. In one hand he holds a sheaf of papers, the other rests on a cork-lined table. Unaware of what is happening he continues to broadcast, a microphone suspended a few inches from his face. Above the studio door a red light with the words 'ON AIR' glows. A smaller sign beneath it reads: '*No Entrar Cuando Esté Iluminada La Luz.*'

A soldier strides up, raises his boot and kicks the door open. The journalist spins round in his chair, tearing off the headphones.

"What the hell...?"

"You out!" says the conscript, his weapon pointing at the man's chest.

The journalist raises his hands and gets to his feet. He is calm and moves deliberately. He does not want to excite or perturb the soldier with his gun. As he approaches the door the youth grabs him and with a kick, propels him towards his colleagues against the far wall. They look nervous. Domingo grins briefly at his companions, but they are unable to share the joke. In the studio he had been asking for the army commander-in-chief General Augusto Pinochet to call the programme, so they could discuss the impending coup. The topic has been the talk of the bars and cafes in Santiago for weeks. All over the city walls have been daubed with the slogan: '*Ya Viene Djakarta*!'. 'Djakarta Is Coming!'. A warning by right-wing activists of the military uprising that toppled Indonesia's socialist President Sukarno. The journalist thought the army chief might wish to enlighten his listeners about the expected military takeover.

The soldiers search the journalists and the copytaker and

secretary are groped and insulted. Maruri is standing by the door with his machine gun, covering his comrades as they collect the prisoners' ID. He wonders where all the Cuban-trained gunmen are. This is just a radio station. A Commie one perhaps, but a radio station all the same. The prisoners look pretty normal too. The usual bunch of lefties and long-hairs. Then he remembers what the officers told him during training: that the really dangerous types are the ones who do not actually look like revolutionaries. People like the president. All smiles and handshakes and fine words. Those guys, they were the worst. Maruri keeps his gun raised, his finger poised upon the trigger.

"Where are the weapons?"

The lieutenant is addressing a bald, middle-aged man with a paunch, who seems to be the most senior of the prisoners. The programme editor looks blankly at the officer.

"There aren't any. It's just propaganda put about by the right-wing press."

In a single, deft movement the officer strikes him with his pistol. The man staggers, but does not fall and blood gushes from an ear.

"Don't lie you sonofabitch!"

"It's the truth I swear!" says the editor putting a hand to his head. "There aren't any weapons!"

The lieutenant raises his gun once more and the prisoners all tense as they wait for the blow. It does not come. Instead an arm reaches out. It is the platoon sergeant.

"Hang on boss! Maybe he's telling the truth."

The thin-faced lieutenant smiles and lowers his pistol.

"OK. Search the place. And you," he says, looking at the editor clutching his bloody ear. "You'd better hope we don't find anything!"

The officer leaves along with his sergeant and most of the platoon. Maruri and two others are detailed to stand guard. Domingo asks his captors if he can smoke. A soldier points the barrel of his gun at him in response.

37

The pain in the janitor's chest is getting worse. He can barely breathe and draws his breath in thin gasps. His mind is hazy and his vision blurred. The old man knows he is having a heart attack, but is too scared to speak out. His companions are unaware and can think only about themselves.

Above the prisoners' heads a rack of 7.5 millimetre reel-to-reel tapes revolve. They had been recording the late night programme. But the only sound the studio microphones have been able to pick up since the soldiers' arrival, is the occasional shout and the hiss of static.

A clatter of hobnailed boots comes down the corridor and the lieutenant appears in the doorway. He has been unable to find any arms and is in a sour mood. As a result the officer has decided to arrest the group. Perhaps they will be more cooperative when they are in custody.

"Take them downstairs!" he says.

The prisoners are escorted below, leaving the lieutenant and the rest of his men alone in the newsroom.

"Right. Let's get to work!"

The soldiers set about destroying the facility. They break open the control desk and editing suites, ripping off panels and tearing out wires and hack at the prefabricated ceiling, pulling out reams of electric cables. A shower of sparks cascades onto the floor and the lights in the room begin to flicker and dim. The row of tapes continues to spin, the trembling audio needles indicating the levels of destruction. Maruri and another soldier enter the studio. The last item that is recorded are their voices and the sound of blows as they break the desk apart with their boots. Finally, they smash the microphones to pieces.

The platoon leaves the place in virtual darkness. A fire smoulders in a wastepaper basket and a shower of sparks spews from a severed cable. The air is filled with smoke and the bitter smell of burnt electrics. The editing suites, the monitors and the racks of tapes, have all been ruined. The floor is strewn with debris and shards of broken glass. In a piece of inspired vandalism, one of the soldiers has thrown a typewriter through the studio window and jagged pieces of glass hang limply from the wooden frame like broken teeth.

Outside the lieutenant orders his prisoners into the waiting trucks.

"Where are you taking us?" asks the editor, holding a crimson handkerchief to his ear.

"You'll find out soon enough."

The prisoners are shoved into the back a lorry. The lieutenant is the last to climb aboard. He bangs on the side of the vehicle with his fist and they depart in a roar. The lorries disappear around the corner and the Plaza de Armas is silent again.

*

The lights in the Moneda are still burning. In the Office of Information and Radio, René Largo Farías is exhausted after a long day. The OIR chief is a stocky, good-natured man with a round belly and a fondness for folk music and beer. Like many in his profession he smokes heavily and an ashtray choked with cigarette butts sits at his elbow. The cup of black coffee on his desk has long gone cold. Forgetting, he picks it up, takes a sip and grimaces. He puts the cup down with an expression of mild disgust and in compensation lights another Viceroy.

Largo Farías sits there smoking and thinking. Something is not right. He can feel it. There is a tension, a heaviness in the air, as though a thunderstorm were approaching. He is sure he can hear a faint moan like a death rattle, the final gasp of someone dying. Largo Farías is not superstitious. He does not believe in ghosts and he certainly does not believe in God. So what is it?

In spite of the phone calls Largo Farías has made, there is no firm evidence that anything unusual is happening.

Cigarette in hand he continues his enquiries, filling in the office logbook as he goes.

0028 hrs: *I call Tomás Moro and am answered by Raul, a member of the presidential bodyguard. I tell him about my concern of troop movements across the country. He promises to convey my feelings to our Comrade President, who is in a meeting with the Minister of the Interior and the former Minister of Foreign Relations.*

0032 hrs: *I try, for the third time tonight, to get in touch with the supervisor of Valparaíso, but I cannot reach him. I can only ascertain that the fleet has embarked for its annual joint operations with the US navy.*

0040 hrs: *Report from the General Prefecture of the Carabineros: 'Nothing unusual on the highways.'*

Largo Farías spends another couple of hours making phone calls and annotating the details. Finally, at 2:30am and still unable to get any hard information, he calls the Director General of Investigations Alfredo Joignant, who is in charge of internal security. Joignant assures him there is nothing to worry about and tells him to go home and get some rest.

Largo Farías dismisses the remaining staff, then tidies up and locks the office. He is the last to leave the building and drives the short distance back to his home. When he arrives he puts his briefcase down in the hall and goes straight to his bedroom and undresses. His wife, Maria Cristina, is fast asleep. Largo Farías raises the covers and slips into bed. His spouse mumbles sleepily and turns over, but does not wake. Her body is soft and warm. He draws up the blankets around them and lies there in the dark, staring up at the ceiling. Despite the assurances from Joignant, he is worried. Something, he knows, is wrong. He can feel it in his bones. Call it a journalistic hunch. But try as he might, Largo Farías cannot find the answer. Eventually, exhaustion overtakes him and moments later he is asleep and snoring.

*

At the presidential residence in Tomás Moro the sixty-five members of Allende's personal bodyguard, the Grupo Amigos Personales or 'GAP', are on emergency alert. They patrol the gardens and keep watch on the streets outside. Some are placed in positions on the roof, where they have a good view of the surrounding neighbourhood, with its low-roofed homes and manicured lawns set back from the road. The naked glare of the street lights reveals nothing except the empty roads. The night air is cold and filled with the pollinated scent of early spring. Blossom lies pale and thick upon the branches of the cherry trees like snow. A dog barks occasionally and sets off others and a wild chorus of howls and yaps erupts. After a time they stop and silence returns.

One of the GAP stationed on the roof is José Huenchullán. He is one of the youngest members of the bodyguard and only twenty. He had been a member of the left-wing paramilitary group Movimiento de Izquierda Revolucionaria, commonly known by its acronym 'MIR', when he was called up to join the presidential corps. It is an elite force and Huenchullán is proud to be able to play his part in supporting Popular Unity, Latin America's first democratically elected Marxist-Socialist government.

Huenchullán looks over the black barrel of a Bren gun at the deserted streets beyond. Beside him lie several clips of ammunition. Four GAP have been placed on this particular section of the roof. Another four are out of sight on the other side. Both groups have been split into two, with each pair facing in opposite directions so as to cover all angles of fire.

The GAP turns to his companion beside him. His friend 'Cuico' is also young but has blond hair, which he combs forward in a fashionable mop. Unlike Huenchullán he comes from a privileged background, hence his nickname 'Posh'. The boy had been taught at a private school, where all the lessons were conducted in English and his family owned a famous vineyard not far from Santiago. The other GAP tease him about his background, to which the boy's response is that all true revolutionaries such as Che Guevara, Fidel Castro and even their own Comrade President, have bourgeois backgrounds. The press have dubbed them 'The James Bonds', an epithet the younger ones in particular are proud of.

Huenchullán addresses his blond-haired accomplice.

"Dude, you got a smoke?"

"Sure," and the youth produces a packet of cigarettes from his jacket. He gives one to his companion and takes another for himself. The blond GAP flicks open his Zippo lighter and the wavering flame illuminates Huenchullán's face.

"Cheers," he says, as the other youth puts his own cigarette to the flame, then snaps the lighter closed.

The GAP sit there smoking and watching, the tips of their cigarettes glowing like fireflies in the darkness. They keep their eyes fixed on the road below. Their orders are to shoot at the first military vehicle that comes down it.

*

In the living-room directly beneath the young GAP, Allende is deep in conversation with his chief advisers. They are the Minister of the Interior Carlos Briones, a respected moderate recently brought into the cabinet to pacify the right wing; Orlando Letelier, formerly the Foreign Minister and now with the defence portfolio; the Director of National Television Augusto 'Perro' Olivares and the president's adviser on education and social affairs, the Spanish born academic Joan Garcés.

Their voices are a low murmur, occasionally crossing over and interrupting each other. The president and his advisers are seated in armchairs arranged in one corner of the room. The light from the lamps is muted and warm. Amid the gentle wash of conversation comes the ticking of an ornamental clock. The long hand moves, the mechanism whirrs and there is a single, silvery peal as it chimes 1:00am.

The walls are lined with rows of books. There are cheap paperbacks, glossy hardbacks and leather-bound volumes covering every subject from politics and medicine (the president is a qualified doctor), to philosophy and poetry. Particularly poetry. Some of them are by his close friend Pablo Neruda, who is now terminally ill at his house on Isla Negra. The president often thinks about him and recently has been re-reading what he considers to be Neruda's greatest work 'Los Versos del Capitán'. The book is a collection of love poems addressed to the poet's wife Matilde Urrutia. Soon the master mariner's voice will be silenced. But his work would live on.

Apart from the books, the room is well furnished. There are paintings by Matta, Guayasamín, Picasso and Siqueiros. Prominently placed on the president's desk is a photograph of Che Guevara, dedicated to Allende. The president had met him in Havana after the 1959 revolution. The Argentinean had given him a copy of his memoir 'Guerra de Guerrillas' and had inscribed it: 'to Salvador Allende, who by other means is trying to do the same. Affectionately, Che.' Looking out from another frame is a photograph of the North Vietnamese leader Ho Chi Minh, his oriental features impassive yet eloquent.

In a corner lies a stuffed Cayman crocodile, a present from Fidel Castro. When Allende's younger nephews and nieces came to stay, he sometimes grabbed the amber-eyed reptile and wrestled with it on the floor, knowing that children only respect adults who have time to play. On a low table by the fireplace is a chessboard. Its pieces arrayed, ready to do battle. The president is a fanatic. He became obsessed with the game when he was a medical student in Valparaíso. His teacher had been an elderly Italian anarchist. The old man had fled Italy in 1922 after Mussolini seized power and the president credited him as the flint which struck the spark and lit his passion for politics.

On Friday Allende had summoned the seven generals of the Santiago garrison to his office in the Moneda for a meeting. He informed the group that he had finally decided to hold a plebiscite, because the political impasse was so bad. The head of the army General Carlos Prats had recently resigned after an incident in which he had drawn his gun at a woman driver, who had gesticulated and spat at him while stationed at a traffic light. In his place the president had appointed General Pinochet. The new army chief was ambitious and something of a non-entity, but he had promised the president his loyalty.

Allende told the generals that he had had enough of the opposition's sniping and accusations of being anti-democratic. The president said that he would announce a plebiscite the following "Tuesday, or Wednesday at the latest." The reason for the delay was that he would have to persuade Popular Unity of his decision over the weekend and that would not be easy.

"No one," he had told them, "will be able to say now that the President of the Republic does not respect the powers of the state."

Unwittingly, Allende had given the rebels the date for the coup. The junta had been plotting for weeks, but because of the aborted Tancazo in June, they were cautious and could not afford another failure. The generals quickly met back at the Ministry of Defence. They needed forty-eight hours to set the blitzkrieg in motion. The coup would begin at midnight on Monday.

The president observes his companions through his heavy-framed spectacles. His sight is poor and the thick lenses magnify his dark eyes. He is sixty-five and looks his age, which is not to say that he does not look well. The Russian poet Yevgeny Yevtushenko once said that Allende has "a country doctor's face." It is an apt description. The president has avuncular good looks, especially when he smiles. If annoyed his jaw slackens a little and his cheeks colour. In spite of his age, hair grows thick and dark upon his head. In contrast to his hair, Allende's moustache is almost white.

"Carlitos," he says, turning to Briones. "What do you think?"

"We should have made an announcement today...sorry, yesterday," the minister corrects himself as he glances up at the clock. "It must be done as soon as possible. Forget whatever MIR and the Socialist paramilitaries want. They are not our mandate. The people of Chile are."

A small, portly man, Briones has a large hooked nose and watery blue eyes. His once blond hair has now turned grey. He is a popular figure and his inclusion by Allende into the cabinet is seen by some as a master-stroke, which may yet save the president's skin.

"The trouble is that MIR and the paramilitaries want a war and the military are quite prepared to give them one," says Letelier, the newly appointed defence minister.

Allende looks across at his cabinet colleague. At forty-one Letelier is young to hold such a senior position. But he is highly intelligent and was recently foreign minister, until the president asked him to take on the problematic defence portfolio, in order to try and keep the military in check. Allende has no doubt that one day his protégé will be president. Letelier has pale skin and red hair and looks more European than Latin. He is raffishly handsome and with his neat moustache and boyish grin, he could pass for a young David Niven. In addition to his worldly charm, the defence minister is a talented musician and at parties often played the guitar and led the singing.

Earlier that evening Letelier had called a press conference in his offices on the ninth floor of the Ministry of Defence. He had invited all the editors from the newspapers and magazines, as well as journalists from television and radio. Once everyone was assembled, he announced the president would be making a speech the following day, which would resolve the political stalemate. His audience was suitably amazed. In the clamour that followed, everyone asked the same question: "will the president be announcing a plebiscite?" The defence minister avoided answering it directly, since he knew Allende wished to make the statement himself. Even so, he left them in no doubt that this was the logical answer and believed the following morning's newspapers and subsequent bulletins would carry the appropriate headlines.

Letelier was confident the government had finally resolved the crisis, but more than one reporter took note of an ominous sign. Not one of the commanders-in-chief of the armed forces was present, an extremely unusual occurrence given that the Minister of Defence was holding a press conference. The answer lay a few floors below where Letelier was speaking, as the rebel generals and their staff added the final touches to the coup, which would begin in just a few hours time.

"MIR and the paramilitaries do not want war, they want a revolution," corrects Allende. "But I have explained to them how Popular Unity intends to enact such a revolution, in a way that does not involve bloodshed. On Sunday I told them that if they're not satisfied with government policy, then they should throw in their hand and go their own way."

"Which they won't do," says Briones.

"I know," and the president smiles. He looks at the others. "But back to the point…is midday too late?"

"Carlos is right. You need to go public as soon as possible. You can elaborate later in your speech at the Chile Stadium," says Garcés, the young Spanish academic.

"But the papers and news bulletins will be full of it. Let everybody digest it and then make the official announcement," counters Letelier, aware of the political value of such a dramatic gesture.

"It's probably too late already," and Briones sighs.

"Something is up. Not a single member of the high command attended your meeting at the MOD and Largo Farías has been calling us constantly from the Moneda, saying he's heard rumours of troop movements..."

"We get these kind of reports hourly..." interjects Letelier, peeved about the Minister of the Interior's reference to the lack of military beef at his press conference. "Look Carlos, I don't like these rumours any more than you do, but I've just called General Brady and he says there's nothing unusual happening..."

"General Brady is a prize asshole," interjects Olivares. The television chief's salty remark breaking the tension as everyone laughs.

The brief moment of levity does nothing to raise Briones' spirits, like Largo Farías he too has an overwhelming sense of impending doom. He does not know why, but it is there. Intangible yet unnerving, like a stranger lurking in a dark alley. The minister looks across at the French windows and the floodlit garden outside. The GAP continue to patrol the borders. The plants are sharp-leaved and the bodyguard emerge and disappear into the undergrowth like phantoms. The glare of the floodlights makes the darkness beyond seem even more impenetrable.

"I agree with Orlando," says the president. "Let's not appear too hasty. It smacks of desperation. I'll announce the plebiscite at midday as planned."

The president then calls General Brady and asks him about unauthorised troop movements in the Los Andes area and is assured the rumours are unsubstantiated. He puts down the receiver and stifles a yawn. The clock on the mantelpiece whirrs and strikes. It is 2:30am.

Allende decides it is time to turn in.

"Let's go to bed, it's late. Tomorrow will be a long, hard day."

The president asks Olivares and Garcés if they would like to stay, since their homes are some distance away and they agree. The group gets up and having wished each other goodnight, the president accompanies Briones and Letelier to the door.

"See you in the morning," he calls out, as the ministers get into their official cars. The engines are started and they drive off, the sound diminishing down the empty street until all is quiet again. There is a chill in the air and Allende shivers in his shirtsleeves as he stands alone on the porch. He looks up at the night sky and sees clouds scudding across the moon's bright face.

The president closes the front door and goes back to the living-room. The others have already gone to bed and he begins to turn out the lights. He looks across at the windows and sees the GAP prowling about in the garden. Allende is glad of them. If only he could rely on his armed forces as he can on these men.

The president wearily shakes his head. There was nothing he could do about it now. He would feel better after a good night's rest and he goes to his bedroom and gets undressed. His wife Hortensia is asleep and he carefully climbs into bed, so as not to wake her. Allende is exhausted, but he cannot help thinking about the speech he is due to give at the Chile Stadium. He had been reading a biography of the Italian nationalist Camillo di Cavour and has written the opening words.

"Women of Chile. I want you to be the first to know that Popular Unity will never forsake democracy. In a plebiscite you, the people, shall decide. Chile shall make herself, by herself…"

*

In the port of Valparaíso, dawn appears over a sullen Pacific. A long, low wave rises and falls and crashes against the breakwater, followed by an endless procession of others. Beyond the waves, the sea lies empty and flat. A thin light steals across its dull surface, turning it to pewter. In the distance the ocean ascends towards the sky and greets it tenderly with a kiss.

Apart from the odd tender and tug, the naval dockyards are bare. At 4:00pm the day before the entire fleet had set sail to take part in annual joint manoeuvres with the US Navy. But this was merely a ploy. Lying just beyond the horizon, they had waited until midnight before weighing anchor and sailing at full steam back towards the coast. Now at dawn ship after ship appears upon the horizon. As the sun rises above the ocean, the entire Chilean navy arrays itself along the coast. The ships line up opposite the shore, their guns pointing leeward.

At prearranged signals naval personnel emerge from their positions and take control of the main junctions in the city. Helicopters judder overhead, flying so low the draught of their rotor blades shakes the tops of the palm trees.

In their homes people begin to stir. They draw back the curtains and peer sleepily out of their windows. Instead of seeing a street, empty except for the postman or a couple of drunks who never made it home, they are confronted by streams of soldiers and military vehicles. Amazed, they switch on the radio to find out what is happening and can only hear a low hiss. They turn the dial back and forth, but there is just whine and static. All the main stations are silent. Outside an officer in a jeep declares through a loudhailer that the military is in control and tells everyone to stay indoors. Some people try and flee, but there is a checkpoint at the highway and they are ordered back, or else detained, depending on their papers.

On duty at Valparaíso's police headquarters, a carabinero colonel stretches and gets up from his desk. His shift is almost over. He walks across to the window and is astounded at the sight. The streets are filled with soldiers and the navy, which should be away on manoeuvres, has returned. The colonel has not been told about any change of plan and he is worried by the aggressive attitude of the troops, who have assumed firing positions and set up gun emplacements. It seems much more than a military exercise.

The colonel goes to his desk and picks up the phone, but finds the line is dead. It explains why it had not rung once during the night. He picks up another and finds that too is silent. So is a third. There is nothing for it, but to call national headquarters in Santiago using the emergency line. After a couple of attempts, the colonel manages to raise the Deputy Director of Carabineros Jorge Urrutia, who has spent the night there because he has only recently arrived in the capital from Concepción.

"Something weird is happening general," says his subordinate. "There are marines in the street and there's no sound on the radio. A1 communications are cut off and the fleet which sailed yesterday, has come back."

"The fleet? You sure?"

"As sure as I'm talking to you. I can see the ships from my window."

He hears a stifled curse down the line.

"What should I do?"

"Stay by the phone and await orders. I'm going to make some calls."

Urrutia then dials the number of his chief José Maria Sepulveda. He asks for further details and tells his colleague to call the presidential residence.

As the Deputy Director is about do this, the phone rings at Tomás Moro. A member of the GAP picks it up. It is the Prefect of Valparaíso Luis Gutiérrez. His message is terse and to the point.

"Tell the president the navy has rebelled."

The GAP immediately informs Allende who tries to speak to the prefect, but the line has already been cut.

III
A CALL TO ARMS

Allende orders the entire bodyguard to assemble outside and returns to his bedroom to get dressed. Hortensia is awake and wonders what is going on. The president slips on some clothes as she watches silently from their bed. He puts on a pair of navy blue trousers, a plain white shirt and a jersey with a diagonal pattern. As he laces his shoes, he sees his wife is no longer asleep.

"It's OK," he says. "I'm going to the palace. Stay here and I'll call you when I get there. I'll leave some GAP with you. Don't leave the house whatever you do."

"What's happening Salvador?"

The president takes a tweed jacket from his wardrobe and puts it on.

"Nothing I can't handle. Don't worry Tencha," and he blows her a kiss and leaves.

The GAP are lined up in the gardens, the early morning mist smoking around their feet while they wait for their commander-in-chief. Allende steps out onto the patio and at an order the men present arms, then stand at ease. They look alert and ready to do battle. The tiredness they felt after a long night of guard duty, evaporating like the dew. The president surveys them all, his hands on his hips.

"Comrades, there's been a naval uprising in Valparaíso. I am going to the Moneda. Some of you will stay here to protect the house and Tencha, the rest will come with me. Those coming to the Moneda, bring all the weapons you can."

The president dismisses them and returns indoors as the GAP fall out and quickly assemble an armoury. There are light and heavy machine guns, boxes of ammunition, grenades and two anti-tank weapons.

Olivares hears the commotion outside, puts on his glasses

and leaps out of bed. Naked, the hairy-arsed television chief throws a towel around his waist, opens the bedroom door and steps into the corridor where he meets a bewildered Garcés, who has just emerged from his room.

"What's going on?" says the Spaniard.

"Fucked if I know."

The president is on the phone, making various calls. He greets his advisers in the hall and tells them there has been an uprising in Valparaíso and they should leave immediately for the Moneda. The pair hurry back to their rooms and get dressed.

Allende calls the palace to let them know he is coming and tells a member of staff to get as many government ministers there as they can. The president then tries to phone some of the military high command at the Ministry of Defence, but cannot get through. The naval uprising appears to have developed into a fully-fledged coup.

Olivares wanders outside and sees the GAP assembling their armoury. He walks up to a group and asks them if they could spare a weapon. Without a word one of the bodyguard hands him an AK47 and a couple of clips of ammunition, before returning to his task. The television chief goes back inside, happily clutching his weapon like a child with a new toy. He stands in the hallway and watches as the president dispenses orders. Olivares is a popular personality and known to all as 'Perro' or 'Dog'. Short and squat, with black unruly hair and a thick moustache, he looks a little wild. The bespectacled television chief stands there grinning and holding his weapon, glad that at last they are going to have a fight.

*

The phone in the Leteliers' bedroom rings. The defence minister's wife leans over and sleepily answers it, her husband having got home shortly before 3:00am. When

Isabel hears Allende's voice, she quickly hands the receiver to her spouse.

"It's Salvador."

"Thanks," he says. "Hi, what's up?"

"The navy's rebelled. Six truckloads of marines are on their way to Santiago from Valparaíso. The carabineros are the only units who respond. The other commanders-in-chief don't answer the phone. Pinochet's not answering either. Find out what you can…"

Letelier asks his wife to call the loyalist head of the navy Admiral Raul Montero and the former army chief General Prats, while he calls his office in his ministry on a special line. Isabel tries but cannot get through, because both men have had their phones disconnected and are now under house arrest. When the minister calls his office in the MOD, he is surprised it is answered by Admiral Patricio Carvajal. The minister does not know that he is one of the main plotters of the coup. Carvajal flatly denies that anything unusual is happening.

"Your information is wrong sir. It's some kind of raid, nothing more. We're trying to get through to Valparaíso now. I'm looking into it."

Letelier is unconvinced. He knows something is awry. He calls Allende back and tells him what the rebel admiral has just said.

"Go Orlando," says the president. "Take control of the defence ministry…if you can get there."

Letelier quickly gets dressed and goes to the kitchen and makes a cup of coffee. As he gulps it down one of his sons José Ignacio enters, dressed in his school uniform.

"Morning Dad, just thought you'd like to know me and some students are going to take over the school today."

The minister cannot help a smile. The school had been closed for days because of a teachers' strike and now his son was a political activist. The smile is strained as Letelier is in urgent need of root canal work. Twice during treatment the previous week he has been called away from the dentist's chair, because of a phone call from the president. The work is unfinished and his teeth remain unfilled. Eating, drinking and even laughing are painful. He does not say anything about the crisis, but gives the boy a hug and tells him to make his own breakfast.

Letelier goes into the sitting-room to get his briefcase, which contain the papers and correspondence he has been working on, including the press release he gave the previous evening at the MOD.

"I'm off," he calls as he prepares to leave, clutching the leather satchel.

At the door Isabel gives her husband a kiss and a couple of aspirin, which he swallows without water and accompanies him into the street.

When they get there they find the ministry car and its driver Jimenez waiting, but no bodyguard. Jimenez, who looks like an overgrown kid, is a giant of a man. He is so big that when he walks, or more accurately waddles, his thighs rub together. The chauffeur looks shifty, refusing to meet their eyes and instead stares at his clod-hopping feet.

"Morning," says his boss. "Where's Marambio?"

Jimenez mumbles that the bodyguard's wife suddenly went into labour and he had to go to the hospital.

"Strange. He never even mentioned she was pregnant."

Isabel steps forward, wraps her arms around the chauffeur's great girth and gives him a hug, which makes his cheeks burn.

"You make sure nothing happens to the minister."

Letelier embraces his wife and he and the baby-faced Jimenez depart, heading straight for the MOD.

*

In his home a few blocks north of the MOD, Largo Farías is snoring. The bedroom is dark, the curtains drawn. Amid the regular resonance of his breathing, the phone on the bedside table rings. The snores cease abruptly and are replaced with a grunt. He raises an arm, gropes for the receiver and picks it up.

"Hello…?"

"René," says a voice. "It's me Iris. Listen, the navy has rebelled and the streets of Valparaíso are full of soldiers."

Hearing this Largo Farías sits bolt upright.

"How do you know?"

"José told me. He's on his way to the Moneda. I couldn't stop him. But please René, stay at home."

Iris is Largo Farías' sister whose husband is José Miguel Vargas, head of press for National TV. The pair have been good friends since university, the OIR chief having introduced Vargas to his sister.

"Thanks. But I have to go to the Moneda. Stay inside and don't answer the door, not even if it's the cops. Sorry, especially if it's the cops."

"René…!"

"Gotta go sis. Take care," he says and leaps out of bed. Largo Farías puts on some clean underwear, then throws on the other clothes he took off just a few hours ago.

Maria Cristina is awake and having heard his part of the conversation, realises there has been a coup.

"Be careful," she says.

Before her husband can reply, the phone rings again. This time it is a friend who tells him the studios at the State Technical University are all smashed and other broadcasting facilities have been destroyed as well.

"Thanks for letting us know comrade."

Largo Farías then kisses his wife and leaves for the Moneda, cursing himself that he ever left the palace in the first place.

*

Allende's last phone call from Tomás Moro is to the head of the carabineros General José Maria Sepulveda, who is known as 'Sepa'. The president tells him to triple the guard on the Moneda and to bring up tank support.

"Mr President, I have already done this."

"I'll be at the palace in twenty minutes. See you there."

"Yes sir."

Even though Allende anticipated a coup, the surprise and swiftness of the rebellion is breathtaking. It is the first full scale military uprising in over a century. June's Tancazo, while a concern, was little more than a damp squib. There had been a quasi-military government under President Arturo Alessandri in the 1920s and again in the 1930s, but Alessandri, although a reactionary, was still a civilian. To find a parallel you had to go back to the civil war of 1891, when the forces of President José Manuel Balmaceda were defeated by right-wing rebels and the military and in despair he had committed suicide in the Argentinean embassy.

Allende also wonders about Pinochet, the grey man he had promoted to replace the hapless Prats. The new army commander had personally assured him of his loyalty that Sunday, when he had held a meeting at Tomás Moro with General Orlando Urbina, the military's third in command. Yet it is possible that Pinochet the faithful servant has already turned, becoming Brutus to his Caesar.

At least Sepulveda and Urrutia are still loyal. The president is glad that he has these two generals and hopes the carabineros as a corps are not involved in the coup. If this were the case, it would be far more difficult for the rebels to overthrow the government. The carabineros come from a predominantly rural and working class background, like many supporters of Popular Unity. Furthermore, soldiers are reluctant to fire on their comrades, whatever the cause. It is a vain hope, although Allende does not yet know it.

*

The president cannot get hold of any of the other leaders of the armed forces for a good reason. They are neither at home, nor at their respective headquarters. Instead each is at their separate battle station. Pinochet is at the military base of Peñalolén in the east of the city, where he has been all night. Hidden in the bowels of a blast-proof bunker, he is studying a *papier-mâché* model of Santiago and its environs. Each tactical military group is marked with a different coloured flag: blue for the infantry, red for the mechanised units and green for the artillery. It took an entire day for his staff to make and paint the model and the army chief is childishly proud of it. Now he is playing war games for real.

To the north are the undulations of the Andes and the skiing resort of Portillo, where the army's winter warfare cadre trained. Pinochet has sent his wife and five children there for safety, in case anything goes wrong. Outside his command post a helicopter is waiting, ready to whisk him away. If the uprising fails he will board the aircraft, make a quick stop to pick up his family, before nipping across the border to Argentina and claiming political asylum.

Pinochet is so engrossed with the model of the city, that he fails to notice an orderly standing at his shoulder. After waiting patiently the man clears his throat and the general turns round.

"Coffee sir?"

The army chief grins, his teeth flashing white.

"Thanks corporal. I need it."

The orderly pours some coffee from a steaming pot and hands him the cup.

Pinochet takes a sip, then places it on the edge of the table and returns to his contemplation. He is good-looking with a neat moustache and distinctive green eyes which, in a certain light, appear blue. He uses them to charm the susceptible, especially subordinate officers and women. His hair is lacquered and greying at the temples, but still lies thick and straight upon his head. The general is not tall, although he is wiry and physically strong. A black belt in karate, his party trick is to split a breeze block with a single blow, which he does every year in front of the newly commissioned officers at the Founders' Day parade at the Military Academy. When excited Pinochet speaks quickly in a high-pitched voice, which others find amusing and sometimes imitate, though never in front of him. Like many Chileans he is religious and attends Mass every day. He has a special devotion for the Virgin and always lights a candle for her in church.

The army chief is thinking about his new status as a rebel. Pinochet wonders how the president will react when he hears the news. He knows that Allende trusts him. Personally, Pinochet likes the president. It is hard not to. Allende has the common touch, an over-used phrase perhaps, but rare for a man in a position of power and rarer still in a head of state. The general had been delighted when the president requested he take over from Prats as head of the army, but his joy was also tempered by the appalling state of the country, which he was being asked to serve. Such was Pinochet's unknown quantity, that he had not been one of the original plotters. Far from it. On Thursday he had told Allende in front of several witnesses: "Mr President you have my unconditional loyalty." He repeated those words again on Sunday at Tomás Moro, but by then he had decided to join the rebels. Earlier that weekend a succession of senior officers had come to his house, telling him that he must join the coup. At first Pinochet hesitated. The army chief knew that if the uprising failed like the Tancazo, he would be court-martialled and tried for treason. But the junta, headed by Admiral José Merino, had convinced him that a coup was the only possible option.

On Sunday morning a group of generals presented the army chief with a document which they urged him to sign, committing him to 'carrying out the military phase with all the forces that you control in Santiago.' On the back one of them had scrawled: 'Augusto, if you don't put all the strength of Santiago to bear from the first moment, we won't be alive to see the future.' Pinochet signed.

The plan had been to arrest the president at home and take him to the MOD. After that the junta's policy on the president's fate was a little vague. There was talk of a plane to fly him and his family to a sympathetic country, such as Mexico or Cuba. Only Pinochet believes this will actually happen. No one has actually said it, but none of the other members of the junta want the president to survive. His demise is something they hope will take care of itself in the time honoured way. A room, a revolver, a bottle of brandy. Whatever happens, none of them except Pinochet believe the president will live to see another dawn.

*

When Letelier arrives at the MOD, he is surprised to find that his usual entrance in a side street is locked. He goes round to the main door and is confronted by a troop of heavily armed soldiers, who point their weapons at him.

"I have orders you cannot enter," says a sergeant.

Letelier bristles. He is a former Military School alumnus and in strict military terms, only the president exceeds his authority.

"I give the orders around here. Now step aside."

"I'm sorry sir, but you're not allowed to enter."

An officer approaches and adds: "if you continue to insist, we shall be forced to execute you immediately."

The defence chief is furious and is about to tell the man to go to hell, when he hears a voice on the other side of the door say, "let the minister inside. It's OK."

The solid wooden doors are opened and Letelier enters. He is confronted by a dozen armed men, including his bodyguard Marambio, whose wife has plainly not just given birth. He feels the sharp jab of a weapon in his back. The minister is taken downstairs to a room in the basement. His tie, belt and jacket are removed. He is searched and then pushed against a wall.

"Put your hands above your head," a voice commands. "You're under arrest."

*

One of the few senior officers who is still loyal is General Alberto Bachelet of the air force. In the dead of night the phone rings. It is next to his wife Angela, who picks it up. The caller is a colleague from the Institute of Teaching at the University of Chile. The man sounds agitated.

"Did you know there's been an uprising in Valparaiso?"

Angela relays the message to her husband, who replies:

"Tell him not to bother us. He should stay calm. Nothing's going on. Nothing."

His wife repeats this to her colleague and ends the call.

Bachelet turns and addresses his spouse.

"These idiots are always imagining things. They're just playing cops and robbers."

He rolls over and they go back to sleep.

It is not for long. At 6:30am the phone rings again. It is an official from the National Distributions Office, of which Bachelet is head. He also mentions that there has been an uprising in Valparaiso. It cannot be a coincidence. The general thanks the caller and tries to contact the MOD, but is unable to get through. He jumps out of bed and puts on his uniform. Then he checks and loads his revolver, before slipping it into his holster.

"Something's not right. I'm going to the MOD," he says to his wife. "I'll call you from there."

Bachelet summons his driver and goes straight to the ministry.

As they travel towards the MOD, the general realises the uprising is not merely confined to Valparaíso. The streets are full of tanks and there are hundreds of soldiers in combat kit.

When they arrive Bachelet alights and walks up the steps of the grand building. The entrance has been heavily sandbagged and there is a machine gun emplacement. The guards salute him and he steps inside.

Usually the place was a citadel of calm. Now it is filled with soldiers all milling about. There is an air of panic, as though everyone has their orders, but no one knows what to do. Bachelet sees another general whom he recognises and approaches him.

"Hey Orlando, what's happening?"

The man he has addressed, General Orlando Gutiérrez, turns round and seeing his colleague, roughly disarms him.

"What the hell do you think you're doing?" says his fellow officer, more surprised than annoyed.

"You're under arrest," and the rebel points Bachelet's pistol at his chest.

"What on earth for?"

The question momentarily stuns Gutiérrez, before he answers.

"There's been a coup, that's what for."

He motions to a pair of soldiers nearby and tells them to take Bachelet to his office and to keep him under close arrest. Sandwiched between them the general is frogmarched up the stairs and taken to his workplace. The soldiers disconnect the phones, put Bachelet under an armed guard and leave. He goes towards the window and looks outside.

In the grey light of early morning, the city is lit by the sodium glow of the street lights. To the north overlooking the Moneda is San Cristóbal Hill. On its crest stands the white statue of the Virgin, her arms raised in benediction towards the city. Beneath the statue is the Municipal Zoo. Bachelet can scarcely believe it. The keepers it seems have unlocked the animals' cages and fled.

*

General Javier Palacios, the Director of Army Instruction, is worried. He is in a jeep racing towards the headquarters of the Second Tank Regiment, in the southern district of Santa Rosa. But it is not the speed at which they are driving, which disturbs the general. It is his orders. The day before he had been instructed by the junta to occupy the Moneda, in case the president took refuge there. In order to do this the Second Tank Regiment has been put under his command. This is the same regiment that played a prominent part in the Tancazo, under Colonel Roberto Souper. Many of the officers, including Souper, have been court-martialled and confined to barracks. As Palacios' vehicle speeds down the tree-lined boulevarde of Avenida Bernardo O'Higgins, he cannot help wondering if these same men will again march on the presidential palace, under the command of an officer they have never even met.

The jeep arrives at the military base and enters through the wrought iron gates. The regiment is on parade in the main square. Palacios gets out of his vehicle and the men stand to attention, waiting for him to speak. He briefly surveys the ranks of soldiers, before declaring in a loud voice:

"We are going to repeat the 29th June!"

The general is answered only by silence. A breeze idly stirs the national flag on its pole. But that is all. There is no noise. No one moves, or speaks. The soldiers are not deaf or dumb, they simply wonder if they have heard correctly. Their commander steps forward and saluting, asks the general if he knows what he is talking about, or is this some sort of joke? For the purpose of secrecy only those directly involved in the coup, have any prior knowledge of it. The rest of the armed forces, including almost all the senior officers, have been kept in the dark.

Palacios turns round. Behind him is a row of Sherman tanks. He climbs up onto one of the armoured vehicles, takes his service revolver from its holster, points it in the air and shouts:

"This tank is now under my command!"

A resounding cheer erupts from the regiment. Rebellion has risen like a phoenix from the ashes. Palacios surveys them all with a smile, puts his pistol back in its holster and gets down. The commander orders his men into their vehicles and the soldiers run towards their tanks and clamber in. A guttural roar rises into the air as the engines are gunned into life and thick, black smoke belches from the exhausts. A stench of diesel fumes fills the parade ground.

With Palacios at their head, the armoured column leaves the barracks and heads towards the presidential palace. Unlike June's Tancazo, this time they do not stop at the traffic lights.

*

At Tomás Moro, Allende is also preparing to leave. The president has divided the GAP into three groups. The first consists of twenty marksmen armed with AK47s. A second group of twenty are to follow, as soon as they have collected more arms and ammunition from another depot. The remaining twenty-five are to stay behind and defend Hortensia. Like the GAP, the president is armed. In his hands he carries an AK47. The weapon is a gift from his friend Fidel Castro and bears the inscription: 'to my comrade in arms Salvador Allende.'

It had been something of a joke between them, the veteran guerrilla commander giving a gun to a pacifist and a democrat. They had used it recently when Castro made an extended tour of the country and had fired at targets on Allende's family farm. Much to everyone's surprise, apart from his own, the Chilean president proved to be the better shot. As a young boy Allende had enjoyed hunting game on the property and his marksmanship had not deserted him.

At 7:20am the first group leaves Tomás Moro. Four bullet

proof Fiat 125s escort the presidential car. In one of the vehicles José Huenchullán, the young GAP who spent the night on the roof, is sitting next to his friend Cuico. The youths had been relieved of their guard duty shortly before dawn, but were too excited to sleep and had spent their time oiling and checking their weapons and playing cards.

Huenchullán is looking out of the car window at the houses and gardens flashing past. It seems as though he is inhabiting a dream, or as if he has taken some hallucinogenic drug. The images rush by in a dizzying array, like a carousel at a fair. Even when he closes his eyes, the colours are astonishingly bright. Around him he can hear voices and conversation, but they are faint and distracted, ambient music to the picture show playing in his head.

The motorcade crosses the Puente Avenida Kennedy and turns into Avenida Santa Maria, which runs parallel to the Mapocho River. Huenchullán reaches into his jacket and takes out a packet of cigarettes. He lights one and turns to look out of the window and watches as the snow-filled waters tumble over the grey rocks.

A few minutes later the presidential group arrives at the Moneda. The eighteenth century government building is ringed by carabineros and armoured vehicles. There are tanks on the lawn. But for the moment these forces are loyal. The group leave the Fiats inside the presidential garage in the adjacent street of Morandé and enter the palace through a side entrance in the same street. Once inside the GAP and the presidential guard, a select group of carabineros chosen both for their height and their physical strength, are organised into defensive teams. A small party of GAP remains with the president for his own personal protection.

Allende goes straight to his office on the first floor and sits down behind the large mahogany desk. The GAP are left by the door and are given strict instructions not to admit any official member of the armed forces. It is a popular order, as there is considerable animosity between the irregular corps and the military. The existence of the GAP has broken a century old tradition, in which the protection of the president had been the exclusive preserve of the regulars. By having the GAP it seemed as though Allende could not fully trust his own forces as head of state. And yet Cardinal Raul Silva, the eminent Archbishop of Santiago, had recently implored the president to disband the group, saying its presence only served to antagonise the military and bolster the right wing.

"Salvador," he had told him. "If you rely on the GAP for your personal protection, you cannot expect any loyalty from the military."

The cardinal's words now seem prophetic.

*

In the quarters of the palace guard on the ground floor of the Moneda, José Sepulveda picks up the phone and calls Urrutia's office at their HQ in the General Directorate, situated in the Norambuena building opposite. He tells his subordinate to come to the palace and to bring "anyone else who is still loyal."

Urrutia gathers three other generals and asks them to accompany him to the Moneda. The group leave the building, cross the Plaza de la Libertad and enter the palace by the Chancellery door.

*

The Presidential Secretary Osvaldo Puccio is in his car on the way to the palace, having been alerted by a phone call from the Moneda. The minister is being taken by his twenty-year-old son, also called Osvaldo, because he has a heart condition and has been forbidden to drive on doctors' orders. As they approach the building, his son sees a newspaper kiosk on the corner of Teatinos and Huérfanos. The front page of the dailies are displayed. The radical left-wing newspaper El Siglo's headline declares: 'Everyone To Battle Stations!'

Seeing this the boy turns to his father.

"Dad, the shit is going to be immense if the Communist Party are using this sort of language."

Puccio knows what he means. The Communists are one of the more moderate parties on the left, despite their name. Now they too were calling for armed resistance. As the car turns towards the presidential palace, they see scores of carabineros and tanks.

"Well, that's something," says the Presidential Secretary, "at least we have friendly *pacos*."

His son parks the car and they walk towards the Moneda and enter the building by the door on 80 Morandé. The palace is seething with activity. The GAP dash to and fro, setting up firing positions and blockading windows as various staff flit about. Father and son go upstairs to the presidential offices. They enter Allende's own suite and he gets up from his desk and greets them cheerfully.

"You here too," he says and pats the boy's shoulder.

"Wouldn't miss it for the world Comrade President."

"Good lad!"

Allende then addresses his chief of staff.

"Call Orlando and tell him to come here immediately. I asked him to go to the MOD, so he might be there. But try his home first."

Puccio and son enter his office and the minister goes to a phone and dials the number of Letelier's house. Isabel answers and says that her husband has already left for the ministry. He then calls the MOD and someone picks up the receiver, listens and puts it down without answering. When Puccio tries again he finds the line is dead. The minister returns to the presidential office.

"It doesn't look good," he tells Allende. "Orlando's wife says he left for the ministry, but when I phoned there was no reply from his office. I tried again, but the line was cut."

The president looks grave. He knows what has happened. His defence minister has been arrested.

A few minutes later Olivares tries to contact General Brady of the Santiago garrison, who has not called back. But he too finds the line has been cut. He calls the MOD and speaks to Admiral Carvajal, who explains the telephone lines to the garrison have been cut, so that Brady can work in peace. The television chief puts the phone down in disgust and turns to Allende.

"Carvajal's full of shit!"

"Tell me about it."

The president realises that of the four branches of the armed forces, only the carabineros appear to be loyal and even then he does not know if it is all, or just part of the force. The men surrounding the palace still obey orders from Sepulveda and Allende hopes the corps within Santiago at least, will remain under the general's command. In total they number some fifty-thousand and are spread the length and breadth of the country. Virtually every *pueblo* has a carabinero post and each is well armed. The corps traditionally recruited from the peasantry and the poorer city dwellers. It is upon this working class background that the president has pinned his hopes. With the carabineros on their side, Popular Unity stood a chance of holding out and forcing a negotiation.

Allende decides it is time to address the nation and let the people know that he is still their president. He picks up a pen and quickly writes a speech, scribbling the words down on a notepad. When he has finished he asks an aide to connect him to the OIR. There is a microphone on his desk, it merely has to be patched to the circuit in the newsroom. Although 'Operation Silence' has effectively cut off all sources of communication two pro-government stations, Radio Candelaria and Radio Magallanes, are still able to broadcast intermittently. The president gathers his sheaf of papers and hushes the room. He talks slowly into the microphone.

This is the President of the Republic. I speak to you from La Moneda Palace. We have confirmed earlier news that a sector of the navy has occupied the city of Valparaíso; the city is now isolated from the rest of the country. This is a revolt against the government and its legitimate authority, protected by law and by the will of the citizens of Chile. Under these circumstances, I call upon you workers to mobilise and occupy your factories and labour posts, but also to keep calm and act with serenity. Up to this moment the movement of troops in the city of Santiago appears normal and the regiment's commander has informed me that the military will stay in their quarters. Whatever the case may be, I will remain in the presidential palace, where I am now, ready to defend the government that I represent in accordance with the people's mandate. I ask the workers to remain vigilant, to follow these events, and to avoid being provoked. Let us see first how the soldiers of Chile respond. They have sworn to protect the government that is the expression of the will of the people and should follow the tradition of loyalty that has given such high standing and prestige to Chile and its armed forces. In these circumstances, I am certain that the soldiers will know what their obligations are and how to comply with them. But whatever the case, the people, and most of all the workers, must act and mobilise the workplace, attentive to the call and to the instructions that their Comrade President may give them.

*

On the 9th floor of the Norambuena building, which is serving as the rebels communications centre, General Arturo Yovane is looking out of the window. From here he has a good view of the Moneda and the tanks and soldiers surrounding it. He is irritated that neither Sepulveda, nor Urrutia have been arrested. Yovane had sent two colonels to detain them that morning. The officers had gone to their apartments in the General Directorate, but the officers had already been alerted and were now in the Moneda.

As Yovane is gazing out of the window General César Mendoza enters the room. The senior rebel carabinero is out of breath and worried.

"What's happening Yovane? It's full of tanks and carabineros around the Moneda. Why haven't they withdrawn?"

"Calm down. It's all under control."

Yovane picks up a two-way radio and calls the officer below to demonstrate the unit's loyalty to their new commander, who is with him. The officer complies and at a given order every man turns and stands to attention, facing the Norambuena building.

"See?" says Yovane.

Mendoza grins and his former good humour returns. Not only is the coup going like clockwork, it is also his birthday. The general is a noted horseman and won a silver medal at the 1952 Helsinki Olympics, as part of the national show jumping team. The carabinero chief is small and dark-haired, with a trim military moustache. He is taciturn by nature and rarely, if ever, made public pronouncements. When asked why he replies in his soft, lisping voice: "he who speaks little, makes few mistakes."

*

Edgardo Enríquez is in his kitchen, making himself a cup of tea. He prefers it strong and, unusually for a Latin, also with milk. "Just like the Queen," the noted anglophile often joked. He is sixty-one and Minister of Education. Previously he had served in the navy as a medical doctor and had reached the rank of captain. He would have been promoted to admiral, but asked to leave the service, so that he could be become rector of the University of Concepción. He had also had several clashes with the Christian Democrat president Eduardo Frei, which prompted his retirement. He lives with his wife Raquel in an apartment in Providencia, a pleasant suburb that borders the more exclusive area of Las Condes. The streets are wide and shaded by plane trees, date palms and jacarandas.

A kind and courteous man, the minister is tall, white-haired and sports a fine moustache. He has the classic looks of an ageing matinee idol and the charm and manners to match. Enríquez and his wife have four children. Two of them, Miguel and Edgardo, are leaders of the revolutionary movement MIR. While the minister is happy to recognise his boys' youthful idealism, he is also anxious about their activities. He knows they will feature prominently on any military 'wanted' list. He also knows that if there is a coup, his sons will be in the thick of it.

Enríquez takes his cup of tea and goes to his study to work. He is drafting a speech which he is due to give that afternoon in the Municipal Theatre, as part of the National Teachers' Day celebrations. Enríquez, in his capacity as minister, will also be handing out diplomas to those who have completed more than thirty years service. The minister works diligently on his draft looking up a quotation here, correcting a point there, in between sips of tea.

At 8:00am the phone rings. It is in the hall and he goes to answer it.

"The armed forces have rebelled," says a friend. "Come to my house and I'll hide you."

"Thanks, but I must go to the Moneda. I must be with the president."

Enríquez feels an extraordinary sense of sadness and loss. The storm clouds, which have been gathering for weeks, now seemed to break about his head in a deluge. There would be no speeches in the Municipal Theatre that afternoon. He goes into the bedroom and tells his wife what has happened.

"I'm going to the Moneda."

"Edgardo are you nuts?"

"Quite possibly. But don't tell the president, or he'll sack me."

Raquel shakes her head. Her husband's sense of humour has always been on the bleak side.

"I'll call you when I get to the palace," he says from the hall as he puts on his coat.

In the bedroom Raquel hears the front door bang and her husband's footsteps descending the stairs. The lift has been out of order for weeks and no one had come to fix it.

The Moneda is little more than a kilometre away and the minister often walked. It was a pleasant stroll and he enjoyed the exercise. But his chauffeur is already there with his official car and drives him the short distance and a few minutes later, he steps inside the palace.

The minister is amazed to see the GAP in firing positions and scores of people going this way and that. The situation appears far more serious than the Tancazo. He ascends the marble staircase to the presidential offices on the first floor.

Allende is on the phone to his ambassador in Buenos Aires. Enriquez hears the president's part of the conversation.

"Yes, there's been an uprising..."

"No. No, everyone's disloyal. I've got many friends with me here and I also have your loyalty and your friendship. But that's it..."

"I'm going to die at my desk. Give my love to Panchita. 'Bye."

The president sees Enriquez and rises to greet him. They are good friends, although not so close that he drops the formal *usted*. Allende is pleased the minister has turned up, but does not want him in the Moneda. Although Enríquez is a former naval officer, he is not the type of person to defend the palace and his responsibilities lie elsewhere.

"Edgardo, I'm going to put out some orders. But you

should go to your ministry because your staff, and there are three hundred of them, refuse to be dismissed. They're loyal like you. Please tell these comrades that I thank them very much, but they must not run unnecessary risks. They must go home. They'll listen to you, if not to me," and the president smiles.

"Very well Comrade President. I'll tell them."

Allende looks at his minister. He is a good man, who has served his country honourably and selflessly.

"Thanks Edgardo. Give my regards to Raquel."

"I will," and Enríquez turns to go.

As he leaves the office the minister realises that he may never see the president again.

At the head of the main staircase a broad-shouldered man with an unruly mop of dark hair is working the bolt of a Bren gun, resting the stock on the marble step. He is in the process of arming it and his hands are covered in oil. It is Perro Olivares. He senses someone else's presence, looks up and grins.

"Hey Edgardo. You here too?"

"So it seems."

"Come to join the fun?"

The minister smiles wanly.

"Journalists arming machine guns. Now I know we're really on our own."

"Why don't you stay and fight?"

"The president has asked me to go to my ministry."

"In that case you'd better do as he says. Each man to his post!"

"Being seeing you Augusto."

"You too comrade. And keep your head down!"

Enríquez nods sagely and descends the marble stairs. He walks through the Cannons' Patio and leaves by the main door. He continues up Avenida Moneda and is pursued by a television crew. He pretends not to notice and carries on walking. But the news team follow and soon catch up.

"Minister," says the reporter, somewhat out of breath, "will the president resign?"

"I very much doubt it."

"Why not?"

"Because," Enríquez says, finally turning and facing his pursuer, "he is the elected president of Chile. And he has to maintain the constitution in order to be faithful to his mandate."

The minister walks on, leaving the television crew behind. He then crosses the road and enters his own ministry building.

*

Shortly after Enríquez has left, other government officials arrive. Soon the presidential office is filled with people and the buzz of animated conversations. Some think the uprising is just another Tancazo and everything will blow over. Others are less sanguine and urge the president to call on the people to resist, or else all will be lost.

The president himself is armed and helmeted. Allende's outward enthusiasm and bonhomie belie the fact he is furious not a single head of Popular Unity has turned up. He presumes they are either cowering at home, or have already made their way to sympathetic embassies. Inwardly he consoles himself that it is only in times of trial, that a man discovers who his friends are.

Several such people have just arrived. Among them are the former Director of Investigations Eduardo 'Coco' Paredes, the psychiatrist Enrique Paris, who is the president's personal physician and an authority on matters of education and science, and Dr Jorge Klein, a prominent Socialist. All of them are valued friends and advisers, even if they do not have actual portfolios.

Allende's voice cuts through the general conversation, as he calls for quiet. He stands in the middle of the room, a tin helmet on his head and an AK47 in his hand. There can be no doubt the president is prepared for war.

"Comrades, first of all thank you for coming. There are some of you whom, quite frankly, I didn't expect to see and there are others who should be here, but who are not. It hardly matters now. What is important is that you must stay only because you want to. Not because you think you have to. I don't want anyone here out of some misplaced sense of loyalty. You all have families. They must be your first responsibility. It's better to leave now while you still can, because later you may not be able to."

The president observes them all, waiting to see who will shrink at his words. Even the most optimistic are left in no doubt as to the gravity of the crisis. A hush envelops the room in a mute mist. No one utters a word. All is still. Outside the streets are also silent. Finally, Paredes breaks the spell.

"Salvador," he says. "We did not come only to leave again. We're here to stay."

"Thank you Coco. I knew you wouldn't let me down."

Allende addresses the room again.

"OK. You all have jobs to do. Go back to your work places and await further instructions."

The president leaves and makes a tour of the palace, accompanied by his bodyguard and coterie of friends as well as his daughters Isabel and Beatriz, known as 'Tati', who have just arrived. They are committed members of Popular Unity and he has been unable to persuade them to seek safety elsewhere. He has told his other daughter Carmen Paz to seek sanctuary with her family at the Mexican Embassy.

Allende surveys the whole of the first floor, checking the firing positions of the defenders and bolstering their morale with his general air of unflappability. The president then goes downstairs and visits the medical unit, which consists of eight doctors. They are hanging around the surgery not doing much and look a little forlorn.

"It seems like you might have some work to do today comrades," he says.

The doctors nod ruefully and after a few further pleasantries, the president continues on his rounds.

*

In the buildings surrounding the Moneda there is a great deal of activity. Snipers loyal to Popular Unity have taken up firing positions at the State and Central bank, the newspaper La Nación, the Ministry of Public Works and also at the Social Security Administration. From these vantage points they have a good field of fire across the two squares: the Plaza de la Libertad and the Plaza de la Constitution, which flank the palace. The snipers have taken up their positions in response to the Major Emergency Alert broadcast by Radio Magallanes, one of only two pro government radio stations still on air, because their mobile broadcast units have so far managed to escape detection.

*

Detective Quintin Romero is sitting on the Pila-Recoleta bus, as it jolts along the potholed roads towards the city centre. The policeman urges the antiquated vehicle on, inwardly cursing each time it gets held up in traffic. He is tense. It is not from fear, but frustration. He presumes the other detectives are already at the Moneda. Romero only learned about the coup from his wife, who heard it on the radio. She alerted her husband who immediately left for the palace. There was no phone in their house and no one had been able to get hold of him.

The Romeros live in Emiliana Zapata, a street situated at the entrance of Recoleta in Conchalí. It is a very different area from the leafy suburbs of Providencia or Las Condes. Here the houses are low built and made from mud bricks and painted in pastel shades of pink, blue and green. The roofs are fashioned from sheets of corrugated iron and weighted with stones, to protect against the winter storms. The occupants come from the lower middle classes: bank clerks, shopkeepers and suchlike. Typical of this class the houses are scrupulously kept, with lace curtains in the windows, scrubbed doorsteps and often a cat or a dog dozing on the patio. Geraniums and succulents cascade from terracotta pots and bougainvilleas festoon the walls and gates, adding a dash of colour to an otherwise drab and treeless neighbourhood.

Romero is the archetypal policeman. He walks with his chest out, chin up and shoulders square. In his face there is no hint of doubt or hesitation. His gaze is direct and unblinking. The detective looks and is tough. Romero is proud to be one of the president's official bodyguards. He imagines, like many who work with Allende, that there is a unique bond between them: one of protector and protected, their destinies as integrated as the pieces on a chessboard. The president and detective are like the king and the knight. And like the horseman, Romero is quite prepared to sacrifice himself in order to save his monarch.

The bus stops at Teatinos just before the palace and the detective alights. There are soldiers everywhere. Romero trots along the street towards the Moneda. He checks the 9mm Browning automatic in his shoulder holster and pats his jacket pocket which has two magazines, one more than usual. In another pocket he also has a Swiss Army penknife. It was a Christmas present from the president. Allende had given one to all the detectives. Romero was fond of it and used it for peeling oranges, which he picked from the trees in one of the palace patios.

The soldiers look at the detective as he passes, but do not try to stop him. Moments later Romero reaches the main entrance of the palace and steps inside.

Despite his concern, the detective is not in fact late. His

commander Deputy Inspector Juan Seoane has yet to arrive. Romero sees his fellow policemen standing in the Cannons' Patio and goes to join them, as they wait for their superior. The men respect Seoane, who is one of the most popular officers in the force. None of them ever questioned an order from him, because he was always scrupulous in dealing with his subordinates. He eschewed favouritism, an important quality in an officer and always appreciated by their men. Seoane was also patient, he never lost his temper or seemed exasperated. Indeed, there was a certain quality about the inspector, which made him stand out from other people. Although no one knew quite what it was. He was conscientious and intelligent it was true, but so were many in the service. The difference was that Seoane seemed to be entirely selfless, as though the wellbeing of his colleagues and indeed the public, were far more important than his own. His men do not know it, but had the inspector not met the woman who became his wife, he would have become a priest.

*

Seoane is in a service Chevrolet rapidly approaching the Moneda. He is late because he had to make a detour to pick up three other colleagues. Approaching the junction of Teatinos and Huérfanos, the inspector's vehicle is forced to halt by a blockade across the street. But the carabineros guarding it recognise the driver and with a smile, wave him through. He continues down Morandé and seeing the side door in the palace is open he parks opposite, next to the Ministry of Public Works. He and his companions quickly leave the vehicle and enter the Moneda.

At the foot of the main staircase the inspector sees the president wearing a tin helmet and clutching an automatic, surrounded by an armed entourage including several GAP. He is momentarily stunned. It is only then that he realises there is a war going on.

"Hi Seoane. Good to see you," says Coco Paredes, his former chief, extending a hand. "Your men are waiting in the Cannons' Patio."

The inspector thanks him and goes off to find them. The detectives are standing in one corner, chatting and smoking cigarettes, which they put out as soon as they see him coming. Seoane pretends not to notice and tells them that as yet he has no orders, but they should join the GAP in their firing positions until further notice. The inspector knows their weapons are no defence against tanks, but does not mention this.

"It is your duty," he says, "to defend the president whatever the circumstances. Even if it means sacrificing your lives."

After dismissing them Seoane goes to the Investigations Office on the ground floor, which the detectives shared with the palace guard. Inside, he picks up the two-way microphone on the desk and speaks to his superior Alfredo Joignant, the head of the Investigations Service, who is in his office in the General Prefecture, situated in the Intendancy across the road.

"Sir," he says. "We're all here. There are eighteen of us in all. I would like to know what the situation is and what our orders are."

"The armed forces have rebelled and are operating under a junta led by Pinochet, Merino, Leigh and Mendoza."

Seoane is surprised by one name in particular.

"Did you say Pinochet?"

"Yes…unfortunately not as loyal as he claimed. But you must remain with your president in defence of the Moneda. Stay with the president and defend the palace. These are my instructions."

"Roger and out," and Seoane switches off the microphone.

*

The last senior government official to arrive at the palace is the former Minister of Defence José Tohá. Seeing him a flock of journalists quickly surround the politician. Tohá is a tall, dark, angular man who sports a neat Van Dyke beard and has a patrician air. With his height and dapper appearance he looks like a heron surrounded by a heaving mass of common gulls, all squawking and flapping and shoving.

"Will the president resign," they chorus, thrusting their microphones beneath the former minister's aquiline nose. Tohá surveys them all and not without a little disdain.

In the past few weeks much of the media have levelled hysterical accusations against the Popular Unity government, calling it anti-democratic and declaring that Chile was set to become another Cuba. They had been neither ethical, nor independent, merely serving as mouthpieces for the military and the right wing.

"President Allende will remain in the Moneda. I have come to take my place with my comrade Salvador. We will not hand over our mandate until elections, which are due on 3rd November 1976."

The former minister moves to pass through the journalists. There is a flurry of notebooks, microphones and more shouting. Tohá magisterially raises his hand. The press pack falls silent, expecting him to say something else, but he simply passes through them and without another word, enters the palace.

*

On the ground floor in the OIR, the staff are gathering as much detail about the coup as they can, making calls and monitoring the two remaining loyalist radio stations. Largo Farías is talking to Veronica Ahumada, one of the journalists in the bureau. She is only twenty-three and is known affectionately as 'La Moneda Chica' or 'Chica' for short.

The journalist is attractive with lustrous eyes, long dark hair and a wide mouth, which she has accentuated with a swipe of red lipstick.

Unsurprisingly, all the men in the palace are in love with her. Ahumada has been working for the president since 1970, when she graduated in journalism from the University of Chile. She shares her office with the Presidential Press Secretary Carlos 'Negro' Jorquera and Olivares.

The OIR chief and his colleague are drinking coffee and smoking cigarettes. He looks on in admiration. He cannot help wondering why some women seem even more attractive when they smoke. Largo Farías watches as the cigarette parts her rouged lips, the mouth opening slightly as a thin trail of smoke wafts out. He observes all this while continuing their conversation, looking into Ahumada's sloe-coloured eyes.

A sudden announcement over the radio startles everyone in the office and cuts through the hubbub of conversation. It is a proclamation from the junta.

In view of the extremely serious social and moral crisis through which this country is passing, the inefficiency of the government in controlling chaos and the steady increase of paramilitary groups trained by the parties of Popular Unity, which will inevitably bring the people of Chile to civil war, the armed forces and the carabineros have decided:

First, the President of the Republic must immediately release all his powers to the armed forces and the carabineros of Chile.

Second, the armed forces and the carabineros are united in their efforts to initiate the historical and responsible mission to fight for the freedom of the country and prevent it from falling under the Marxist yoke and to ensure the restoration of order.

Third, the workers of Chile can be assured that the economic and social achievements which have been reached to date, will not undergo any fundamental change.

Fourth, the press, radio stations and television channels serving Popular Unity must suspend their functions as news media forthwith- otherwise they shall be punished.

Fifth, the people of Santiago must remain in their homes in order to avid becoming victims.

Signed by Augusto Pinochet, José Merino, Gustavo Leigh and César Mendoza.

*

In his office Allende listens to the pronouncement from a speaker connected to the OIR, as he slowly turns a pen in the fingers of his right hand. It is the first official confirmation of the coup. The president curses softly when he hears Pinochet's name. So, the head of the army had indeed turned. Allende wonders when it happened and assumes that it must have been over the weekend. This single act of treachery angers the president more than anything else.

After the announcement finishes, Allende calls the OIR on the intercom and tells them he wished to respond. A few minutes later the president gives his answer to the junta's proclamation. He speaks calmly and without notes. The broadcast is disjointed and interrupted by static as the military try and jam the signal.

The situation is now critical. We face a coup d'état launched by the majority of the armed forces...I have not sought this. I am not a martyr. I have struggled for social justice and to do the job that the people asked me to do... But let them understand this very well, those who wish to roll history back and disavow the will of the majority of the people in this country... I have no other alternative. Only with bullets will they stop me from realising the project of the people of Chile...I shall not give up. But if I die, the people will keep going, with the only difference that perhaps things will get a lot harder, a lot more violent... I will remain in La Moneda. I intend to resist with what I have, even at the cost of my life…

*

Neruda listens to the president's address in his house on Isla Negra, as the sea crashes onto the beach below. They have been friends for many years and the Nobel laureate was recently Chile's ambassador to France, but returned through ill health. Now he is dying of cancer. A veteran of the Spanish Civil War, Neruda is once again witnessing the forces of oppression triumph over the popular will. But he never thought it could happen in his own country. The poet's political sympathies are well known and because of this the military have taken precautions. A road block has been set up and no one has been allowed either in or out. Neruda and his wife Matilde are alone and isolated.

The poet sits at his desk by the window, a poncho made from alpaca wool wrapped around his shoulders and watches as the grey sea swells beneath a greyer sky. He sips the herbal tea *mate* through a silver straw and enjoys its mild aroma. He can hear the ceaseless scrape of the surf, the melancholic sigh of tide upon shore. Neruda is at peace. He possesses the calm self-awareness of the dying, who know there is no God and that death is merely life's last disappointment.

The radio continues to broadcast. Beyond the disembodied voice the sound of waves mingles with the sharp cry of gulls, as they wheel and tack above the ocean. The poet sits there thinking about his old friend Salvador and of the times they spent together, discussing their dreams for a socialist Chile which would be truly just and democratic. Now such dreams were dust.

The poet sighs, or at least thinks he has. It is difficult to know whether the small involuntary gasp comes from a deeper, inner pain, or from the relentless surf outside, for both seem to echo the other. He takes another sip of *mate*. Open on his desk are his memoirs. He thought he had finished them, but this morning he has been adding a postscript. Neruda has said it all before in his poetry, but now he finds that he is saying it again.

> *Death lies in our cots:*
> *in the lazy mattresses, the black blankets,*
> *lives at full stretch and suddenly blows,*
> *blows sound unknown filling out the sheets*
> *and there are beds sailing into a harbour*
> *where death is waiting, dressed as an admiral.*

*

At Tomás Moro the remaining GAP keep a close watch on movements in the surrounding streets and gardens. The road is blocked by military vehicles and soldiers are deployed at either end. So far no shots have been exchanged between the opposing forces: both groups content, for the time being at least, to observe each other through binoculars. The twenty-five GAP have been deployed in separate sections, each with a commander and man the same firing zones established the night before.

Hortensia is in the kitchen, busying herself making coffee for the bodyguard, whose thirst seems to be insatiable. The doorbell rings and a GAP answers it. He returns to say that Miria Contreras, otherwise known as 'La Payita', the president's personal secretary, has arrived along with her two sons. Hortensia thanks him, wipes her hands on a cloth and goes to greet them. La Payita and her husband are old family friends and live next door. It is a curious relationship since everyone knows that Miria Contreras is also the president's mistress. But both families appear to be reconciled to this state of affairs and continue with their daily lives, as though nothing has happened. In the hall the women embrace and the president's wife also kisses the boys, who are both in their teens. Hortensia tells La Payita that her husband has already left for the Moneda.

"Why don't you stay here with me?"

The president's secretary smiles.

"Thank you. But Salvador will be expecting me at the palace. I'll leave Max here to protect you."

Max is fifteen and the younger of the two boys and when his mother says this, he puts an arm affectionately around Hortensia.

"Don't worry aunty," he says. "I'll take care of you."

The president's wife beams and gives him a hug. It is good in times like these to have such friends. La Payita looks at Enrique, who is three years older than his brother.

"As for you young man, you can come with me," and the president's secretary thanks the first lady and prepares to leave.

Hortensia and the secretary's younger son wave them off from the porch and watch as the car disappears down the street.

Max then goes and joins the GAP, who take him under their wing and teach him how to present arms and strip an AK47. The president's wife returns to the kitchen and listens to the radio for further news. The phone rings and she answers it. Hortensia is relieved to hear her husband's voice.

"The navy has rebelled and the city if full of tanks and soldiers. I don't know how long we can hold out. But you must stay at home and please Tencha...keep calm."

"I'll try..."

"Tati and Isabel are with me. They're fine. How are things?"

"I'm OK. La Payita was here, but she left for the Moneda."

"Couldn't you make her stay?"

"No. She insisted on going. Enrique is with her and Max is here."

"Fine, I'll tell her to go home as soon as she arrives. Please don't worry. A kiss..." and Allende finishes the call.

The president's wife returns to the kitchen and sits at the table. She is trying her best to stay calm, but finds it almost impossible. Her nerves have been shredded by the previous weeks and she fears for her husband and daughters. It is fortunate for Hortensia's state of mind that she is unaware the air force chief General Gustavo Leigh, has just sent the following terse message to the MOD.

We bomb the Moneda at eleven.

*

Outside the presidential palace the GAP who went to fetch further arms and ammunition appear, but are immediately arrested by the carabineros. With them are La Payita and her son. They were unlucky enough to arrive at the same time and the boy is also detained. The president's secretary berates the soldiers, as they escort Enrique along with the GAP into the presidential garage.

"Leave him alone! Assholes! Get your hands off my son! He's just a kid!"

The carabineros ignore her and once inside the garage, they try and arrest her too. But the formidable La Payita will have none of it. She kicks and claws her way out of their clutches and warns that there will be "hell to pay" if they so much as touch a hair on her son's head. She demands to use the phone and calls the president, who tells her to enter the palace by the main door and not by 80 Morandé.

"The soldiers have arrested Enrique!" she wails.

There is little the president can do, although he assures her otherwise.

La Payita walks round to the main entrance, where she is joined by Allende's naval attaché Captain Jorge Grez, who has also just arrived. He greets her cordially and is given a withering look in return.

"It's all your fault!" she says.

Inside the palace La Payita catches sight of Juan Seoane and takes him to one side, imploring the inspector to do something about her son. He tells her it would be better if she asked one of the generals, as he doubts he is senior enough to make any difference. Distraught, the president's secretary sees Jorge Urrutia and begs him to secure her son's release.

"I'll see what I can do," he says.

The general goes to the Investigations Office and makes some calls. A few minutes later he emerges and sees La Payita has not moved, her expression caught amid the twin horns of hope and despair.

"I'm sorry. The carabineros refuse to obey my orders. Mendoza has everything in hand."

When she hears this La Payita breaks down and grasps the general, sobbing into his tunic.

Urrutia does his best to calm her. He looks at Seoane and motions for him to come forward. The inspector takes hold of the president's weeping secretary and tries to comfort her. The general then goes off to the Oranges' Patio, where he can hear Sepulveda encouraging his men. He steps out into the paved courtyard, with its cluster of gnarled orange trees and takes his superior to one side.

"Sepa," he says. "Why don't you have a word with the president? You're the DG. He trusts you. Why don't you tell him to compromise? Because there's no way we can win."

Sepulveda observes his subordinate.

"The president, more than anyone, intends to see out his mandate. He is not going to resign. You heard his broadcast didn't you?"

The Deputy Director of Carabineros nods.

"Well then?"

Urrutia looks at his colleague, but does not reply. He has his answer. His duty is to remain in the palace with his president.

*

Captain Grez ascends the main staircase to the presidential offices and finds Allende seated at his desk. He looks up and seeing his naval attaché quips:

"Once again, problems in your fleet captain!"

Allende is leafing through several sheets of paper, ready to make another broadcast to the nation. Magallanes is now the only pro-government radio station still on air and the president wants to make the most of the opportunity, before it too is silenced.

Grez is anxious to speak with his commander-in-chief on his own. But Allende is surrounded by his close advisers and the GAP and the aide realises he will have to wait for a more opportune moment. He looks across the room and sees the air force attaché Colonel Eduardo Sanchez and his military equivalent Commander Sergio Badiola. He goes over to them and his colleagues greet him with worried smiles.

Earlier that morning Sanchez had been instructed by Admiral Carvajal to try and persuade Allende to leave the Moneda, with the promise of safe conduct out of the country for both him and his immediate family. A DC-6 was on standby at the military airfield of Los Cerrillos, in the south of the city. The colonel had been told he would personally pilot the craft, either to Buenos Aires or La Paz.

As the president makes another broadcast, Sanchez informs Grez and Badiola about the plane. All three attachés agree the offer of safe conduct might be enough to convince Allende to leave, if only they can have a word with him in private. They look across at the helmeted president seated at his desk, flanked on either side by the GAP. Light falls through the French windows and illuminates the group, leaving the corners of the room in shadow like the chiaroscuro of an old master.

*

In the offices of the OIR, the staff are listening to another junta proclamation from Norambuena. Veronica Ahumada jots it all down in shorthand.

Citizens are hereby warned that any act of sabotage of national activity such as businesses, factories, or transportation facilities shall incur the most dramatic punishment possible at the place of occurrence and at the complete discretion of the local authorities. It is the duty of citizens to keep intact the wealth of the country by reporting to the police immediately, the names of all who paralyse production, or engage in labour activities of any sort whatsoever.

When the announcement has finished, Ahumada picks up her notebook and goes upstairs to the presidential offices. Allende is at his desk discussing tactics with his advisers. He glances up as the serious-faced young woman enters and cannot help a smile. Ahumada looks attractive even when she frowns. The journalist informs the president about the recent junta broadcast and then reads him her notes. Allende listens and tells her not to worry, he will be making another statement soon.

"You only have to say the word Comrade President," she says and with a swing of her hips, Ahumada turns and goes click-clacking out of the room.

As she departs one of the GAP standing by the windows calls out.

"Chief, the tanks and carabineros are withdrawing…"

Allende gets up and goes to see for himself. He looks out of the window and discovers the bodyguard is not exaggerating. All the armoured vehicles are pulling back.

"Cowards!"

The president had hoped that at least this force would remain loyal. Now he has nothing except the GAP, the detectives and the remaining palace guard. Angrily he summons Sepulveda.

The general arrives in his office and the president turns on him.

"What the hell's happening?"

"The carabineros are withdrawing Mr President."

"I'm not blind! I want to know why?"

"They're following orders."

"Whose?"

"Not mine sir."

"You're the DG aren't you? These are your men!"

"Mr President, I'm afraid they're following orders from Norambuena."

Allende swears furiously and dismisses the officer with a wave of his hand. He addresses those around him.

"OK. We're on our own now. Any ideas?"

There is a brief silence, then Paredes speaks.

"Salvador, why don't you make an announcement and get the people out onto the streets. Call on them to march on the Moneda. They will protect you if the carabineros can't, or won't."

Paris, Olivares and Klein are among those who agree with the former Director of Investigations. They are some of the most radical of the president's entourage and think it is time he faced down the military with the country's most valuable asset. Its population.

"Coco's right, the soldiers won't shoot unarmed civilians," says the television chief.

But not everyone agrees. Briones, Puccio and Tohá head the group of advisers who are strongly against the idea, which they believe will tip the country into civil war.

"If people march on the palace there could be a massacre. There's no guarantee the soldiers won't fire on them. If that happens there'll be a bloodbath," says the Minister of the Interior.

The opposing sides begin to bicker as they try and outflank each other, until Allende raises a hand and his voice silences them all.

"OK everyone…enough. I agree the people are my mandate. But no one can say for sure what the military will do. The soldiers could well fire on the crowd and if that happens, I shall be responsible for their deaths. As their president that is unacceptable. I shall ask the people to resist, but not to sacrifice themselves. We shall fight on. The longer we hold out, the more likely the military are to negotiate…"

A phone ringing on the desk interrupts the president. A GAP answers and informs him it is Admiral Carvajal. Allende indicates that he wished to talk with the rebel officer and the bodyguard hands him the receiver.

"Mr President?"

"Speaking."

"Carvajal here."

"What do you want?"

"Look, it's pointless resisting. Why don't you give up?"

"You vulture! You've been conspiring to do this for a long time!"

"Please Mr President, let's try and be civil. You will have to leave the palace sooner or later. Why waste life?"

"Waste life? You've got some nerve admiral!"

And Allende hands the phone back to the GAP, who terminates the call. Seeing this Captain Grez and his two colleagues, who have been standing by patiently all this time, approach their commander-in-chief.

"Mr President," says Grez, "can we have a word?"

"Of course captain, by all means."

"In private."

"Certainly. We'll go to my study."

The three attachés follow the president, along with a handful of GAP and enter. It is a small, neatly furnished room, which he used when he did not want to be disturbed. Allende often took siestas there on the sofa. Others also arrive and he turns and addresses them.

"Would you be so kind all of you as to leave?"

Everyone files out except for Paredes, who hesitates by the

door. The president looks at his friend and smiles.

"That includes you Coco."

The former Director of Investigations departs and Allende takes off his helmet, puts down his gun and sits at the bureau. Four members of the GAP stand behind him, their AK47s slung across their chests. The officers pull up chairs and sit facing the president. Allende removes his glasses, yawns and rubs his eyes before replacing them. He looks tired.

"Gentlemen?"

"Mr President, you must soften your attitude if you wish to live," says Grez, a note of exasperation in his voice. "How can you expect to hold out against the combined might of the armed forces?"

"Not for ever captain. But the longer we hold out, the better position we'll be in to negotiate."

"I don't think the junta wants to negotiate," says Badiola. "They're going to bomb the palace at eleven."

"So they say."

"I'm sure they mean it."

"Let them. The President of the Republic does not surrender."

"There is a plane, a DC-6, ready and waiting at Los Cerrillos," says Sanchez. "Admiral Carvajal has asked me to pilot it personally. He says you can take your family and whoever else you want with you."

Carvajal has not actually said this to Sanchez, he has told him only that Allende can leave with his immediate family. The junta have no intention of letting the president anywhere near the plane, it is simply a means of getting him to surrender. Sanchez is unaware of this and genuinely believes in the junta's promise of safe conduct. The air force attaché added the part about an entourage, because he knows a DC-6 can seat up to fifty people and hopes that by broadening his remit, Allende might be persuaded to leave.

"Colonel, you can be quite certain I shall not flee my

country as a fugitive."

"Mr President at least consider it."

"I already have and the answer is 'no'. The only way they are going to get me to leave the palace is to carry me out... feet first."

There is a shocked silence as the three attachés consider Allende's words. They know that he is deadly serious. Then Sanchez speaks.

"Mr President...there is one other thing."

"What is it?"

"In spite of my personal loyalty to you as president and my oath to the constitution, I cannot fire on my own comrades-in-arms. I wish to be relieved of my duties."

The other attachés both murmur their assent.

"Very well gentlemen. I understand. You and your men are free to go."

They stand and Allende replaces his helmet and takes up his weapon and leads the way back to the presidential office. He tells everyone the officers are leaving and that no one should impede them. The attachés thank the president and say goodbye and descend the stairs. They go to their quarters and order the remaining personnel under their command to withdraw. The GAP take their weapons and the group leaves the palace by the door on 80 Morandé.

Sanchez, Badiola and Grez walk with their men across the Plaza de la Libertad towards the MOD on the other side. The square, which only half an hour before had been full of tanks and troops, is now deserted in anticipation of the bombing by the air force. Along the Alameda, which divides the plaza from the buildings on the other side, soldiers congregate in the depths of the earthworks. The trench is thirty metres deep and fifty metres wide and runs as far as Providencia. It is part of the new metro, which is under construction. But there are no workers today, only soldiers. The conscripts peer up at the attachés as they pass by on duckboards and ascend the steps of the MOD. Once inside the building they go straight to Admiral Carvajal's office on the fifth floor. They have already informed him they are on their way and the admiral is waiting for them.

"Well," Carvajal says when they arrive. "Is the president going to leave?"

"No sir," says Sanchez.

"Not even with the plane?"

"I'm afraid not admiral. He seems determined to stay on and fight."

Carvajal looks disappointed. It is exactly what he feared. For one thing it complicates matters and means the day will be more drawn out than the junta had anticipated. Also, he does not want the air force to bomb the Moneda. He is particularly proud of the building and has been ever since he visited the palace on a school trip and imagined himself one day sitting behind the presidential desk.

"OK. What about the Moneda defences?"

"There are about fifty GAP, detectives and carabineros still inside. A few of the civilians are armed as well," says Badiola. "But it should be possible to storm the building after it has been bombed."

"What ordnance do they have?"

"As far as I could see mostly small arms and grenades. They may have one or two bazookas and a couple of heavy machine guns."

Carvajal thanks the attachés and dismisses them. He goes to his desk and decides to call the Moneda again. Perhaps the president has reconsidered the offer of the plane and changed his mind. It is worth a try. He picks up the phone and asks to be connected to the palace. He waits and hears it ring before the phone is answered. The voice on the other end says the president is making a tour of the building, but he will try and connect him. The admiral waits, the plastic cool against his ear.

Allende is in the surgery chatting with the doctors of the medical team, when a GAP tells him that Carvajal is on the line. The president goes to the phone and picks it up. The admiral sounds most conciliatory and repeats the offer of safe conduct for him and his family. Allende listens. When Carvajal has finished, the president gives him his answer.

"Stick it up your ass!"

He then replaces the receiver and continues chatting with the doctors, as though nothing has happened.

*

Allende returns to the presidential office to make his last statement to the nation. He sits helmeted at his desk, surrounded by his followers including his daughters Isabel and Beatriz, who have barely moved from his side all morning. There is an expectant hush in the room, as though everyone is aware of the dramatic and historic nature of the announcement. The president holds up the sheaves of paper that compose his speech and peers through his thick-framed spectacles, as he prepares to make what everyone knows must be his final broadcast. He sounds resolute, his voice grave.

My friends, this will probably be the last opportunity that I have to address you. The air force has already bombed the towers of Radio Portales and Radio Corporación. But my words are not spoken in bitterness, rather in disappointment. Let there be a moral judgement on those who have betrayed the oath they took as soldiers and commanders-in-chief: Admiral Merino, who has appointed himself commander-in-chief of the navy, Mr Mendoza, an abject general who only yesterday declared his loyalty to the government and who today has appointed himself Director General of the Carabineros.

In the face of these events, all that remains for me to say to the workers is: "I shall not surrender." Placed in a crucial moment of our history, I will pay with my life for the loyalty of the people. And I tell you that I am certain the seed which has been planted in the conscience of thousands and thousands of Chileans, shall not be uprooted. They are strong, they are all able to subdue us, but social processes cannot be detained by either crime or force. History is on our side and it is made by the people.

Workers of my country, I thank you for the loyalty you have always shown me, the confidence you have placed in a man who was a mere interpreter of your deep yearning for justice, who pledged his word to defend the constitution and the law and who has kept it. In these final hours before my voice is silenced, I want to make one point. It was the united reactionary forces of foreign capital and imperialism that created the climate for the army to break their tradition.

I wish to speak most of all to the modest women of our land, to the peasant women who believed in us, to the working women who wished to work more, to the mothers who knew of our concern for their children. I address the professionals of our country, who kept on working despite the sedition encouraged by professional colleges, elitist institutions which sought to defend the advantages a capitalist society grants them for its own ends.

I address the youths of Chile, those who sang, who gave their joy and fighting spirit to the struggle.

I address the men of Chile, the workers, the peasant, the intellectual, all of whom shall be persecuted. In our country fascism has been present for some time- evidenced in the terrorist actions which blew up bridges, cut railway lines, destroyed pipe lines, all done while those responsible remained silent. They were compromised and history shall judge them.

Radio Magallanes will surely soon be silenced, and the calm tone of my voice will no longer reach you. It does not matter. You shall continue to hear it. I shall always be with you, and you will remember me as a dignified man who was loyal to his country.

The people must defend themselves, but not sacrifice themselves. The people shall not let themselves be destroyed nor demolished, but they shall not let themselves be humiliated either.

Workers of my country, I believe in Chile and her destiny. Other men will survive this bitter and grey moment in which treason is trying to gain the upper hand. Just remember, sooner than you think avenues shall again be opened, down which free men shall march towards a better society.

'Long live Chile! Long live the people! Long live the workers!' These are my last words. I am convinced my sacrifice shall not be in vain. I am convinced that, at least, it shall serve as a moral judgement on the felony, cowardice and treason which lay waste our land.

*

At his rebel command headquarters in El Bosque, General Gustavo Leigh is listening to the president's broadcast. He shakes his head incredulously. The man was a romantic fool. On his desk is a model of a Hawk jet, which had been presented to him as a gift by a former British military attaché who had advised the Chilean government on the purchase of the aircraft. The general picks up the model and admires it and recalls a recent conversation he had with the president at the annual celebrations for Air Force day. Leigh took umbrage when his commander-in-chief made some disparaging remarks about his beloved Hawks during a fly past.

"Don't worry general," Allende shouted in his ear, as the jets hurtled overhead. "Next year I promise you'll have some proper planes, Russian MIGs, and not these pieces of junk!"

Leigh was affronted both by the comment about his air force's capability and by the offer of military hardware from a Communist country. The general replaces the model and smiles to himself.

"Now that quack will see just what these little jalopies can do!"

He leans forward and presses a button on the intercom. He wants to contact General Pinochet at his base in Peñalolén. To do this Leigh has to talk via the Military Academy, since a communications error means the two cannot speak directly. Each of Leigh's messages has to be retransmitted to the army commander via the academy and vice versa. The air force chief asks his aide to connect him to the military school. He is concerned about Radio Magallanes. The conversation with Pinochet is stilted, because of the delay in transmitting each message.

"Post 2 to Post 1 are you receiving?..."

"Post 1 copy, over..."

"The president has just made another statement..."

"I know. I heard," says Pinochet. "Our signals can't block it because there's a mobile unit out there somewhere. We've sent a search and destroy mission ... They're triangulating the signal ... When they find it they'll block it for sure ..."

"The sooner the better..."

"Couldn't agree more old boy ..."

"Copy, Post 2 over..."

"Post 1 roger and out ..."

*

At 10:00am gunfire erupts around the presidential palace. It is not known who started firing first, but both snipers and soldiers now actively engage each other. In the presidential offices everyone takes cover, although the shooting is not directed at the palace. Outside the troops come under concentrated fire from gunmen hidden in the surrounding buildings, including the Entel tower. From his vantage point on the roof of the MOD, General Palacios orders a tank to advance towards the building and fire several salvoes in retaliation. The air around the Moneda is filled with dust and the concussion of explosions.

*

In the Ministry of Education, Edgardo Enríquez is sitting at his desk, away from the window. He can hear the whine of bullets as they ricochet against the building's walls. The minister remains at his desk and continues working. There is a knock on his door and his secretary enters and tells him two employees would like to see him.

"Please show them in."

Enríquez is confronted by a pair of youths, who cannot be out of their teens. In spite of their age, there is a look of fierce intent about them.

"Comrade Director," says one. "We're members of MIR, like your sons. We wish to defend the ministry against any attack by the armed forces."

The minister nods calmly, as if he has been asked for no more than a request for annual leave.

"Gentlemen, your resolution is commendable. But how, may I ask, do you propose to defend the ministry?"

The youths proudly produce pistols from their jackets. They are 9mm Browning automatics. Enríquez says nothing and motions for them to come towards the window.

"Let me show you something and whatever you do, don't touch the blinds."

The boys go to the window and peek cautiously through the slats. The minister stands next to them. Outside scores of soldiers shelter behind barricades and tanks, firing up at snipers in the surrounding buildings.

"Now just what are your pea shooters going to do against that lot?"

The young paramilitaries say nothing and feel a little foolish. Enríquez takes them away from the window and out of the line of fire.

"I want you to empty your pistols' magazines and throw

the guns into the building's incinerator. You must empty the magazines first, or else the ammunition will go off. If the soldiers hear that, they'll think there are snipers in the ministry. And then we really will be in trouble."

"Yes Comrade Director. Sorry."

"Don't apologise. I commend you both for your fortitude and bravery."

The employees thank him and leave. After the youths have departed, Enríquez tells his secretary what has happened.

"That, surely, was the last audience in a democratic government until God knows when." He sighs wistfully. "Perhaps the youth of Chile can still save this country."

The secretary departs and shortly afterwards a fusillade of bullets shatters several windows in the ministry. Enríquez leaves his office and orders all his employees to quit their desks and to take cover in the corridors.

"Normally I would send you good people home. But I fear it's more dangerous outside than in."

The minister returns to his office and continues to sign papers. He will not be distracted from his work, like a captain who refuses to leave the bridge of his sinking ship. The papers he is signing are long service diplomas, which he was due to confer upon senior teachers that afternoon in the Municipal Theatre. On the back of each he writes: 'signed during the assault on the Moneda and the ministry by the armed forces.' Under this declaration he writes the date and his signature: Edgardo Enríquez F.

As he is signing these diplomas, a hail of bullets smashes the office windows. The shots whizz past the minister and strike the opposite wall with a resounding crack. He realises from the trajectory of the gunfire, that soldiers must have gained access to the building opposite. It is possible there are loyalist gunmen on the ministry roof. Enríquez realises he should call his wife and let her know what is happening.

"Hi, it's me. Fighting has broken out around the Moneda. Don't worry, I'm OK. Whatever you do don't go outside, it's dangerous."

"When are you coming home?"

"I'm not sure. The president has asked me to stay at the ministry. I'll call again soon."

"Please be careful…"

"I will. Love you, 'bye."

There is a knock on his door and Enríquez's secretary enters with a cup of coffee and some biscuits balanced on the saucer. The minister thanks her and takes the cup and forbids her to enter his office again.

"You must stay in the corridor with the others."

"But what about you?"

"I'm not in the line of fire, whereas the door is."

The secretary does not answer and departs with a worried look. Enríquez leans back in his chair and sips his coffee. He takes a biscuit from the saucer and munches it, listening to the sounds of gunfire reverberating in the plaza below.

*

At Los Cerrillos a dozen Hawker Hunters are lined up across the airfield. Painted slate grey these ground attack aircraft form the backbone of the Chilean air force. Two pilots in flying gear walk out across the asphalt and clamber into a pair of waiting Hawks, which have been fuelled and armed for their mission. The riggers strap the men into their seats and close the Perspex canopy over their heads. The pilots check the electronics and give a thumbs up and the ground crew descend their ladders and unclip them from the fuselage. The aircraft engines are engaged and put to half throttle, as a group of fellow officers stand at the edge of the runway. They had all drawn lots for the mission and each man wishes he were piloting the aircraft. A small thrill courses through them when they hear the scream of the jets' turbines and watch as the air quivers in their wake. The planes turn and taxi along the apron. With their low hanging wings and skinny legs they look like monstrous hornets, as they pause briefly on the runway. Then, with a final roar, the Hawks race across the asphalt and ascend into the air. The jets rise quickly into the cloudy sky and soon are no more than specks on the horizon. In less than a minute they will be over the Moneda.

*

In the heart of a forest overlooking the city, a platoon advances stealthily. Figures in olive green move silently through the eucalypts and pines, their boots treading warily upon the leafy floor. The air is cold and damp and there is a strong smell of resin. The officer gives a signal to halt. He has seen something and points due north.

Private Maruri cranes his neck and looks in the same direction, but trees and foliage obscure his view. To his right other soldiers have seen whatever it is their commander is pointing at and make their way towards him. Maruri follows, his heart pounding. The platoon congregate around the officer, who waits until everyone has assembled.

It is the same thin-faced lieutenant who led the patrol the night before, when they destroyed the facilities of Radio Nacional. After the raid the soldiers had returned to their barracks at the Tacna Regiment and were granted a few hours rest. Then at 7:30am Maruri's platoon were ordered to seek and destroy the mobile broadcast unit of Radio Magallanes. It is this vehicle which the officer has spied on an escarpment a hundred yards ahead. A signals unit has managed to trace the source of its emission to within a single square kilometre and for the past hour, Maruri and his comrades have been combing the coordinates on a map.

The lieutenant addresses his men, keeping his voice low. "We proceed as before and remember, keep your distance. There may be booby traps. When we get to within thirty metres of the vehicle, stop. I'll proceed and demand their surrender. They're sure to be armed, but they're wanted alive. So no shooting unless absolutely necessary. Is that clear?"

The soldiers nod dumbly.

"Any questions?" The officer observes his platoon, who are no more than boys. All solemnly shake their heads. "Right," he says. "Let's go!"

The lieutenant leads the way, his platoon strung out on either flank. Maruri stays close by. He feels safer that way. Talk of booby traps unnerves him and he thinks it is better to be near the officer, because the man is a professional and will be able to spot any danger before he can. If the private was anxious before they started, now he is terrified. Beneath his combat gear his body is drenched with sweat. He looks nervously about. The entire undergrowth seems to be wired. Every bush, every branch presaging death. The conscript walks grimly on, his face set with fear.

Something snaps beneath Maruri's foot and he freezes. Slowly, he raises his boot. It is only a twig. He swallows hard and continues, his heart fluttering up and down his rib cage like a trapped bird. The private grips his machine gun and mutters a constant mantra under his breath.

The officer raises an arm and the platoon halts. Maruri drops down to one knee, relieved he has made it this far without tripping a device and having his balls blown off. He pushes up the brim of his helmet and wipes his brow. He tries to spit and finds he has no saliva. But he does not dare release his grip on the weapon and reach for his water bottle. Beside him the lieutenant observes the white truck. A tall aerial disappears into the branches and on its roof a dish revolves.

The officer raises a megaphone to his mouth. His amplified voice sounds unduly loud in the stillness of the forest.

"This is the army.... You are completely surrounded! ... Come out with your hands up ... No one will be harmed!"

The soldiers crouch and wait. Nothing. The dish on top of the truck continues to revolve. No noise comes from the vehicle and the rear door remains firmly shut. A wind gently stirs the leaves and bushes. Everything is quiet. Above the canopy of trees, the sky is powder grey. The lieutenant watches. Maruri looks at him. Even he seems worried. This is hell. Screw their orders. They should start shooting and get it over with.

The officer raises the megaphone and repeats his message, his voice echoing among the trees.

Again they wait. Again there is no response. The lieutenant licks his lips and swears quietly. It is proving to be more difficult than he imagined. What if the men refuse to come out? Should he shoot at the truck? No. His orders are to take them alive. His platoon glance nervously at each other. The officer does not look at them and stares intently ahead. The truck is parked on a crest, the trees massive and silent around it. The lieutenant raises the megaphone again but before he can speak, the rear door of the vehicle swings open and three men emerge, their arms raised above their heads. They look about to see where the soldiers are.

"Turn around and put your hands against the sides of the truck!"

The men obey and the officer advances, holding the megaphone in one hand and his pistol in the other. Behind him the soldiers rise in a single khaki wave. Maruri can barely put one foot in front of the other, he is so scared. He is quaking all over like a horse in an abattoir. The safety catch of his machine gun is off, his finger poised upon the trigger. He does not trust these guys one bit. If one of them so much as farts, he is going to waste him.

The soldiers advance slowly towards the vehicle and its occupants. Suddenly a man trips and falls, discharging his weapon. Another soldier cries out in shock, as the ricochet hits him in the leg. Thinking it has come from the truck, he fires his machine gun at the vehicle before collapsing on the ground in agony. Everyone, including Maruri, starts shooting. He swears wildly as he does so, the sound of gunfire ringing in his ears.

The lieutenant is shouting, but in the confusion he has dropped his megaphone and his platoon cannot hear above the din. Maruri continues firing at the truck, his machine gun bucking in his hands as he empties an entire magazine. When it is spent he fumbles in his webbing for a fresh clip and only then does he hear the lieutenant.

"Cease fire for fuck's sake! Cease fire!"

The amplified words of the officer are well-timed and take immediate effect. The gunfire stops and the soldiers all look around. The men from the truck are nowhere to be seen. The lieutenant gets to his feet and with his pistol raised, runs towards the vehicle. Maruri follows him. He feels calmer now, relieved even. The shooting having expelled all his tension and fear.

The private reaches the truck and sees three men sprawled upon the ground. None of them move. Blood drips quick and dark upon the leaves. Maruri stands there transfixed. He has never seen a dead man before, let alone someone who has been shot. He is amazed at how still and lifeless they are. Their eyes stare blankly at the sky, their mouths agape. And the blood! There is so much of it.

IV
TO REMAIN IS TO DIE

General Jorge Urrutia is marshalling his men in the Cannons' Patio. With him is his adjutant Captain Espinoza. The officers look at the faces of the few carabineros that remain. It is plain the men do not want to be there. Their comrades have already deserted, obeying an order from General Yovane at Norambuena. These others remain simply out of a sense of loyalty to the Deputy Director. But they would rather he gave them the order to retire.

Urrutia has no intention of either leaving the Moneda, or dismissing these men. Instead, he wonders where the other three generals who arrived with him have gone. Neither can he find his chief José Maria Sepulveda.

"Come with me to the palace guard," Urrutia says to his aide. He then turns and addresses his men. "The rest of you wait here until I get back."

The general walks towards the main entrance. On his right is the guardroom. He looks inside, but the place is empty and he continues on towards the front, where some GAP are on duty at the great wooden door. Urrutia opens a smaller entrance in its side and looks out across the Plaza de la Constitution and sees about two hundred people cowering around the base of the La Nación building. They stare fearfully up at the sky, waiting for the planes to appear and the bombardment to begin. The staccato sound of small arms fire echoes across the square.

Urrutia closes the entrance and returns to the guardroom. A phone rings and he goes to answer it. He asks who is calling and the question is repeated to him and so the general gives his name and rank. On the other end is General Yovane.

"Still there Urrutia?"

"Seems like it."

"Your orders are to withdraw your men from the palace. The air force is going to bomb the Moneda."

"The only orders I obey are from the president," and Urrutia puts the phone down. As soon as he does so it starts to ring again. But he ignores it and leaves the room, the phone pealing plaintively behind him.

The general returns to the Cannons' Patio, along with Espinoza. Urrutia wonders what he should do and decides to inform Allende that most of the palace guard have left. He tells the remaining men to wait and he and his aide ascend the marble stairs to the presidential offices on the first floor. They find Allende at his desk, surrounded as always by his advisers and the GAP.

The group are discussing how long they can hold out and whether they can rely on the paramilitaries to come to their rescue. Spread out across the president's desk is a plan of the palace and next to it lies a map of the city. On one side is Allende's weapon. They are trying to work out from which direction a military assault is most likely, so that they can place defenders accordingly, since the palace area is large and the personnel few.

A shadow falls across the table and the president looks up and sees Urrutia and his adjutant before him.

"Ah. Just the fellow I wanted to see. General, how many of your men can we count on?"

The Deputy Director is momentarily struck dumb by the question. He does not know what to say because the entire palace guard, except for a handful of men, have disappeared. The president looks at him and is plainly waiting for answer. Urrutia realises he might as well tell the truth.

"Just me and Captain Espinoza. Other than that I'm not sure. There were some men in the Cannons' Patio."

"What do you mean were?"

"Mr President, most of the palace guard have left and the few that are here want to retire. I don't know what's going on at the Intendancy either. General Parada was there, but

I've heard nothing from him since I arrived."

Urrutia hesitates. He wants to say something else and is unsure the president will appreciate it. He looks across at the heavily armed bodyguard and back at his commander-in-chief.

"Mr President…"

"Yes?"

"Sir, the situation is extremely grave. The GAP must not open fire. If they don't shoot, the armed forces won't either. But one round from the palace and all hell will break loose."

"You seem remarkably sure about that general. Have you seen what's going on outside?"

"I know. But if the GAP start firing, it will only provoke an assault. If we hold our fire, there's still a chance to negotiate."

Urrutia waits, uncertain as to the president's reaction. The GAP look menacing. They are desperate to fight.

"You've a case general," Allende says and addresses his entourage. "Comrades, no one is to open fire unless I authorise it."

The president then picks up his weapon and the group leaves the room to make another tour of the building.

The general and his aide are left alone in the office. They exchange looks. Urrutia gives an expression which suggests they might as well follow and they wander out into the corridor. In the passage the officers see La Payita approach with a silver tray full of drinks, the glasses clinking together as she walks. She smiles radiantly.

"General, so nice to see you're still here. And you too captain. Please, have a drink," and she offers them the tray. The officers each take a glass and Allende's secretary beams as they raise their drinks. "Whisky for heroes!" she says and continues on her way, leaving a trail of perfume floating in her wake.

They watch her go, clutching the glasses in their hands. Neither feels remotely heroic.

The officers knock back their drinks and go downstairs to tell their men about the president's order prohibiting shooting without his authorisation. But when they enter the Cannons' Patio, they find it empty. The carabineros have all disappeared. Urrutia is surprised. Cowardice it seemed was contagious. The general goes to the main gate again, opens the side entrance a fraction and peers outside.

He sees an intense firefight between a tank and a group of government supporters holed up in the Hotel Carrera. Shell after shell explodes against the building and blocks of masonry tumble with a rush into the street below. The once carefully tended lawn has been churned into a muddy battlefield by the tracks of armoured vehicles. The air is choked with dust and echoes to the crash of explosions. Urrutia closes the door and realises he must speak with the president again. He walks across to the Oranges' Patio and finds him standing in the shadow of the Chancellery, on the north west side of the palace.

"Mr President," he says. "I've just had another look outside. The situation has deteriorated. There's a raging battle going on in the Plaza de la Constitución. With your permission I'd like to go to the Intendancy and see if any carabinero personnel are there or not, because there's no one here now except me and my adjutant."

The president looks at his loyal general.

"Sure, go. And if there are any carabineros left, tell them to come here. And if General Parada's there, tell him to come as well."

Allende departs and Urrutia watches him go. It is the last order he receives from the president.

*

Together the general and his aide make their way to the door on 80 Morandé.

"Right Espinoza," he says, when they reach the entrance.

"We'll go singly. I'll go first."

Urrutia reaches for the door handle. On the other side he can hear the irregular clatter of automatic weapons. He has never been under fire before. The general sees the medal ribbons on his tunic and realises that, for the first time in his life, he is about to earn them. He takes a deep breath, opens the door and rushes into the street. In front of him is a Sherman tank, the commander's head poking out of the turret.

"Lieutenant!" he shouts. "Cover me! I'm going to the General Prefecture!"

The tank commander takes the 50-calibre machine gun mounted on the turret and opens up, directing his fire at the Ministry of Public Works opposite. There is also shooting coming from the Workers' Insurance building on the other side of the Intendancy. The lieutenant traverses his weapon and begins to fire at that as well. Dust spurts in neat rows as bullets smash into stone walls. Plate glass windows shatter and fragments cascade in a long crystal stream into the street below.

Urrutia bows his head and sprints across Morandé towards the four-storey mansion on the other side, bullets pitting the air as he races up the steps. In the safety of the hallway, he stops to catch his breath. Moments later Espinoza arrives.

"Fucking hell!"

The general looks at his aide. He knows what he means.

"Stay here," he says. "I'm going to find Parada."

Urrutia makes his way to the General Prefecture, his footsteps echoing loudly across the marble hall. Within its walls the sounds of the gun battle outside are muted and distant, as if a television were playing in another room. He is upset the other generals and carabineros in the palace have deserted. Even Sepulveda appeared to have left. Oaths of commission apparently counted for nothing these days. A tide of despondency surges through the general, as though he mourned some great and irreparable loss. Feeling hopeless and depressed, he ascends the stairs and enters the grand colonnaded offices.

Parada is sitting alone at his desk, shuffling through some papers. He looks up and sees his superior approach, his uniform creased and dusty.

"What's up Jorge?"

"I've just come from the Moneda. The president wants to know how many men are with you."

"Twenty, more or less."

"That's not much."

Parada gives a look of resignation. Urrutia understands. Everyone appears to have given up.

"That it then?"

"Got any other ideas?"

"The president wants you and your men to come and defend the palace."

"He's mad. He should surrender."

Urrutia is unsure what to do and is torn between a natural instinct for self-preservation and loyalty to his commander-in-chief. When did one supersede the other? Try as he might, the general is unable to solve his dilemma.

"I need a piss," he sighs.

"Use my toilet," says Parada. "It's in the corridor on the right."

Urrutia walks down the passage and wearily opens the door of the bathroom. As he urinates a bullet shatters the window and whistles past his head. He ducks involuntarily and misses the bowl, splashing the marble floor. The general quickly moves away. A sniper in the opposite building must have spotted him.

Urrutia grabs a towel, wipes his hands and crawls out of the bathroom. In the safety of the corridor he stands up, discards the cloth and returns to Parada's office.

"You almost had one less carabinero," he says and explains what has just happened.

The general knows that any attempt to return to the

Moneda would most likely be fatal. A great weight bears down upon his shoulders and he fears it will crush him. Urrutia can feel his bones creaking, his joints about to give way. Any moment now his spine will snap and he will be ground into the dust and pulverised. He realises that he must give in, if he is to survive. It is every man for himself.

"There's no point staying here. It's too dangerous," the general says. "The air force is about to bomb the palace. I want you to retire with your personnel. Everyone should return to their respective units."

Parada obeys and orders the men under his command to return to the Second Commissariat. Urrutia and Espinoza also leave and make their way back to the carabinero headquarters at Norambuena.

To avoid the battle in the plaza they go by the east side of Avenida Moneda, towards Bandera and head south. The general and his aide pass several bodies lying in the street. On the steps of the Union Club they see another corpse and Urrutia realises the death toll of the coup is only just beginning. The officers continue and cross Alonso Ovalle. Espinoza suddenly halts and grabs his companion's shoulder. He points to a sniper on a balcony. The man has his back to them and is facing down the street.

"Should I shoot?"

"No," says the general. "He hasn't seen us. And if we fire, we'll only draw attention to ourselves. Let's keep going. We're almost there."

They continue past the building of the Clarín newspaper, which is ablaze. Flames pour from the windows in a fierce roar. The air is filled with soot and charred newspapers flit across the road. A sudden gust of wind catches the pages and sends ashen wings floating up into the sky. At the other end of the street is the General Directorate.

Cheered by the sight the officers make a final bid for safety, as they dodge past burnt out vehicles and shuttered shops. They reach the car park unharmed and approach the imposing stone entrance. A group of soldiers in battledress guard the front door, their weapons at the ready. The men see the general and his aide and salute smartly as they step inside.

Urrutia thanks Espinoza and goes upstairs to his own office and locks the door. He sits down at his desk. He is alone. He looks at the papers spread across the polished surface of the mahogany bureau. Most are orders waiting to be counter-signed by him. They are all irrelevant now. The general picks up the papers and throws them into the bin. Pens, pencils and other writing paraphernalia also strew his desk and with a single sweep of his hand, he scatters them onto the floor. Urrutia sits there and stares at the shiny wooden surface of his desk. Although it is clear, the general realises that his conscience is not. Allende had asked him to go to the General Prefecture to get reinforcements and return to the palace. Instead he has disobeyed the president, in order to save his own skin.

*

The GAP in the presidential garage have been placed under an armed guard and sit on the floor with their hands behind their heads. Throughout the morning conscripts have routinely beaten and kicked them. An officer arrives and orders the men to their feet. Their hands are roughly bound behind their backs and they are taken next door to the Intendancy and marched outside into a courtyard. A platoon of soldiers stands nearby. The leader of the group Domingo Blanco, known as 'Bruno', realises what is about to happen. They are going to be executed. He turns and addresses the officer.

"Let the kid go," he says, looking at Enrique, who is shaking and close to tears. "He's nothing to do with us."

The captain is unmoved

"I don't give a shit, orders is orders."

"He's not a GAP! He's just a fucking kid. He's La Payita's son!"

"You're all the same to me asshole...so shut it."

The GAP, including Enrique, are put against a wall. Some of them call out and ask the soldiers why they are about to slaughter fellow Chileans. Their leader silences them with a shout.

"Viva Allende!" he says.

"Viva!" they answer.

The soldiers present arms and take aim. As they do so Bruno steps forward and shields Enrique with his body. The captain sees what is happening and orders the GAP to move aside. He refuses and so the officer raises his pistol and shoots him dead. He turns and gives the order to fire and the courtyard resounds to the crash of a fusillade.

*

On the first floor of the Moneda, Quintin Romero is on guard duty in one of the presidential offices. The stocky detective is looking out of the French windows facing onto the muddy acre that was the Plaza de la Constitución's lawn and which is now a battleground. He is on guard duty with another colleague and two members of the GAP. One of them is Daniel Gutiérrez, known as 'Jano', a ruggedly handsome man with a mop of dark hair. Romero does not know the name of the other GAP, although he recognises him. The youth came from an aristocratic background, his family owning a famous vineyard. He is poised behind a heavy machine gun, the barrel of which pokes through the bars of the balcony. He looks young. The GAP is slimly built with straight blond hair and wears a white polo neck. Beside him lies a black leather jacket.

A lieutenant arrives and tells Romero his stag is over and to take a break. The detective thanks the officer and pulls out a packet of cigarettes and offers it to Jano and his colleague who both accept. He also takes one for himself. He calls across to the boy at the window, but the GAP declines with a shake of his head and continues to watch the battle outside, the Bren gun's stock in his shoulder.

Romero strikes a match and lights his comrades' cigarettes. He puts the flame to his own and someone says "third light" and they grin at the old military saw. As the men stand there smoking, the president appears flanked by his bodyguard. Paredes is also with him and so too are Olivares and Paris. All of them are armed. Allende thanks the detectives for remaining in the palace. He is impressed by their devotion to duty.

"The rest of the armed forces can go to hell!" he adds.

They do not know what to say and smile. Allende wishes them well and departs. Romero is touched by his thoughtfulness. The entire country was at war and yet the President of the Republic still had a few kind words to say to his detectives.

Moments after Allende and his entourage leave, a burst of gunfire shatters the French windows and blazes across the room, forcing the defenders to the floor. The rounds are mixed with tracer and the curtains quickly catch alight. The firing continues and splinters of woods spin through the air as plaster rains down from the ceiling, the rounds whining about their heads. The men grab cushions and try to put out the flames, bullets ricocheting around them. Romero looks across at the open window and sees the body of the young GAP slumped across his gun. His white polo neck is peppered with holes and a pool of blood edges across the floor.

Romero and the other detective try to reach him, but it impossible to get close while gunfire flashes across the room. The flames in the fabric take hold and the place begins to fill with smoke. The detectives tie handkerchiefs around their faces and increase their efforts to put out the conflagration. Jano is cursing with fury. He picks up a bazooka and crawls towards the smashed windows. He desperately wants to knock out the tank that is shooting at them. The GAP seizes a blue serge cape which belonged to the president and throws it over his shoulder, protecting him from the weapon's recoil. He kneels, takes aim and fires, the backdraft sending a shock wave rippling through the air. The shell sails over the tank and explodes harmlessly on the muddy lawn. Jano swears in desperation. He cannot get close enough to the window to get a proper shot.

In the middle of all this mayhem, the phone on the desk rings. Romero crawls across the room, pulls it off the top and sits with it under the bureau.

"Hello."

"Who's this?"

It is Hortensia Allende. Romero recognises her voice.

"A detective from the guard Madam President."

"What's happening?" she says, hearing gunfire crackle in the background.

"The soldiers are attacking the Moneda."

"Where's Salvador?"

"He's downstairs with some people."

"Who's with him?"

"Paredes, Olivares and some others."

"Please tell the president I'm going to leave. I'm going to leave the house."

"OK," says Romero.

Hortensia hangs up. She takes her bag and goes to the hall to collect her keys. She is about to depart when one of the bodyguard stops her. The first lady cannot leave the residence, because the soldiers surrounding it have also begun to attack. The GAP tells her to stay in the kitchen as it is the safest place. Hortensia goes and sits beneath the table and listens as the bodyguard return the soldiers' fire. Her eyes well with grief and tears splash her blouse. But the tears are not for herself, they are for her husband and their two daughters in the Moneda.

*

Inside the palace the president has organised teams to douse the fires, which have broken out all over the building. People stand in lines and pass buckets of water to and fro, the person at the head of the chain hurling the contents onto the flames. Hoses are quickly produced. The palace is full of running, shouting people. Clouds of steam and smoke fill the rooms and corridors and pools of water inch across the floor. A steady stream cascades down the main marble staircase and runs into the entrance hall.

As Allende directs operations from the Oranges' Patio, he catches sight of a good-looking youth with blond hair. He is small, with a trim moustache and pale blue eyes. In his hands is a FAL machine gun. He reminds the president of a young Douglas Fairbanks Jnr. He knows the person well. It is Osvaldo Puccio's eldest son.

"Osvaldito," he says. "Be a good lad and see if any uniformed men are defending the palace."

"Of course Comrade President."

The youth makes his way towards the Ministry of the Interior, where most of the firing is coming from. As he wanders blithely across the Cannons' Patio a voice yells out.

"Don't be a damn fool! Run!"

The younger Puccio dashes to the nearest doorway, leaps inside and goes upstairs to the first floor. As he ascends the stairwell, the sound of gunfire increases. The defenders are grouped together on the north side of the building. The youth enters the Ministry of Foreign Affairs and sees the GAP and the detectives firing from the windows. The floor is littered with empty ammunition clips and spent bullet cases. Occasionally there is a roar and the whole building shudders as another tank round strikes the palace. One of the GAP fires a missile from a bazooka, the weapon's backdraft tearing a curtain behind him. Strewn around the defenders' feet are open boxes of grenades and ammunition.

A detective pauses to discard a magazine from his AK47 and puts in a fresh clip. He looks up and sees Puccio transfixed in the middle of the room and calls angrily across to him.

"Are you going to stand there all fucking day or what?"

The youth apologises, goes to a window and peers out. A troop of soldiers slowly advances behind a tank. He does not hesitate and puts his machine gun to his shoulder and starts firing.

As the younger Puccio is upstairs fighting, Allende asks his father to find out if there is anyone in the General Prefecture across the road. The president wonders what has happened to Urrutia. He should be back by now. The Presidential Secretary picks up a phone and dials the number and is answered by General Julio Rado, the carabinero chief of Santiago.

"Is Alfredo Joignant there?" asks Puccio.

"No. He's under arrest."

"What about Jorge Urrutia?"

"He was here apparently. But he's gone. General Parada has also left. The building is now occupied and under my command."

"You must be very proud of yourself," says the minister.

Puccio tells the president what has happened. None of his armed forces are loyal. Not even the carabineros. Allende's face reddens and his jowls tremble.

"Cowardly shitheads!"

*

The battle continues to rage around the Moneda. In the presidential offices there is a discussion among the remaining ministers and governmental advisers. All agree they cannot hold out much longer and want to try and negotiate a truce, before the palace is bombed. The problem is how to persuade the president, who is now actively defending the building. Briones suggests Tohá calls the Ministry of Defence and speaks to Admiral Carvajal. As a former defence minister he knows the admiral well and the two, while not exactly friends, are at least cordial with each other. The Minister of the Interior knows Tohá will be diplomatic with the rebel officer. Perhaps Carvajal would consider a ceasefire, while they talk to Allende. The former minister agrees it is worth a try and goes in search of a phone that is still connected.

After several attempts Tohá finds one that does work and dials the number of the ministry. It rings briefly and is answered by a junior official.

"Can I speak to Admiral Carvajal please."

"Who's calling?"

"José Tohá."

"Just a minute."

There is a pause, then Carvajal comes on the line.

"Mr Tohá, what a pleasant surprise! How are you?"

"Fine thanks admiral. And yourself?"

"Couldn't be better. So, what can I do for you?"

"Admiral, I have a request. I wonder if you would grant me ten minutes to convince the president to leave the palace before we are bombed."

"With the greatest of pleasure Mr Tohá."

"If I may ask another favour, will you stop shooting so that we can continue our conversation undisturbed?"

"I would be more than willing. However, we are under fire both from the palace and from snipers in the surrounding buildings. We have no choice, but to respond."

"Of course, but who knows. Maybe an order from you and…"

"Unfortunately they are unwilling to listen to an order from me and time is running out. The air force has already been sent on its mission. The planes are circling as we speak."

"Admiral, I have tried everything in my powers to convince the president and…"

"Well, throw him out by force!"

"Ah, that would be difficult. You see he has a machine gun. Why don't you try talking with him admiral? Perhaps your arguments will be more convincing than mine."

"What? I, talk with Allende? You can't ever talk with that man. All he ever does is insult you!"

"Very well. I'll see what I can do," and Tohá hangs up.

The former minister goes back to the presidential offices and rejoins the group.

"How'd it go?" asks Briones.

Tohá wags his head sadly.

"Not good. Unless we surrender now, they will bomb the palace. The planes are already here."

The officials sit there in silence. The situation looks dire. The junta's decision to bomb the Moneda is no empty threat and doubtless they will all be killed. The group realise the only solution is to convince the president to surrender. The problem is that Allende no longer seemed to be the same man. Since the shooting began and possibly since that morning, he appeared to have abandoned dialogue in favour of an armed response.

As they discuss various options, Briones wonders if the president was actually realising a long suppressed revolutionary vocation. He had always espoused a democratic path to socialism. Perhaps Allende now believed that it was impossible and had decided to take up arms against the forces of reaction. Whatever the reason, Briones is certain the president will not surrender.

Arturo Jirón, the former Minister of Health, cuts across the general conversation.

"Comrades, we might as well tell the president what we think," he says in his languid baritone.

The others agree and Jirón volunteers to go to the offices of the Private Secretariat, where Allende was last seen fighting. As he approaches the north wing, the sounds of battle intensify. A tall, elegant man Jirón enters the ministry on his hands and knees, his head bowed against the percussion of battle. He sees the president lying on the parquet floor, his legs splayed in a firing position. Allende has his machine gun to his shoulder and fires in controlled bursts through a shattered French window. The former minister shouts to get his attention, but the noise is deafening. Since he cannot be heard above the din, Jirón crawls towards the president and grabs him by the ankles.

"What the hell!" and Allende turns round to see who is molesting him. "Ah, it's only you Jiróncito."

"Hi chief, can I have a word?"

"Can't you see I'm shooting!"

"I know, but some of us want to talk to you."

"Can't it wait?"

Jirón shakes his large, shaggy head.

"No."

Allende sighs and removes his glasses and wipes them on his sleeve, then replaces them.

"OK. You go first, I'll follow," and with his weapon in his hands, the president crawls out after his former minister.

Allende and Jirón make their way back to the presidential offices. When they arrive Tohá tells the president about his conversation with Admiral Carvajal and the junta's avowed intention to bomb the palace. But the president refuses to be swayed. For one thing, he does not believe the air force will bomb the Moneda and even if they do, it is better to remain inside.

"Comrades. You know what this palace represents: the Chilean constitution. More than one hundred and fifty years of democratic tradition."

"To be quite honest Mr President, I don't think democratic tradition rates that highly on the junta's list of priorities right now," says Briones.

Even you Carlos, even you? Allende thinks, but does not

say.

"In that case let them bomb the palace and the world will see exactly what sort of people they are."

The others are astounded to hear this and can only look on in silent disbelief. Some even wonder at the president's sanity. But he has a point. It is safer inside than out and the longer they resist, the greater the pressure on the junta to negotiate.

There is nothing else to be said and telling them all to remain firm, Allende leaves the group and returns to the offices of the Secretariat. He walks down the corridor and pauses at the door of his private study, where he had spoken earlier with his three attachés. The president steps inside and sits down on the sofa. He had forgotten how much he appreciated the little room. It was a haven away from the constant grind and worry of government, where he could be alone and think. Even the noise of battle did little to diminish its tranquillity. Allende removes his helmet, props his weapon against the sofa and considers what his ministers have just told him. The country was at war. He had done everything in his power to prevent it, but now it was too late.

As he sits there in solitude, the president reflects on the irony of it all. When he informed the generals of the Santiago garrison on Friday of his decision to hold a plebiscite, he had inadvertently given them a date for the coup. They had to strike before he made the announcement. Allende swears silently in frustration. The generals must have been plotting for weeks. All those last ditch negotiations with the Christian Democrats and the military had been pointless. The junta were simply waiting for the right moment. It dawns on the president that, for the first time in his life, he has been outmanoeuvred politically. His mistake was to believe the armed forces would remain loyal. If not to him, then at least to the constitution. He knew now why they wanted a war. They wanted to get rid of Popular Unity and everything that it stood for. And for that they needed a coup.

Allende sighs. It was too late for regrets. Perhaps he should end it all now? Just as Balmaceda had done all those years ago, when he took his life in the Argentine embassy. He knows his own death would bring an abrupt end to the coup and most likely prevent a civil war. The president looks at the weapon beside him. It would be quick certainly. Just place the gun under his chin and pull the trigger. But... that was just what the military wanted. All the talk about a plane and safe conduct was eyewash. He knew they would never let him leave. They wanted him dead. Well, he was not going to give them that satisfaction. At least not yet.

Allende is determined to fight on. He will save the last bullet for himself. The president gets up from the sofa, takes his weapon and returns to the fray.

*

Largo Farías climbs the stone staircase which connects the offices of the OIR on the ground floor, to the presidential suite on the first. Allende wished to make an announcement to everyone inside the palace and has summoned all remaining personnel. He enters the Toesca Salon, named after the Moneda's Italian architect and sees the president dressed for battle, wearing his tin helmet, a machine gun in his hands. The lofty, panelled room is full of government officials, advisers, members of the GAP, the detectives and remaining civilians. There are about seventy people in all.

Allende sees that everyone is assembled and his voice silences the room.

"The women and those of you who are unarmed must leave. I order our female comrades and any other civilians to abandon the Moneda. I want them to leave. I am not going to surrender, but I do not want empty sacrifices. Revolutions are not made with cowards at their head. That is why I am going to stay. Those who remain must have weapons and know how to use them. The others must go."

The president observes the room. No one speaks. Largo Farías notes this all down mentally. Allende is determined to stay on with his bodyguard and supporters and do battle with the armed forces. The air resonates with tension, as though a great bell has tolled and its solemn note has yet to fade. Everyone looks at the president. It seems as if he has crossed a personal Rubicon. To remain is to die. The silence is broken by the gentle voice of José Tohá, who again tries to persuade his friend to negotiate with the junta. Allende's reply to his former defence minister is emphatic.

"I refuse to leave the seat of government. I shall fight on until the end. They will have to carry me out dead."

He says the words calmly and is composed. There is a sense of restraint and self-possession about the president. Whereas before he had seemed exasperated at each new turn of treachery by the armed forces, now he has come to terms with the situation. Allende knows he cannot expect any further support either from the armed forces, or from individual units of carabineros. Even the small contingent that was with him had now deserted. He has insisted there should be no popular uprising, or crowds marching on the Moneda. The president realises he is alone. Surrounded by supporters and friends perhaps, but alone.

Standing there in front of the gathering, Allende possesses an aura of quiet determination. He is at peace with himself because he knows that once a man has made up his mind to die, the rest of his life is easy.

The president dismisses the group and orders all documents, which might compromise members of the government or other radicals, to be burnt. A large pile of papers is heaped in the conservatory of the Winter Patio and a GAP puts a match to them. A few desultory flames appear and the documents begin to flicker and burn as the fire takes hold. Soon the whole pyre starts to roar and a plume of smoke rises through a vent in the conservatory roof.

Allende returns to his office with his entourage. He presses the intercom that connects the Moneda to the MOD and asks to speak to General Ernesto Baeza, one of the senior rebel officers. He waits and soon the official is on the other end. The president asks if he can delay the air force attack, in order to let the women and other civilians go. Baeza tries to persuade him to surrender, there is still time. Allende refuses.

"General you have betrayed both your oath of commission and your country. I hope you won't betray what a man must be to a woman. At least respect them enough for this."

"Of course," says Baeza.

The president then asks to speak to Carvajal.

"Admiral," he says. "I want you to let the six women here leave the palace. Among them are my daughters, one of whom is pregnant. It is your duty as a human being to allow them to leave."

"I understand perfectly. We'll let them leave."

"I want a vehicle and an officer for their protection."

"Fine, I will send a vehicle with an officer."

"I want you to give me your word of honour that you will not shoot them."

"Who on earth is going to shoot them?"

"There are some who might do it. Fascists."

"What fascists are you talking about? There are no fascists here, only patriots."

"You know what I mean. I want your word."

"Mr President, you have my word."

Allende breaks off the communication and goes to find his daughters to say goodbye. They are waiting with the other women in the office of Enrique Huerta, the Palace Intendant and head of the GAP. With them are the OIR team and Largo Farías. The president appears at the doorway, flanked as ever by his bodyguards.

"General Baeza has given me his word that there will be a ceasefire for a few minutes, to allow all of you to leave."

"Papa, you still believe the word of a general!" says Isabel.
"I believe it."

"They will take us hostages," says Beatriz. "They will kill us!"

The president turns and looks at his eldest daughter.

"It would be better if they did kill you then rather than now, because history will judge them not only as traitors, but also as murderers of women. Please, you must leave both of you. Isabel, you have a mother and sister to take care of. Tati, you have a child and your husband in the Cuban embassy. You must be with him."

Nevertheless, both sisters are determined to remain. Their father is moved to pity, but knows he cannot let them stay.

"Please, if you don't go now I shall be forced out into the street with you. And that is just what the military want."

Largo Farías and the others remain silent and uneasy witnesses. Everyone knows the two women will never see their father again. Isabel looks as if she is about to collapse. She is deathly pale, her chin trembles and her dark eyes are filled with tears.

Unable to restrain her grief she begins to cry and sobbing, embraces her father before leaving the room. Beatriz lingers a few seconds more, staring at her father as if trying to place the moment precisely in her memory. Then she hugs the president tightly and follows her sister outside.

The others also leave and Allende takes them to the entrance on 80 Morandé. He opens the side door and waves a white handkerchief. He turns and with a final embrace, the president kisses his two daughters for the last time.

*

The decision to delay the bombing until 11:30am has to be relayed to the two Hawks circling above the palace, which are just about to attack. On the fifth floor of the MOD there is a collective sigh of relief, when the planes are seen to withdraw. Carvajal and the other generals with him still hope Allende might surrender, although there is little likelihood of this happening. The fighting around the Moneda has resumed and because of it, no vehicle or officer comes to collect the group.

The women leave the palace along with the staff of the OIR. Together they cross the road in a monkey run while soldiers and snipers exchange fire, the air crackling around them. As they run Beatriz feels contractions in her belly. The group splits up and the sisters manage to reach the lobby of a nearby hotel. Breathless, they go up to reception and ask the startled manager if there are any rooms available. He nods and opens a large leather bound ledger and takes out a pen. But when he hears their names, his face freezes. The manager promptly snaps the ledger shut and shoos them out, saying the hotel is fully booked.

*

The president is glad he has persuaded his daughters and the other civilians to quit the palace. The idea they might be killed because of their loyalty to him is anathema. He is anxious that all personnel not involved in the defence of the Moneda should leave. Only the diehards need remain.

Allende talks to the chief medical officer Oscar Soto and he agrees. Together they go to dispensary where the doctors are assembled and the president tells them it is time to go. But they refuse.

One of them, Patricio Guijón, speaks for all.

"Mr President. If there was ever a time when I can demonstrate what kind of man I am, then this is it. I'm staying."

The others murmur their assent and Allende realises he can do nothing about it.

"Very well comrades. I accept your decision."

The president and Soto then leave, along with the

bodyguard. One of them is Jano who grins and claps Guijón on the shoulder as he departs.

"Good for you doc!"

*

There are others beside the doctors, whom Allende wants to evacuate. One such person is Joan Garcés, his Spanish born adviser. He wants the academic to go, not only because of his youth, but also because he wants him to live so that he can speak about his presidency and vouch for the Popular Unity government.

Allende finds his friend in the Winter Patio, chatting with Paredes and Olivares. He takes him to one side and addresses the earnest, bespectacled man who has served him so well.

"Joan, I'm sorry to have to say this, but you must go. You cannot stay here."

The Spaniard is shocked, as though his moral and physical courage has been impugned.

"Salvador, I won't…I refuse. My place is here with you. "

But the adviser can see from Allende's expression that he resolutely disagrees.

"No. You shall bear witness to my presidency and the work of Popular Unity. You cannot do that if you are dead. That is what you have to do and that is why you must leave."

Even so, Garcés is in no mood to be browbeaten and continues to protest.

"Salvador, I have been with you since the beginning. There are thousands, millions of Chileans who can bear witness to Popular Unity and to the truth. I am not going to leave the palace like some whoreson absconder!"

Allende smiles. The man from La Mancha always had a memorable turn of phrase.

"You can and you must. If you want me to order you to do so as your president, then I will. But I'm asking you as a friend. A loyal and trusted friend. You are young, you have much work ahead of you..."

"Please, Salvador..."

"No, I insist."

Allende then embraces his adviser.

"Thank you comrade and take care," and the president walks away.

The others go with him and Garcés watches them leave. It is the last he sees of Allende. The Spaniard looks about. He is on his own. He goes towards the entrance on 80 Morandé and does as his president ordered.

*

The OIR is now deserted except for Largo Farías. He picks up the logbook on his desk and goes downstairs to one of the cellars to await the bombing. As he sits alone in the dusty subterranean cave, he takes the opportunity to commit to paper what Allende told everyone in the Toesca Salon. On the back of the book Largo Farías writes a message to his wife and their seven-year-old daughter. He has no doubt that he will die. As he is writing a farewell note his boss Carlos Jorquera, the Presidential Press Secretary, appears at the door clutching a bottle of Johnnie Walker and two crystal glasses.

"Care for a drink comrade?"

Largo Farías looks up at his colleague and smiles.

"Just what the doctored ordered," and he puts the book aside.

Jorquera sits down and pours them each a slug of whisky. The pair clink glasses.

"Cheers," they chorus.

The journalists nurse their drinks in silence. Each knows what the other is thinking. They are like the condemned in their cell, waiting for dawn and the rattle of the gaoler's key in the lock.

Largo Farías sighs and leans back against the wall. Neither man speaks. It is a silence of hopeless anticipation. Every act, every movement wearies them. Even breathing is a burden. All they can do is accept their fate, clinging to what little is left of their life like drowning men to a piece of flotsam.

Jorquera stares at the ceiling and turns the glass of whisky slowly in his hand. He hears a woman's footsteps approach and is surprised to see La Payita. The press secretary thought she had left with the others. The journalists greet her with smiles and she sits down beside them.

Above they hear Allende's voice call out.

"Paya, Paya? Where are you? Come on, you must leave now."

La Payita puts a finger to her lips and smiles conspiratorially at her companions. They say nothing as the president continues on, calling out her name.

Later, Jorquera and La Payita depart, leaving Largo Farías alone in the cellar. The place starts to fill with smoke, which makes his eyes smart. He wonders where everyone has gone. As he sits and ponders, the smoke worsens. He decides he would rather be blown to pieces than slowly kippered to death and leaves the cellar and climbs the stairs to the first floor. He walks through the deserted presidential gallery with its marble busts of Chile's leaders and descends to the Winter Patio, where the bonfire is still burning.

Largo Farías looks at the smouldering pyre. It is an apt metaphor for what is happening to the country. Even now, he cannot help reporting. A monologue runs drily through his head.

There are just minutes to go before the air force attacks the Moneda. President Salvador Allende remains inside. Despite the threat of bombardment, he refuses to leave the seat of government. "They will have to carry me out dead," was his response to a former minister's request that he surrender. It seems the president will make good his intention...

A voice behind the journalist interrupts his thoughts.
"What are you doing here you idiot? Go home."
He turns round and sees Olivares standing there, an AK47 in his hands.
"You're going to be more useful outside than stuck in this death trap. Here they're about to blow everyone to bits. Go on, fuck off."
The television chief starts to hustle him towards the door on 80 Morandé.
"What about you Perro?"
"My place is with the president. Besides, I'm bullet proof."
When they reach the entrance, Olivares opens it and pushes his friend outside.
"And be sure to keep your hands up!" he says, as he slams the door shut.
Largo Farías finds himself alone in the middle of the street. He stands there with his hands up, expecting someone to shoot him. Nothing happens. Slowly, the journalist walks away, his arms raised above his head. The Plaza de la Constitución is deserted, the soldiers having fallen back in anticipation of the bombardment. It is eerily quiet. Even the pigeons have fled. The only sound is the wind moaning in the telephone wires and his footsteps, as he crunches across the broken glass that litters the road. Nobody appears, or challenges him. After a few more yards he lowers his arms and walks the remaining seven blocks back to his house in Alonso Ovalle. When Largo Farías gets home, he opens the front door and is embraced by his sobbing wife and child.

*

Allende is holding counsel in the Toesca Salon. He is still trying to get as many people as possible to leave the palace before the bombardment begins, including the detectives who have stayed resolutely with him all morning. Their commander Juan Seoane enters the room. He has been told the president wants a word. He sees Allende seated upon the great mahogany table, his legs dangling over the side. He approaches his superior and salutes.

"Mr President?"

"Inspector, you are to leave the palace with your men. I shall stay here and fight on with the GAP."

"Sir, I have only one order from the Director General of Investigations Alfredo Joignant and that is for me and my men to stay with you and defend the palace."

"You're relieved of that order."

"I refuse to be relieved."

Allende allows himself a small smile.

"I knew you'd stay Seoane. But tell your men they're free to go."

"Yes sir."

The inspector leaves and goes downstairs to the palace guardroom, where the detectives are waiting and repeats the president's order to his men. But they all reply that they too wished to remain. One of them explains why.

"This is our question," he says. "We have to stay."

Seoane understands and like the president, accepts their decision. Feeling hungry he goes off to the kitchen to get some food. The inspector makes himself a cheese sandwich and a cup of coffee. He eats quickly. He has had no breakfast and has been up since dawn.

*

At his military headquarters in Peñalolén, General Pinochet is confused. He has mistaken Allende's plea for a ceasefire, as an offer to surrender. He is concerned because as far as he knows, the bombardment has not been called off. As the women and the OIR team leave the Moneda, Pinochet contacts Admiral Carvajal in the MOD.

"Patricio," says the army commander-in-chief, "the sooner the president leaves in the plane the better. He can take all the chickens he wants…"

"No, not the GAP. They're too dangerous…"

"OK, not the GAP. But from the Moneda to the plane old boy, keep the leash good and tight…let's not have any problems. We'll deal with the GAP ourselves. But we must get him onto that plane. Once he's out of Chile, it can fall out of the sky for all I care…"

Carvajal chuckles, but realises the general has got his facts wrong.

"Augusto, he's not surrendering…"

"Not surrendering?…"

"Affirmative. Only the women and non-combatants are leaving. I've just spoken to the president myself. We'll have to go in and get him ourselves. Maybe after the bombardment…"

"Post 1 copy that. Roger and out…"

Pinochet switches off the intercom and strokes the edges of his trim moustache. He is impressed by Allende's resistance. He had always wondered how the president would react to the coup and suspected he might make a stand. But he did not think he would hold out for so long, or that he would show such resolution in the face of an aerial bombardment. Surely the president can be persuaded to surrender? Despite Carvajal's own failure, Pinochet is convinced he can get Allende to leave the palace. Simply flatter him and tell him that he has put up a brave fight, but there is no point in causing unnecessary deaths.

"Put me through to the Moneda," he tells a subordinate. "I want to speak to the president."

The connection is made and after a while Allende comes on the line.

"What do you want?"

Pinochet, in his best butterscotch voice, tries to persuade the president to give up. He has fought valiantly and is a brave man, but any further resistance is futile.

"I do not make deals with traitors and you, General Pinochet, are a traitor!"

"Now then Mr President…"

"Don't 'now then' me you sonofabitch! If you had an ounce of self-respect, you'd be here defending the Moneda. Not holed up in some concrete bunker with your maps and battle plans!"

The army commander-in-chief is surprised at the vehemence of Allende's response, but continues to be emollient.

"Mr President, what's it serve you staying? You'll have to give up sooner or later."

"Surrender is for cowards and I am not a coward! The real cowards are you lot, conspiring like gangsters in the dark of the night!"

Allende terminates the conversation and Pinochet is left holding the receiver. The general replaces it and thinks. He cannot understand why the president refused to leave in the plane. Perhaps he wanted to be killed. Pinochet does not particularly wish Allende to die, but neither does he care too much if he lives. He simply wants him out of the way. It would be so much easier if the president took the plane.

V
THE PALACE IS BOMBED

In the Moneda everyone is tense as they wait for the air force to begin their attack. Allende is in the cellar below the Winter Patio. Beside him is La Payita. Realising his secretary was never going to leave, the president has agreed she can stay. Among the others in the cellar are Paredes, Olivares and Paris. Osvaldo Puccio and his son are also there, as well as some members of the GAP.

A few minutes later another group arrives, but find there is no room. One of them, a former minister of foreign relations, says he knows of a cellar in his previous ministry and they dash across the patio towards the Chancellery. But the ex-minister cannot remember exactly where the cellar is. As the group search frantically from room to room, they encounter a minor official and an operative from the OIR, who were unable to escape with the others. The civil servant is better informed than his superior and shows them the way to the cellar, although they have to kick down a door to get to it.

The place is several metres below ground and is not really a cellar, but a boiler room. At least it is safe. The group sit down and wait. A naked bulb glows above their heads, its wattage unable to penetrate the corners of the room which remain in shadow. The air is foggy and there is a lingering smell of dust and oil. Beside them the boiler hums and gently ticks. No one talks. There is a sense of dreadful expectation, like troops waiting for the shrill blast of a whistle before they go over the top.

A dozen GAP and detectives take cover in the Counsel Room on the first floor, which looks out onto the Cannons' Patio. Below them two GAP stand guard by the massive front door, waiting to repel any infantry should an assault immediately follow the bombing. They lean casually against the walls and smoke cigarettes, their weapons pointing at the door.

On the west side of the palace, some of the medical team and a few others install themselves in a small passage on the first floor, near the Salon Independencia that runs parallel to Morandé. The place is unlit and windowless. They sit silently in the gloom. It is so dark they cannot see each other's faces. The only thing they can hear is the low sound of their own breathing and the faint rustle of clothes as someone shifts to a more comfortable position. All are convinced they will die.

Sitting in the cellar, young Osvaldo Puccio notices a carabinero sergeant with the presidential group. The man is well built and the only uniformed soldier left in the palace. Allende also sees him and gets up and gives the man an embrace. The policeman smiles bashfully and looks away. The NCO had refused to leave with the others, electing to remain with his president.

Shortly before midday the military issue a further communiqué although the people inside the palace, cocooned as they are in their makeshift shelters, do not hear it.

We have been waiting for the surrender of Salvador Allende since 10:30am and since this hasn't happened we have begun an aerial and territorial attack upon the Moneda. With this action we seek to avoid further bloodshed. Signed, the Commanders-in-Chief.

In the cold, grey skies above the palace the Hawks, which have been circling for the past hour, prepare their bombing run. The planes dive and flying fast and low across the Mapocho, turn and release their first salvo. The rockets streak towards their target, leaving a long vapour trail in their wake and explode in the north-west wing of the palace. A great roar shakes the building and a cloud of dust and smoke erupts. Soon the Moneda is alight and begins to burn fiercely. The attack is relayed live on national TV. Across the length and breadth of the country people sit watching their televisions, transfixed as flames and smoke billow from the shattered government seat.

One horrified observer of the bombing is the air force general Alberto Bachelet. Under arrest in his office in the MOD, he has a direct view of the Moneda. He stands at the window watching the destruction. His own air force, his own comrades in arms are wilfully desecrating the presidential palace. It is more than an act of treason, it is sacrilege. The soldiers guarding him laugh and cheer as each bomb detonates against the building. Bachelet trembles silently beside them, his eyes brimming with tears of helpless rage.

*

In the cellar below the Winter Patio the last remaining carabinero suddenly drops his rifle and flees in terror, slamming the door behind him. The other occupants cover their heads with their hands and do not move, as the rockets continue to rain down. Young Puccio looks at his father who seems remarkably composed. The Presidential Secretary had experienced aerial bombardments many years before. During World War II his own father had been Chile's ambassador in Berlin and the family had endured countless Allied air raids. But he never thought he would experience such a thing again. Father and son sit there and listen to the sound of explosions and feel the building shake upon its foundations.

As the bombs begin to fall, one of the detectives is caught unawares. David Garrido is running down some stairs in the search for more weapons and ammunition. The blast picks up the bodyguard and knocks him backwards, blowing the shoes off his feet. He lies dazed and winded on the staircase as the palace erupts around him.

In the Counsel Room a rocket strikes the ceiling and engulfs the place in a ball of fire. Among those seeking shelter is Quintin Romero. The force of the blast throws the detective to the ground. Stunned, he can hear the screams of men burning. They are hysterical, high-pitched screams. The smoke is blinding and he can barely breathe. Romero staggers to his feet and grabs a table for support. Next to him his colleague José Sotomayor also gets up. They are trapped as the fire separates them from the passage. The flames roar and leap as men twist and turn in their final agony.

The detectives' only means of escape is behind them but the heavy oak door, which leads to safety, is locked. In desperation they kick at the panels, the fierce heat of the flames at their backs. As the bombardment continues, their endeavours become ever more desperate. After a succession of heavy blows the frame begins to give and, with a final splintering of wood, the door breaks open. The detectives rush through, only to encounter another door on the other side of the room. But this time the panels are made of glass instead of wood. Romero takes out his automatic and smashes a pane with the butt. He puts his hand through the shattered glass and unlocks the door and the pair rush across the room and crawl under a table to wait for the bombing to end. They sit and catch their breath. No more screams come from the Counsel Room. The only sound is the spit and crackle of flames.

*

The younger Puccio has been counting the explosions. After seventeen strikes there is silence. Suddenly it is all over. The survivors get to their feet and dust themselves down and go outside to survey the damage, scarcely able to believe they are still alive. They look about and see the palace is in ruins, with fires burning along the upper storeys of the north wing.

The bombardment over, Romero and Sotomayor crawl out from under their table and make their way downstairs to the ground floor and the Ministry of Foreign Relations. They enter one of the Chancellery offices. It is large and comfortable with an en suite bathroom and a view onto the Oranges' Patio. The detectives discuss what they should do. They are completely cut off from the rest of the palace, because of the fire. Both men realise it would be best for them to surrender. But if they go outside they could be shot, either by soldiers or by loyalist snipers lurking in the rooftops of adjacent buildings. The clatter of gunfire resumes, as rebels and loyalists engage each other once more. There is nothing else for the detectives to do except wait.

Smoke billows through the palace as fires continue to burn. Outside, a white fog creeps across the ground and seeps into the offices of the Foreign Ministry. The army has fired tear gas canisters into the building and the detectives, who have no gas masks, begin to cough and choke. The pall of gas worsens and they realise that if they do not leave the place, they will suffocate. They go to the bathroom and dip their handkerchiefs in water and tie them around their faces. The tear gas hurts their eyes and makes them stream. The detectives go back to the room, coughing and wiping their eyes and hear shouts and the distant sound of blows.

Soldiers advance through the Chancellery room by room, kicking down doors and calling out for anyone to surrender. The sounds increase steadily. Romero and Sotomayor look at each other and put their hands above their heads. This is it. In a few moments they will both be dead. The door bursts open and a troop of soldiers rushes in. The detectives brace themselves, expecting to be cut down in a hail of bullets.

"Identify yourselves!" demands the platoon commander, his pistol pointing at them.

"Detectives Romero and Sotomayor," says Romero.

"Anyone else with you?"

"No…they're dead."

The officer approaches and the detectives begin to lower

their arms.

"Keep your hands up!"

The men stiffen and do as they are told. Romero looks at the shoulder flashes on the soldiers' battle dress and realises they are from the elite Infantry School regiment. The sort who shoot first and ask questions later. The detective decides to make their job as easy as possible.

"We're armed," he says and opens his jacket, so they can see his pistol. The captain steps forward and removes their weapons and gives them to a soldier. He takes their badges and ID and checks these, before handing them to another man in his platoon. The officer continues to frisk them and in one of Romero's pockets he finds the Swiss Army penknife, which had been given to him by the president.

"Can I keep the knife? It's personal."

"No. You're both under arrest."

The detectives are taken outside along with the others, who sought shelter in the Chancellery boiler room. They have all been affected by the tear gas and it is a relief for them to be able to breathe freely once more. One of the soldiers standing guard asks the detectives what they were doing in the palace.

"Defending the president," says Romero.

"Did you shoot?"

"Sure. Wouldn't you?'

The soldier does not reply and the prisoners are escorted across the Plaza de la Libertad and taken into the Ministry of Defence.

*

In the Moneda, Allende returns to the presidential offices. He orders the GAP to open all water outlets in an attempt to dampen the fires, which burn fiercely in the north-west wing and along the southern façade of the building. The men rush about turning on taps and unravelling fire hoses along the corridors. Pools of water inch across the floors and stairs become waterfalls.

The president organises the remaining GAP into new firing positions and concentrates his forces around the presidential offices and the principal reception rooms. The army has renewed its assault on the palace and the defenders run from room to room, firing from the windows to keep the soldiers at bay. Olivares lets out great whoops of joy as he empties the magazine of his weapon from a window.

"This is just like the Alamo!"

Breathless with excitement, he turns and leans against a wall. He removes the spent ammunition clip from his AK47 and throws it away, then reaches into his pocket for another. The wild-haired television chief looks about and grins like a loon. He has never enjoyed himself so much. At last they are fighting the fascists. It was going to be a fight to the death and he was going to die inside the palace along with his comrade Salvador. The president is nearby. He has a bazooka on his shoulder and is aiming at a tank on the corner. Allende pulls the trigger and Olivares yells encouragement.

"That's right Salvador! You show the sonsofbitches!"

The president cannot hear him because of the roar of gunfire and with a mad shout, Olivares turns and begins shooting at the soldiers in the street below.

*

After the Moneda mission the Hawks return to their base at Los Cerrillos. The pilots unstrap themselves in their cockpits and climb down from the aircraft, to be greeted like conquering heroes by the rest of the personnel on the base. They are carried shoulder high from the airfield to the officers' mess, where everyone congratulates them. As they celebrate and the pilots have champagne poured over their heads, another pair of Hawks are on their way to bomb the

Allende residence at Tomás Moro.

The soldiers assaulting the presidential home have withdrawn in anticipation of the bombardment. For the last forty-five minutes a helicopter has been hovering overhead, to enable the pilots to pinpoint the target more accurately. Just after 12:30pm the planes swoop down, firing their rockets at the house. Everyone in Tomás Moro takes cover where they can: under tables, in cupboards, beneath beds. One of the GAP even installs himself beneath the kitchen sink.

Hortensia phones the Moneda crouching under her husband's desk, as rockets explode around the building. Amid the din she speaks to a detective who says the president is defending the palace with all his might. He tells her that some of his comrades have been killed and others are wounded. They desperately need more forces. But this is all the president's wife hears as the phone suddenly goes dead. It is the last communication she has with the palace.

The Hawks continue their bombardment of Tomás Moro. Several rockets land in the soft earth of the garden and fail to detonate, or else explode beyond the grounds. But some do hit their target, shattering windows and splitting walls. Inside, the GAP and the president's wife brace themselves as the building is rocked by the concussion of the bombs.

A few minutes after it has started, the mission is complete and the planes peel off and return to base. In the ensuing silence, the survivors pick themselves up. Three bombs have made direct hits and barely a window pane is undamaged. Smoke drifts through the house and garden. The air is filled with dust and reeks of cordite. Hortensia crawls out from under the president's desk and pulls pieces of plaster from her hair. The GAP also emerge from their shelters and together they gather in the living-room.

It is a miracle that no one has been killed and only one of the bodyguard is slightly wounded. Hortensia tells the GAP they must go to the Moneda and help defend the president.

There is no point staying at Tomás Moro. The bodyguard agree and after embracing the president's wife, they leave the residence. But the soldiers surrounding the house have already begun to advance and most of the GAP are arrested before they can get away. A few do manage to escape but realising the Moneda is unreachable, they go to ground.

After the GAP's departure Hortensia wanders unhappily from room to room, surveying the damage of her home. The floor is covered with lumps of plaster and shards of broken glass. Bullet holes pit the walls in crazy pointillist patterns and torn canvases hang limply from shattered frames. The place is littered with discarded ammunition, empty grenade boxes and gas masks.

The president's wife looks sadly at some photographs strewn across Salvador's desk. There is a picture of her husband at his investiture and other assorted family snaps. She begins to put them upright, wiping the dust from each frame as she does so. A sudden noise behind Hortensia startles her and she turns round.

"Sorry Madam President," the man says. "I didn't mean to frighten you."

It is Carlos Tello, the presidential chauffeur. He has managed to evade the road blocks and made his way to the house from the garden at the back.

"Madam President you must leave. The army will come soon. The car's parked nearby."

Hortensia looks at the small, dark-haired man standing implacably before her. Carlos Tello. Loyal, brave Carlitos. What he says makes sense, but she cannot bear to leave her home.

"Really, I can't."

Tello draws a step closer and smiles shyly, revealing his gold fillings. His eyes shine with desperation and he clasps his hands beseechingly like a monk.

"Madam President we must go. The soldiers will come back at any moment."

Hortensia looks at the chauffeur and knows that if she refuses to leave, he will remain with her. And when the soldiers arrive, they will both be arrested. As the president's wife, she is unlikely to be harmed. She cannot be so certain about Tello.

"First, I must pack some things…"

"Madam President there is no time," he says with a sad shake of his head.

The first lady looks at the photos on the desk next to her. She picks up two of them. One is of her husband at his investiture, dressed in his morning coat and wearing the red, white and blue presidential sash. The other is a family group taken by Salvador using a self-timer on holiday some years ago, when the children were still teenagers. With these photos clutched to her breast, she turns to her chauffeur.

"I'm ready."

Tello leads Hortensia outside. They cross the cratered garden with its piles of freshly turned earth and walk through the deserted grounds of the Sacred Heart Convent at the rear. In the school's forecourt is the limousine. The chauffeur opens the door for his charge, as though spiriting away Chile's first lady is all part of his daily routine. He shuts the door beside her and gets in the vehicle.

"Where do you want to go?" he asks, starting the engine.

"Take me to the house of Felipe Herrera."

Herrera is a respected economist and head of the International Development Bank in Chile. He and his wife Inés are old family friends.

*

At Los Cerrillos the pilots who bombed Tomás Moro are debriefed. Unlike the Moneda sortie, the mission has not been a success. Instead of striking the Allende residence, four rockets have hit the Chilean Air Force Hospital, twenty blocks north of the target.

"The windows' glare confused me," says the guilty pilot as his superiors enquire about the error. "Was it bad?"

A senior officer explains the rockets struck a wing of the hospital. One landed in the basement laundry, a second on the first floor, a third on the terrace and a fourth in the garden.

"Fortunately, the only casualty is a nurse who broke both her legs," the officer says. "Perhaps you can send her some flowers."

*

In the south of Santiago lies the industrial sector of La Legua. It is a working class district and staunchly pro Popular Unity. At the Indumet factory the Socialist paramilitary leaders have gathered to talk tactics. The factory has long been a radical stronghold and the leaders have been there with their supporters since early morning. Apart from discussing their options, they listen to the infrequent bulletins from ham operators on a VHF radio. With Radio Magallanes now silenced, the only news they have been able to obtain is from clandestine operators swapping scraps of information. They have also been in regular contact with the Moneda and have spoken both to the president and Coco Paredes.

Allende has forbidden them to carry out any measures of popular resistance while he remains in the palace, explaining that he wants to avoid bloodshed. There have been some heated exchanges between the president and the paramilitary leaders, who have made it quite plain that they are prepared to sacrifice their own lives, with or without his permission.

At their home in downtown Gran Avenida, Edgardo Enríquez's sons wait patiently for the remaining Socialist leaders to arrive. Miguel, the principal leader of MIR, is dark-haired and handsome like his father and sports a Zapata moustache. He is also a qualified doctor and specialised in neurosurgery, before deciding to take up the armed struggle. His younger brother Edgardo, who acts as his lieutenant, looks almost identical and they are often mistaken for twins. At midday the Socialists finally turn up and the group arm themselves and leave for the Indumet factory, except for Edgardo who stays behind to keep watch.

The group reaches the complex shortly afterwards, having avoided a number of patrols by taking the back streets. They pass through the steel gates and enter the main compound and proceed to the operations room on the second floor. After they have all greeted each other, Miguel Enríquez takes control and calls the Moneda. He speaks to Paredes who asks him when they are going to come and help defend the palace. But the messages have been conflicting. Allende has asked them not to engage in acts of popular resistance. Now the former head of Investigations insists they march on the seat of government.

"What exactly does the president want us to do?" asks Miguel.

"Things have changed. And not for the better. We need all the people we can get," says Paredes.

Miguel can hear the sounds of gunfire in the background. It appears the situation around the palace has indeed worsened.

"OK. I'll speak with the others."

The MIR leader then tells his companions what he has just heard.

"What are we waiting for? Let's go," says Ariel Ulloa, one of the Socialists.

In spite of his comrade's eagerness, Miguel does not want to rush things. For one thing he has not received a direct order from the president. Also, there are only a handful of them at the Indumet factory. To try and reach the palace with such a small force would be suicidal. It is better to wait until they have as many supporters as possible. He is hoping for several hundred paramilitaries.

"We need to gather as big a force as we can," and he surveys his comrades with his dark eyes. "We'll wait until one o'clock. We can meet up with people then."

Ulloa takes out a piece of paper and begins to draw a rough diagram. He explains that they could approach the palace in two groups, running parallel to each other. The Socialists could go by Avenida Santa Rosa, while those from MIR could travel via Avenida Cochrane. As they discuss the route a comrade suddenly puts his head round the door and shouts:

"Everyone grab your guns! We're surrounded!"

Chairs are knocked over with a crash as the leaders race to pick up their weapons and head for the door. The carabineros have surprised them by using local transport, instead of military vehicles. It was only when they began to pour out of the buses, that the paramilitaries realised what was happening. The soldiers quickly encircle the factory and a carabinero officer with a loudhailer tells the paramilitaries to give themselves up.

They answer him with a volley of shots and the officer throws himself to the ground, along with the rest of his men who return fire.

Inside the main building the leaders rapidly descend the steel stairs, while bullets ricochet across the factory floor. There is a resounding clash of metal upon metal, as if some demented god were hammering away in the underworld. Bullets whine and ping off girders, causing sprays of sparks. A man called Leon is hit in the thigh and falls. Ulloa and another companion grab an arm and drag their wounded comrade to safety.

They join the others at the rear of the factory and pause for breath, the din of battle ringing in their ears. Amid the hellish cacophony the group briefly discuss their options. They decide the best way to escape is to make a break all at once and divide themselves into three groups, each taking a different route out of the complex. The paramilitaries have an advantage over the soldiers in that they know the layout by heart.

At a signal the men all rush outside, their weapons blazing. As they make their way across the dusty ground, the group separates. Leon, realising that he is slowing his comrades down, tells Ulloa and the other man to let go. They take cover behind some empty oil drums and the wounded paramilitary slots a fresh magazine into his AK47. He puts it to his shoulder and settles himself against a drum.

"OK," he says.

The other two make no move and their comrade turns and looks at them angrily.

"My leg's fucked! Now go!"

Ulloa and his companion need no further encouragement and sprint for the perimetre fence, Leon's AK47 clattering behind them. Bullets sing around their ears and kick up spurts of dust, as they race and weave across the open ground. Ulloa's comrade cries out and falls, but he does not stop and keeps on running. The chain link fence is only metres away. He drops his weapon and scales it with a single vault, landing in a heap on the other side. The paramilitary is winded by the fall, but he jumps up and sprints past the lines of buses and carabineros and disappears into the surrounding neighbourhood.

The area is crawling with soldiers. A jeep with a mounted machine gun races across a junction, a soldier firing over the head of the driver. Ulloa dives down another street and continues running. He comes to a crossroad and stops and pauses for breath, resting against a telegraph pole. His chest heaves with exertion and he spits drily into the dust. There is a shout and the paramilitary spins round and sees soldiers rushing down the street towards him, their weapons drawn.

"Hey you!" they shout.

Shots whistle past Ulloa's head as he darts down an alley and too late, he realises that it is a dead end. He is trapped. He quickly jumps over a garden fence and opens the back door of the nearest house. A shocked elderly couple look up as he passes through their kitchen and leaves by the front. The paramilitary hurdles three more garden fences and pounds on the door of another house.

"Open up! It's the police!"

An ancient, birdlike woman with snow white hair appears and Ulloa leaps inside and slams the door shut.

"But you're not the police!" the old lady protests.

The intruder smiles and puts a finger to her lips.

"Not a word grandma, thanks."

The soldiers follow their quarry through the first house, the bemused couple still sitting at their kitchen table as the platoon stomp past. They too leave by the front door and look up and down the road, but the man they were chasing has disappeared into thin air.

The officer stands there looking aggrieved, as if he has just been robbed.

"Sonofabitch!" he says. "OK," he tells his men. "He can't have gone far. Let's search the houses one by one."

*

At Tomás Moro the neighbours casually inspect the damaged presidential residence, like the curious at the scene of a traffic accident. A gaping hole yawns in the roof and the front door leans sadly from its hinges. It is not long before the more adventurous step inside and emerge carrying various trophies. Others take their cue, pilfering whatever souvenirs catch their eye. After all, it is not every day that you can help yourself to a president's personal belongings. Some neighbours try to prevent it, but the looters are many and the honest few.

"He's ruined the country! He owes it to me!" says one indignant man as he is stopped with an oil painting in one arm and a television under the other.

"Why don't you go and rob the houses of the Christian

Democrats or the military," says the neighbour who has waylaid him. "After all, it's their fault not his."

The looter brushes him aside, telling him to mind his own business and stalks off with his booty. Finally, some soldiers come and seal off the residence.

As they stand guard the president's sister Laura Pascal arrives, believing Hortensia is still there. When she learns the first lady is not, she angrily asks the soldiers what they have done with her. The conscripts pull faces and reply they have no idea where she is.

"Let me inside!" she says.

"No one's allowed to enter. Orders," says a sergeant.

"But it's our house!"

The NCO remains unmoved and refuses to let her in.

Hearing the altercation, the same neighbour who had words with one of the looters approaches. The man takes Laura back to his home, which is opposite the Allendes'. They sit down in the living-room and his wife asks the maid to make them all some coffee.

"I'm sorry," says the neighbour. "I tried to stop them, but it was impossible."

"It's OK. You did more than most would."

"Some people have no respect for others. It's shameful," adds the neighbour's wife.

The maid appears carrying a tray with a silver pot and some cups and puts it down on the table and leaves. The wife pours the coffee and they sip their drinks and agree that it is extraordinary such a thing could be happening in a country like Chile. They just cannot understand. It was as if the nation had willingly pressed the self-destruct button. It was madness, really it was. There was no other word for it. Madness.

Laura finishes her coffee and thanks the couple for their kindness and hospitality. They get up and the husband sees her to the door and again apologizes for the looting of Tomás Moro.

"Listen, if there were more people like you, none of this would have happened," and Laura kisses the good neighbour on the cheek.

The president's sister walks to her car and gets in. She starts the engine and drives away in a tearful daze, not knowing what has happened either to her brother or his family.

VI
DEATH ALONE

In the Moneda, amid the fog of tear gas and smoke and the crash of gunfire reverberating all around, the president is sitting under his desk. With him are the General Government Secretary, Fernando Flores, the Under Secretary for the Interior, Daniel Vergara, and Osvaldo Puccio and his son. Allende has agreed the three ministers should go to the MOD as a delegation, in order to try and negotiate a truce with the junta. They have also heard the air force is now bombing the poorer areas of the city, in particular La Legua and La Reina, where resistance has broken out. The president wants the high command to stop the attacks and begin talks. Having refused to leave the palace despite the bombardment, he hopes the junta now realise that he will not surrender unconditionally. Allende also understands that power lies in their hands. As a compromise he is willing to step down from the presidency and put in his place a person who is acceptable to all sides. He is thinking of someone like Carlos Briones, who is widely respected as a moderate. The military would be able to keep whatever concessions they have already obtained. There would be no reprisals or recriminations. For their part the junta would have to guarantee to hold free and fair elections within a year.

Allende tells the emissaries that he will only resign, if all three of these conditions are met. The others agree the demands are not unreasonable. Inwardly they are glad that at last the president appears to be seeing sense. They also believe it is just possible the junta will agree to their proposals. But Allende does not share their optimism. The president knows the desire to negotiate is a hopeless one. It is a bluff in a round of poker and he is out of cards.

In his office on the fifth floor of the MOD Admiral Carvajal receives a message from the Moneda, saying the president now wished to negotiate. He picks up the microphone of the two-way radio on his desk, to inform Pinochet of the development.

"Post 5 to Post 1, are you receiving me?..."

"Post 1, loud and clear ..."

"This is Admiral Carvajal. Can I speak to General Pinochet please? ..."

"One moment admiral ..."

There is a pause while the aide calls across to Pinochet, who is standing over his model of the city and its regions and plotting the progress of his forces. The general goes over to the desk and speaks into the microphone.

"Patricio. What's up? ..."

"We've just had contact with the Moneda. Puccio called. Allende now wants to negotiate. He's sending three emissaries: Flores, Vergara and Puccio. We'll collect them at the entrance on 80 Morandé. There's no way we're going to talk. We'll arrest them instead..."

"If we do that, the president certainly won't negotiate..."

"The time for that's long gone. Either he comes out with his hands up, or we go in shooting and bring him out feet first..."

There is a pause as Pinochet reflects. If they go in shooting, Allende will end up becoming a martyr. And that is something none of them want.

"Maybe we can persuade the emissaries to tell him it's all over ..."

"We can try, but he won't budge ..."

"OK. Your call ..."

"Roger that. Post 5 out ..."

*

In the palace Augusto Olivares goes to the bathroom under

the staircase, which leads up to the state rooms on the first floor. He does not bother to shut the door. As he urinates the head of the medical team Oscar Soto passes. The doctor sees the television chief's broad shoulders, topped by his head of black hair as he stands over the bowl.

"What a pisser eh?"

"Sure is!" says Olivares and he flushes the toilet with a watery roar.

Soto smiles and is halfway up the stairs, when he hears a single shot ring out. Immediately the doctor rushes back down. Olivares is lying slumped on a chair in the staff dining-room, blood pouring from a head wound. In his hand is a pistol. The doctor hesitates. He is momentarily stunned as he watches a pool of gore creep across the tiles. Behind him Carlos Jorquera appears. Seeing his friend lying there covered in blood, he turns round and shouts hysterically.

"Perro's killed himself! Perro's killed himself!"

Two other doctors from the nearby medical unit, Patricio Arroyo and Patricio Guijón, arrive and moments later the former health minister Arturo Jirón. The doctors take Olivares by the arms and lay him down on the floor. There is a neat hole in the television chief's right temple, through which his pink and scrambled brains are visible. Olivares is not quite dead and his eyelids flutter briefly, opening and closing like butterfly wings. Jirón squats on his heels and takes the dying man's head in his arms and cradles it tenderly. Blood spills from the wound onto his shirt, but he does not notice. Instead he looks deep into Olivares' dilated pupils. It seems as though he is staring into infinity. The former minister peers into the television chief's dark eyes until the last moment, when he finally expires and the light within flickers and dies.

Jirón releases Olivares' head and lays him gently on the floor. The doctor checks the man's pulse and nods to his colleagues, confirming what they already know. Perro Olivares is dead. Seeing this Jorquera slumps down beside the body, puts his hands to his face and begins to weep. No one speaks. Soto puts an arm around his colleague's heaving shoulders and tries to comfort him.

The former minister leaves the distraught press secretary in the care of the other doctors and wearily climbs the stairs to tell Allende what has happened. The president is in the midst of a firefight in the Salon Independencia and is shooting through a shattered window, the spent shell cases spilling from his AK47 onto the polished parquet floor. Jirón crouches down and calls out his name, shouting above the rattle of gunfire to make himself heard.

The president stops shooting and turns. Jirón tells him what has happened. Allende says nothing. He simply stares back in disbelief. He stands there blinking behind the heavy frames of his glasses, as though trying to recall some distant memory. The president wonders if he has heard correctly. El Perro? Dead? It was impossible. But the look on Jirón's face tells him otherwise. Allende nods and slings his weapon over his shoulder and follows the former minister downstairs.

He enters the small dining-room and sees the body of his friend and fellow combatant, lying in a pool of blood. Beside him is Jorquera, his face streaked with tears. Allende goes over to the press secretary and lays a hand on his shoulder.

"Poor Negro…" he says.

Jorquera looks up, but he is too distressed to speak. The president brings him to his feet and hugs him. It is too much for the press secretary and he begins to weep again. Allende continues to hold him and the two of them sway gently together in a long, slow dance of grief.

The president breaks from the embrace and calls for a minute's silence in memory of their dead comrade. They gather in a circle around the body, their faces downcast as they become lost in their own reflections. The religious among them pray. Sounds of gunfire echo in the stillness of the dining-room.

After a full minute Allende replaces his helmet and walks

back upstairs, his face resolute. At the top of the stairs he turns and gives a thumbs-up.

"This is for you Augusto!" he says.

*

As the president returns to do battle, the three emissaries and the younger Puccio approach the door on 80 Morandé with a white flag and tentatively open it. Immediately several shots strike the panels in rapid succession and the elder Puccio slams the door shut.

"We're never going to get out of here, even with our hands up!" he says.

Puccio goes upstairs to his office and calls General Baeza in the MOD, telling him the shooting has not stopped and that it is impossible to leave the building. Baeza promises to send an armoured car. The Presidential Secretary returns to the ground floor and a short while later a half-track arrives outside the entrance. Two soldiers rush out and tell the emissaries to open the door, while their comrades give them covering fire.

Vergara leaves first. The others swiftly follow, with the younger Puccio last. The four are bundled into the back of the vehicle and soldiers are placed between them. The half-track quickly departs as bullets pit the steel exterior and drives down Avenida Bandera, in order to avoid the earthworks along the Alameda. A few minutes later it comes to a halt outside the MOD and the group is escorted out. As they rush up the steps of the building, a volley of shots rings out and one the soldiers falls down dead.

The men hurry inside and are met by a naval lieutenant. He notices the Presidential Secretary is carrying a gas mask and asks him where he got it.

"The Moneda."

The officer takes it from him.

"Cheers. It'll make a nice trophy."

He sees Puccio smiling and his brow furrows.

"What the hell's so funny?"

"You can't get war trophies here, you can only get them over there," and the minister points to the smouldering palace on the other side of the plaza.

Furious, the lieutenant pistol-whips the emissary who staggers and clasps his head. His son remonstrates with the officer, only to be shoved back by a soldier.

"Fucking Commies!" says the lieutenant, as he stalks off with his souvenir.

The emissaries are taken upstairs to an office where they are confronted by Generals Baeza, Nuño and Díaz and Admiral Carvajal himself. The younger Puccio is left under guard outside. Carvajal immediately starts to hurl abuse at the ministers. His rage is such that he shakes with fury and as he berates them, his jowls tremble and gobs of spit fly from his mouth.

"You are nothing but a bunch of whores who've led Chile to the brink of disaster!"

The three emissaries are so amazed, they say nothing.

"At least we can save this country but, by God, you're going to pay for it. You're responsible for all the shit that's happening. Especially you!" he says, jabbing a finger at Flores. "You're one of the worst!"

Díaz also has a go and begins to berate the treasury minister.

"You dirty, Commie bastard! You're going to suffer hell for this!"

He seems even angrier than Carvajal, if that is possible. The admiral's outburst appears to have struck a chord of hatred that has simmered for months, or even years, and which only now is he able to exorcise. As Díaz's invective increases the guards start to slap and jeer the emissaries, who stand there rigid with fear, convinced they are about to die.

Puccio finally summons up the courage to speak and addresses Carvajal. After the tirade of the two senior officers, the Presidential Secretary's voice seems oddly serene, his words calm.

"Admiral, we have come to parley with you. We have been sent by the President of the Republic and you personally agreed to the meeting. You said the junta were interested in negotiating. Now you are hitting and abusing us instead of talking. If you don't want to listen to what we have to say that's fine. We'll go straight back."

Puccio's gently spoken words have their intended effect and General Baeza shoots an accusatory glance at his colleagues.

"It's OK Osvaldo. Sorry and please, tell us your message."

The Presidential Secretary looks at him. He is glad that at least one of the high command seems to have kept his head.

"It's Fernando who has the message," he answers. "You'll have to ask him."

"OK. Go ahead," Baeza tells the treasury minister.

Flores informs the defence chiefs of the president's demands while they listen. When he has finished they quit the room, leaving the emissaries alone with their guards.

"Thank God for that," whispers Vergara when they have gone. "I thought we'd had it."

"Hey! No talking," says a soldier, poking the Deputy Minister of the Interior in the ribs with his machine gun.

Presently Baeza returns and announces that Flores and Vergara are to remain in the MOD, while Puccio is to go back to the Moneda with the junta's reply.

"Our conditions are as follows," says the general. "There is to be unconditional surrender. President Allende and his family are to leave the country immediately together with Briones, Letelier and you Puccio. The junta will decide later what happens to the rest."

The Presidential Secretary asks for a piece of paper, so that he can write all this down. He explains the military will have to sign it, if the demands are to carry any weight with the president. Puccio is then handed a piece of paper and Baeza leaves again.

As the emissary finishes copying down the junta's conditions, Baeza enters the room once more, this time accompanied by his fellow generals and Carvajal.

"There's no need to return now," announces the admiral beaming, "the president has just this moment surrendered!"

The three men look at each other. They do not believe a word of it, but there is nothing they can do.

"Puccio don't worry about your son. I'll have my driver take him home," says Nuño. The Presidential Secretary smiles gratefully. His son's loyalty has been unimpeachable, but he has no business being involved in his father's political travails. He should be safe at home with the family.

The emissaries are then dismissed and led downstairs, Vergara being singled out for abuse by the guards.

"Hey Barnabas!" they mock. "Tell us everything is coo-ool and nothing is going to hap-pen."

'Barnabas' is Vergara's nickname and a particularly odious character in a popular British television drama, to whom he bears an unfortunate resemblance.

The prisoners are put in separate rooms and shortly afterwards Puccio's son joins him. The Presidential Secretary tells him what happened in the meeting.

"Doesn't look too good does it?"

"No," agrees his father. "At least Nuño says his driver will take you home."

"I'll tell Mum and the boys not to worry."

"Yes, do that. I'm sure they'll release us soon. If not today, then perhaps tomorrow."

"How's the head?"

"Oh. It's OK," and the elder Puccio rubs the spot tenderly. "Just a flesh wound," he says, smiling.

There is silence as father and son sit there, each wondering what the military intend to do with them. Later, the door opens and an officer enters. It is the same man who pistol-whipped the Presidential Secretary. The lieutenant stands there flanked by some guards. He seems surprised that Puccio's son is still with him.

"You again?" he says, looking at the youth.

"Yes...?"

"What the hell are you doing here?"

Before the younger Puccio can reply, a guard explains that General Nuño has promised to have the boy escorted home. His superior looks appalled, as if he has been asked to pick up dog shit.

"Not if I can help it! I know all about little Osvaldo Puccio. He's a filthy Mirista and he's not going anywhere!"

The officer turns on his heel and leaves along with the guards. When they have gone the Presidential Secretary puts an arm around his son to reassure him. Both realise they are about to be separated and might not see each other again. Neither of them speak and Puccio's arm remains wrapped around his boy's shoulders. Presently, the lieutenant returns.

"Come with me," he announces. "You're going to be interrogated."

The Presidential Secretary can only look on helplessly as his son is hustled out of the room. The youth manages a brief backward glance, before the door is shut behind him.

Puccio is left on his own. He shakes his head in disbelief. He just cannot understand. They had come to the MOD to negotiate, but rather than talk the military have locked them up. Now, to make matters worse, instead of taking Osvaldo home as they had promised, they were going to interrogate him. The thought is far more painful to the minister than the blow he received to his head. He touches the bruise tentatively with his fingertips and feels a lump the size of a hen's egg beneath his scalp. This hurt he can endure. What really concerns Puccio is his son. Although he is twenty, to his father he is no more than a boy. The Presidential Secretary is convinced he will never see him again. It is more than he can endure and he clasps his hands in prayer.

"Dear God," he whispers. "Please don't let them kill him."

*

General Jorge Urrutia is in his office at the carabineros headquarters. He has not moved for the past hour and sits at his desk staring into space. He glances at his watch and sees it is now 1:00pm. He realises he has not eaten all day and decides to go to the Carabineros Club for lunch. The general puts on his cap and makes his way downstairs. It is only a short distance away and he decides to walk. The club is a fine old neo-classical building, which formerly belonged to a wealthy senator.

The general ascends the flagstone steps and is greeted at the door by one of the white jacketed orderlies, who takes his hat and gloves. He goes inside and enters the Cochrane Lounge, where he orders a whisky and soda at the bar. Urrutia takes his aperitif and downs it quickly, then orders another. He drinks this one more slowly, the spirit and the old world atmosphere working its charm. The room is hung with nineteenth century portraits of Chile's military leaders, including the British admiral Lord Cochrane after whom it is named and the nation's other great hero Commander Arturo Prat, who was killed in the War of the Pacific in 1879. The general takes his glass and goes towards some leather armchairs in a corner. In one of them a carabinero officer sits with his back to him, facing the tall windows which look out onto the courtyard. It is Urrutia's chief, José Maria Sepulveda.

"Where on earth have you been?"

"I could ask you the same," and he puts down the magazine he has been flicking through.

"The president told me to go to the General Prefecture to see who else was there. I thought you'd left."

"I was in the Chancellery talking to Mendoza on the phone. I tried to persuade him to stop the bombing, but he didn't want to know. He kept insisting I join the rebels. The president ordered me to leave just before the bombardment began."

Urrutia nods and sees Sepulveda's glass is empty.

"Care for another?"

"Why not? Might as well poison myself."

His friend smiles.

"Better than hemlock. What'll it be?"

"Tanqueray and tonic, with a dash of Angostura. No ice. Thanks."

The Deputy Director calls over a waiter, who takes the order and departs. He returns with the drink on a silver tray, which he places on the table along with a bowl of pistachios. Urrutia is about to sign the chit, when Sepulveda stops him.

"Please put it on General Mendoza's tab," he says.

The waiter grins broadly and leaves.

Later, a carabinero colonel enters the lounge. He recognises the two generals in the armchairs and approaches them.

"The shit you've done today!"

"Really? And have you seen the Moneda lately?" says Urrutia, who finishes off his whisky and puts the empty glass down on the table.

The rebel officer is offended by the remark and without another word, he walks off to the bar. Other senior carabineros arrive and the disgruntled colonel points out Urrutia and Sepulveda, sitting on their own in the corner. The officers go over to them. They are more polite than the colonel and invite the generals to join them for lunch. Urrutia is astounded. These men have overthrown the constitutional government and are responsible for bombing the presidential palace. They have broken their oaths of commission and are guilty of high treason and yet they expect a pair of loyalist generals to dine with them, as though they had done nothing more than play on opposing football teams.

"I'm sorry," Urrutia says and he rises from his chair. "I

only came here for a drink. Really, I don't feel like lunch. In fact I'd better be getting back to headquarters."

"Got a lot of work to do?" asks one of the officers, a glint of sarcasm in his voice.

Urrutia ignores the slight and wishing them all well, he says goodbye to Sepulveda who remains. The general cannot wait to get out of the stifling confines of the club and its old boy bonhomie. Instead of being reassuring, the chummy atmosphere now makes him want to choke. Urrutia needs air, clean fresh air. He hurries outside, brushing past the orderly who is waiting with his cap and gloves. The general stands at the entrance and breathes deeply. The whisky has made him light-headed and the buildings around him start to spin. He feels as though he is losing his mind and remains motionless as he tries to gather his senses. After a few deep breaths Urrutia's equilibrium returns and feeling better, he walks back to Norambuena.

On arrival, the general goes straight upstairs to his office and once inside, he locks the door and sits down at his desk. The trip to the club had been a mistake, although he is glad he saw Sepulveda. At least old Sepa was all right. How he had managed to remain so calm with those other generals, Urrutia has no idea. He had felt like screaming. Those bastards! The nerve, the absolute nerve. 'Stay for lunch dear chap'. 'Have another drink why don't you?'. 'Excuse me while I bomb the palace!'

The general bangs his desk in frustration.

"The country has gone mad!" he shouts, his voice echoing flatly against the white walls. No one can hear him. He is alone.

"Oh God...oh God," Urrutia moans and he puts a fist to his forehead.

The general wishes he could end it all now. Then he lowers his hand and smiles. It is as though a cloud has lifted and what was obscured by fog, is now revealed in bright sunshine. There was something he could do that would make a difference. He wonders why he had not thought of it before. It was easy. He takes out his service revolver from its holster and inspects it with grim appreciation. 'Problem solver,' they called it in the force.

Urrutia raises the weapon and places the barrel in his mouth. He can taste the gun oil, feel the cold steel against his tongue. He closes his eyes and in his self-imposed blackout, waits for the moment when he is ready to pull the trigger. He waits. And he waits. But the moment does not come. The general removes the gun. He is weeping. His shoulders heave and hot tears roll down his cheeks and he begins to sob. He puts the pistol down and opens his eyes and daylight enters his head once more. Daylight which he never expected to see again.

Everything was hopeless. Urrutia realises he does not even have the courage to commit suicide. He sits in his chair, staring at the revolver on the desk. The general is still sitting in the same position two hours later, when a carabinero unit bursts in and arrests him.

*

In one of the presidential offices a two-way radio bleeps. A GAP answers and a voice asks to speak to Inspector Seoane. The bodyguard calls across to the senior detective, who picks up the microphone. On the other end is an officer from carabinero headquarters.

"Is the president dead?" asks a voice.

"No, the president is very much alive."

There is a pause, as though this latest piece of information is a surprise to the caller. The voice then continues.

"Look, Chief Inspector Carrasco wants to speak with you."

Carrasco, who is third in command of Investigations, comes on the line.

"Seoane, tell me is the president well?"

"Seems fine to me."

"He hasn't gone..." and the chief inspector lowers his voice, to make sure no one else can hear. "He hasn't gone a little crazy?"

"Crazy? No. Angry, possibly."

"It's just that I was wondering about his mental stability."

"What do you mean his mental stability?"

"Well, why's he still fighting?"

"Because he's the president. Or at least he was when I last saw him."

There is an audible sigh from Carrasco. The inspector's penchant for sarcasm is a new one to him.

"Seoane, you know what the situation is. The palace is surrounded by tanks and soldiers. All four branches of the armed forces have rebelled. Give yourselves up. You'll save a lot of lives, including your own."

"I only take orders from the president."

"What about the other detectives?"

"They only take orders from me."

Despite the inspector's cussedness, Carrasco persists. He understands and respects his subordinate's loyalty, but does not want either him or his men to die needlessly, which they will do if the military storm the Moneda.

"Look, both Sepulveda and Urrutia have been sacked. I'm now in command of Investigations on the instructions of the MOD and the junta..."

"Congratulations."

"This is no time for jokes."

"Then stop shooting."

"That's the whole point of this damn call!" and Carrasco's voice rises, before he checks himself and speaks calmly again. "Seoane, tell the president I can organise a ceasefire, so you can all surrender. I promise no one will be harmed."

"Fine, I'll do that."

The inspector switches off the mic and goes off to look for the president, leaving a detective next to the radio in case Carrasco should call while he is gone.

He discovers Allende at the end of a corridor near the Salon Independencia, where some of the doctors and civilians had taken cover during the bombardment. The president is accompanied by his friends and bodyguard and the remaining personnel, who have gathered there for safety. The passage is mostly in shadow because the electricity has been cut and clouds of smoke and tear gas drift eerily about like fog on a winter's day.

Seoane sees Paredes and gives his former boss the message. The ex-Director of Investigations goes over to Allende. They have been holding out in the vain hope that MIR and the Socialist paramilitaries are on their way to relieve the Moneda, although they have heard no news from either group since midday. They do not know about the firefight at the Indumet complex and that the men have either been killed or taken prisoner, or else have gone to ground.

"Salvador," Paredes says. "I don't think the paramilitaries are going to come. No one can leave their houses. We're alone in the Moneda.

"I know."

Allende realises that since they have had no word from the three emissaries: Flores, Vergara and Puccio must also have failed in their mission. Since all negotiations have proved fruitless, the only alternative is to stay on and fight. Even so, the president is anxious to avoid any unnecessary deaths, especially after Olivares' suicide, and wants the remaining civilians and detectives to leave. Amid the sporadic crackle of gunfire and the fog of tear gas and smoke, Allende turns to Paredes.

"Coco, tell everyone I want them to leave."

"Sure, I'll do that."

Paredes approaches the medical team and asks them to get ready to depart and to pass the message on. He then goes back to Seoane, who has been waiting patiently and tells him to keep the lines of communication with Carrasco open.

The inspector returns to the office and as he enters the two-way radio bleeps again. He switches on the mic. It is Carrasco.

"Seoane?"

"Speaking."

"Tell the president I've spoken with the forces surrounding the palace. Everyone can leave so long as you do so singly and with a white flag."

"OK," says the inspector.

He goes back to the darkened, smoke-filled corridor and this time relays Carrasco's message to Allende himself. The president nods and looks satisfied. It is what he wanted to hear. At least those who leave now can do so without getting shot. But in case some refuse to go, Allende decides to announce that he is surrendering as well. For one thing he knows it will be the only way to get the indomitable La Payita out of the palace. He gets to his feet and calls out to everyone in the passage.

"Listen. I want you all to go downstairs. The Moneda is surrounded and we cannot continue like this. If we stay, we'll all be killed. We have to surrender. There is no alternative. The military have promised not to harm anybody. They have given their word. You must leave singly. La Payita will go first and I shall be last."

The civilians and defenders line up and start to leave and the president stands at the top of the stairs, shaking each one by the hand and thanking them for their loyalty. The doctors, the detectives and the remaining government officials all begin to depart. The group slowly descends the stairs, which lead down to the entrance on 80 Morandé. It is hard to see because of the smoke and they all go carefully. Oscar Soto passes by a window and a bullet shatters the glass, sending him diving to the ground. The head of the medical unit is unhurt and his companions pick up their shaken colleague and dust him down and continue their descent. On the ground floor one of the doctors takes off his white coat and wraps it around a broom and the group prepare to leave the palace.

Allende and his bodyguard remain behind. Several are injured and have bound their wounds with rudimentary bandages. The president observes them all proudly. They have fought like lions against overwhelming odds. That morning some of them were no more than boys. Now they are men. He tells the GAP to resume their positions on the upper floor and brace themselves for the final assault. Then he goes off to the Salon Independencia.

"I shan't be long," he says and closes the door.

*

The group of civilians gather on the ground floor. As they approach the door, Patricio Guijón realises that he is witnessing history and has nothing to show for it, not even his gas mask. He had taken it off when he removed his white coat to improvise a flag of truce, which they had hung from one of the windows. The doctor does not need the mask anymore, but as he waits in the hall he reflects: 'this is the first time I have been in a war. My sons might want a memento. I'll get my mask which I left in the corridor.' And without a word he turns and makes his way back upstairs.

It is dark and the corridor is filled with smoke. There is nobody about. The doctor searches for his gas mask, but cannot find it and concludes that someone else must have picked it up. Then he remembers there were some lying around in the Salon Independencia. He could take one of those.

Guijón approaches the wooden door and opens it. He sees the president sitting on a sofa with an AK47 placed between his legs, the barrel under his chin. Allende does not look up. Instead he pulls the trigger and two rounds are fired in rapid succession, the force knocking him backwards. His cranium splits open and his brains splatter onto the wall behind. The doctor rushes over to the stricken president and instinctively takes his pulse. It is pointless. Allende is already dead.

*

The last of those to descend the stairs hear the shots and rush back. As Guijón kneels beside the body, a group of people enter the room. Among them are Arturo Jirón and Oscar Soto. Coco Paredes and Enrique Huerta are also there, as is one of the president's bodyguard called 'Ignacio'.
"What the hell happened?" asks the GAP.
"The president shot himself," says Guijón, visibly shaken.
The others look stunned. No one expected this. Allende said he would surrender along with them. Now he was dead. They stand there for a moment in silence and then begin to leave. Paredes turns, raises his fist and calls out.
"Viva Chile! Viva Salvador!"
Others echo the words as they depart and the room empties except for Guijón, who remains alone beside the president's body. He does so out of a sense of duty and also because shooting has started again, as the remaining GAP fight on.

*

General Palacios and his forces from the Second Tank Regiment are gathered around the evacuated Office of Administration on Avenida Moneda. He is waiting for more firepower to arrive, before he begins his assault on the door of 80 Morandé. The fighting has been fierce. It has already cost him several men to get this far. The general looks at the soldiers surrounding him. That morning they had refused to believe there had been a coup, until he climbed onto a tank and took command. Although Palacios knew the whole of the armed forces were behind the uprising these men, who had already risen during the abortive Tancazo, must surely have doubted it. Nevertheless, they had followed him without question and proved their valour in battle. The general surveys their youthful faces, some barely shave, and he is proud of them.

The tanks Palacios has been waiting for arrive and ordering them to give his unit covering fire, he advances towards 80 Morandé. The general hurries across the street and sees a white coat hanging from a balcony. Perhaps they will not have to fight their way in after all. But the remaining defenders on the first floor take no notice of the flag of truce, hanging limply from the palace window like some piece of discarded washing, and open fire. The rest of the platoon joins Palacios and he motions to a pair of soldiers carrying sledgehammers to come forward and do their work.

In the hallway the civilians are about to open the door, when the solid wood reverberates to the thud of heavy blows and begins to splinter, before collapsing on its hinges. Soldiers kick the broken panels aside and charge in. At their head is Palacios, shouting and waving his pistol, one of the lenses of his glasses shattered.

"All of you, get your hands in the air!"

The soldiers are pumped with fear and adrenaline. They shove the civilians against the wall, cursing and striking out indiscriminately with their boots and rifle butts. Once the people are lined up and searched, the situation becomes calmer. The general begins a head count. There appears to be about forty, including the detectives. He orders them to be taken outside and they are made to lie face down on the ground.

*

In the Salon Independencia, Patricio Guijón sits next to the president's corpse. He sees Allende's weapon and pushes it away. He does not want to be mistaken for a defender. Guijón wishes now he had not taken off his white coat, which was the only thing that visibly identified him as a doctor. There is shooting along the upper floors of the building, as the remaining GAP continue to do battle and Guijón realises it is safer to stay where he is.

The ceiling of the room is in flames and the smoke makes it difficult for the doctor to breathe. He sees an abandoned gas mask nearby and holds it to his face. There is barely any oxygen left, but it helps. The rattle of gunfire and the crash of exploding grenades echoes along the corridor. The doctor remains beside the body of his dead president, listening to the sounds of fighting and drawing shallow breaths from the mask.

Suddenly the door is kicked open and a burst of gunfire sends Guijón sprawling across the floor.

"Don't shoot! Don't shoot!" he cries, waving his arms frantically. "I'm a doctor!"

A group of soldiers stand in the doorway, the smoking muzzles of their weapons trained upon him. Around their necks they wear orange cravats. They are from the Infantry School regiment. One of them comes forward, his machine gun pointing directly at the terrified figure.

"Don't shoot…please! I'm just a doctor!"

"What's your name?"

"Patricio Guijón. I'm from the palace medical unit."

"Show us your papers!"

Guijón fumbles inside his jacket and produces his identity card, together with his palace pass, which he hands over. The soldier inspects the papers and seems satisfied. He does not return the items and instead puts them in the top pocket of his battle smock.

"Who's this?" and he points at the body sprawled across the sofa. The doctor notices the twin chevrons on his upper arm. The man is a corporal.

"The president," he says.

The NCO moves closer and inspects Allende's shattered face.

"Shit, it is too! Quick," he tells a subordinate, "go and get the captain."

*

A burst of gunfire from upstairs sends Palacios and his men diving to the ground. The general realises that not everyone has given up. Pistol in hand, he leads his unit up the stairs to the first floor and follows the sound of gunfire. The group makes its way towards the presidential gallery on the north side of the palace, where the remaining GAP are putting up a desperate last stand. The defenders shout obscenities at the soldiers and encourage each other as they leap out from doorways and dash from cover to cover. The sound of battle and profanity fills the air.

The soldiers advance as the GAP retreat from room to room, firing all the time. Inside the presidential gallery Palacios suddenly finds himself face to face with a young defender. There is an instant as the adversaries look at each other before the boy opens fire, missing the general, but wounding a sergeant in the stomach beside him. A lieutenant quickly steps forward and returns fire with his own weapon. He keeps shooting and empties his magazine at the GAP. A bullet ricochets and strikes Palacios in the hand, as their adversary falls to the floor. The general stands there clutching his wound and looks down at the defender who almost killed him. The GAP has a long tear in his trousers, exposing a red-stained bandage. Palacios is amazed that he could stand, let alone fight.

A soldier sees the general's bloody hand and offers his handkerchief.

"Here, use this sir."

"Thanks," he says, wrapping it tightly around the cut. "I'm OK. It's just a scratch."

The young GAP at their feet is seriously wounded. It is José Huenchullán, the boy who spent the night on Tomás Moro's roof along with his friend Cuico, the first defender to die that day. Palacios kneels down and asks the youth his name and he replies faintly.

"Where are you from sonny?"

"Colonia Boroa."

"I know that place! It's near Temuco. Very beautiful. I go there sometimes for my holidays. You got any papers?"

"Sure, they're in my pocket. Excuse me if I don't get 'em out…it's kinda difficult to move."

Huenchullán has a sucking chest wound and speaks in a gurgling whisper, his lungs slowly filling with blood. Palacios reaches inside the GAP's leather jacket and removes the papers, which he checks. The general sees from his date of birth that he is only twenty.

"Why on earth didn't you give up?" he asks, as he pockets the ID.

"We made a pact sir…to fight on to the last…," and the boy smiles wanly. "Besides…who wants to live forever?"

Palacios sees that the youth is fading and gets to his feet.

"Get him to hospital quickly," he tells the soldiers.

Huenchullán is carried away and the general and his unit continue. The shooting, although still spirited, is noticeably less. The general estimates there must only be a handful of defenders left. When he reaches O'Higgins Hall, the place is in flames. He orders his men to try and save the furniture and seeing the Liberator's sabre, he rescues the weapon and hands it to an aide.

There is a final exchange of fire and the last of the defenders are overcome, as they run out of ammunition and find themselves trapped by Infantry School forces, who have advanced up the stairs behind. The remaining GAP are disarmed, put under escort and taken downstairs. Palacios, pistol in hand, walks back through the burning hall as soldiers run to and fro, removing pictures and valuable pieces of furniture. He wonders where Allende has got to and it occurs to him that in the confusion, the president might have escaped.

A handsome, blond-haired officer approaches the general and salutes him.

"Captain Roberto Garrido, Infantry School."

"What is it?"

"Sir, the president's dead."

"You sure?"

"Yes. His body's in the Salon Independencia. Looks like he committed suicide."

Palacios is surprised. He doubted Allende would have allowed himself to be taken alive, but even so the knowledge of his death comes as a shock.

"OK, let's go."

Garrido leads the way and takes the general to the state room. They enter the Salon Independencia and Palacios sees Allende's body lying slumped on the sofa, his legs splayed and his cranium shattered. The wall behind is covered in gore. On the floor lies an AK47. Standing nervously to one side is a civilian.

"Who's this?"

"A doctor from the medical unit. We found him here."

Palacios merely nods and turns to a signaller with a radio set.

"Get me the MOD."

The soldier makes the connection and hands the receiver to the general.

"Attention Post 5. Combat Unit Blue. Over…"

"Post 5 receiving. Proceed…"

"This is General Palacios. I wish to speak to Admiral Carvajal…"

There is a moment before Carvajal comes on the line.

"Hello..."

"The Moneda is secure. The president is dead…"

"Dead?..."

"Yes, his body's here. Suicide we think…"

"Any witnesses?..."

Palacios looks at Guijón beside him.

"One that we know of..."
"Is he a civilian?..."
"Yes. He's a doctor from the medical unit..."
"Take him under escort to the MOD immediately..."
"Roger and out..."

The general hands the receiver back to the signaller and addresses the pale faced medic.

"I've got orders to send you to the ministry. Don't worry, nothing's going to happen. You're going to be debriefed that's all."

The doctor is too scared to answer. His light brown eyes are fixed and staring like a hypnotised rabbit's.

*

Palacios leaves the Salon Independencia and descends the stairs to the entrance on 80 Morandé. A dejected Guijón follows, flanked by some soldiers and the group emerges into the street. The general tells him to stand to one side and goes off to issue orders to his men. With his back to the palace wall, the doctor surveys the scene. The Moneda prisoners are lying on the ground, their arms stretched out. Soldiers stand over them and mock, the barrels of their weapons pointing at the captives' backs.

A female voice cries out and Palacios turns round.

"Who the hell's this?"

"It's Miria Contreras, the president's secretary sir," says a lieutenant, who recognises La Payita as she staggers to her feet, falls and then rises again. She begins to sob and grabs Palacios by the arm, clawing at him hysterically.

"No! No! No!" she cries.

Momentarily the general is at a loss as to what he should do and embarrassed, he gently removes her hands from his uniform.

"Calm your self madam please," he says and turns to the officer. "Get her out of here for heaven's sake!"

The lieutenant motions to some soldiers nearby, who grab the president's secretary and carry her kicking and screaming to an ambulance. They bundle the woman into a waiting vehicle and shut the doors. Inside the ambulance La Payita continues to howl.

Suddenly another prisoner on the ground starts to moan. The man curls up into a ball and makes desperate gagging noises. Palacios hears this and tells two doctors lying nearby to find out what is wrong. Patricio Arroyo and Jose Quiroga, both members of the palace medical team, go over to the man who is now gasping and writhing in agony. It is Luis Gonzalez, otherwise known as 'Eladio'. He is one of the youngest GAP and only nineteen. As the doctors look into his eyes to check the dilation of his pupils, they realise he is faking. Arroyo and Quiroga exchange glances. It is only for a moment, but it is enough. The doctors look up and tell Palacios the man has a ruptured appendix and must be operated on immediately.

"OK, take him to the Military Hospital," orders the general.

Arroyo and Quiroga are joined by two other colleagues and together they haul the still convulsing Eladio to his feet and carry him to the same ambulance, which contains La Payita. Arroyo tells the driver not to go to the Military Hospital, but to the civilian Central Post of Public Assistance instead. The vehicle then departs its lights flashing and siren wailing.

The soldiers tell the medics to get back on the ground. The rest of the prisoners are ordered to their feet and escorted to the main entrance, opposite the Ministry of Public Works, where they are made to lie down again.

Arturo Jirón turns his face to see who is next to him. It is Oscar Soto.

"We're fucked comrade," he says.

"We will be if you don't shut up," comes the terse reply.

*

Guijón feels embarrassed that his colleagues in front of him are forced to lie prostrate, while he is able to stand. They were after all non-combatants like him and he decides to tell Palacios. The general seemed a reasonable man. In the Salon Independencia he could simply have produced his revolver and shot him. No one would have ever known.

"Sir, may I have a word with you."

"Of course, what is it?"

"My colleagues in the palace medical unit. They shouldn't have to lie in the street. They're just doctors like me."

Palacios observes the fresh-faced medic. Guijón is not wrong in his assumption of the general. He might be a rebel, but the officer has not forgotten the responsibilities that a soldier has towards civilians in a time of war. He realises that some of those in the Moneda must have been there simply out of a sense of duty, like the doctors.

"OK, tell them they can come here."

Guijón goes over and informs his four colleagues that they can stand. The doctors cross the street and join the general. Quiroga sees Palacios' wounded hand and dresses it, using a fireman's first aid kit. He tells him the cut is not serious, but that it will need stitches.

The general thanks him and admires his fresh bandage. Arroyo, ever the smoker, asks Palacios if he can have a cigarette.

"Sure," he replies.

"Want one?" and the doctor offers his packet.

"No thanks, don't smoke."

"Quite right. Bad for your health," says Arroyo who promptly lights up. As he puffs away he remembers his colleagues who are still under guard. "General, there are some others in the medical unit by the main entrance. Can they come and join us as well?"

"Certainly," says Palacios.

Arroyo is escorted to the front of the building and tells his colleagues they can get up. Hearing this Danilo Bartulin, Arturo Jirón and Oscar Soto, all rise to their feet. But Arroyo forgets that Coco Paredes, Enrique Paris and Jorge Klein are also doctors, since they were advisers and not part of the medical team. These three remain on the ground with the rest of the prisoners.

When the other doctors join Palacios, he collects all their IDs and announces they can go home.

"Except for you," he says, looking at Guijón. "You have to come with me to the MOD."

One of the firemen nearby approaches the general and reminds him that Jirón was formerly the Minister of Health and he too is made to stay.

A jeep is brought round and the members of the medical team are driven back to their homes. As it moves off another military communiqué is broadcast from Norambuena. The corporal driving the vehicle tunes the radio to get a better reception and the words ring out and flat and clear from the speaker.

The occupation of the Moneda has made secure the authority that has been imposed by the armed forces and the carabineros of Chile for the good of the country. It brings forth new hope for the country this springtime and we ask citizens to show their loyalty by flying the flag in front of their houses. This liberation and reordering of Chile is nothing but a cause for joy in this month, in which we commemorate the men and women who sacrificed themselves to give us our freedom.

The communiqué finishes and martial music is played. A few spots of rain begin to splash the windscreen and as it increases, the corporal switches on the wipers. The doctors in the back are numb with relief. They can scarcely believe they are on their way home. Amid the metronomic swish-swash of the wipers, comes the jaunty sound of a military brass band.

*

The ambulance arrives at the Central Post of Public Assistance Hospital and discharges La Payita and Eladio, who are then separated. The president's secretary is shown to a small room, where an attendant asks her name and she gives him a false one. The man then leaves and later a nurse, Maria Lizama, enters.

She takes one look at the woman's filthy, tear-streaked face and decides the first thing her patient needs is a tranquiliser, which she makes in a glass. Lizama gives it to La Payita who drinks the cloudy concoction. She downs the contents in a single gulp and looks up at the nurse, the mascara around her large brown eyes smudged by tears.

"Look," she says, "I need to tell you something."

The nurse puts a finger to her lips. She does not want to know. It is better for her patient to rest. Whatever it is she has to say, can be said later.

"Don't worry. You're in good hands here."

"You don't understand. I'm Allende's secretary Miria Contreras. I'm La Payita!"

Lizama is stunned and lets out a gasp, a mixture of surprise and concern, as if she had suddenly snagged her finger on a thorn. She never suspected her charge was so close to danger.

"I just to want to know about my son," the president's secretary continues in the same desperate tone. "They took him prisoner this morning along with some GAP, when we arrived at the Moneda."

La Payita's eyes fill with tears and she begins to sniffle, wiping her nose on the cuff of her blouse, because she has no handkerchief. It is in her handbag, which she left behind at the palace. The president's secretary turns away and twists her hands hopelessly in her lap, her eyes and nose streaming. Lizama tries to calm her and says she knows a doctor in the hospital who can help.

The president's secretary is not really listening and gazes out of the window, as she thinks about Enrique. He was just a kid. She realises she should never have taken him with her to the Moneda. What was she thinking? He should have stayed behind with Max at Tomás Moro.

Outside soldiers take cover behind the tall, grey trunks of some palm trees and shoot at the snipers in the San Borja buildings opposite. Bullets crack and pit the air and force the staff at the hospital entrance to take cover. A voice distracts La Payita and she turns away from the window.

"Are you injured?" asks Lizama.

"My right knee hurts," she says, looking down at her leg.

The nurse rolls up the trouser and sees a livid bruise just below the kneecap. The injury happened when La Payita feigned nervous collapse in the street. Lizama presses it gently to see if there is a break. Her patient winces and the nurse thinks there might be a fracture. The president's secretary dissolves into tears again.

"I don't know where my son is, or even if he's still alive…please help!"

"Listen," says Lizama. "I'm going to speak to that doctor I told you about. He'll know what to do. Don't worry, I shan't be long."

At that moment the door opens and another doctor enters the room. He looks across at the nurse.

"This patient being attended to?"

"Yes, she's fine. Just upset. She's about to be discharged," says Lizama, hoping the man will go.

The doctor nods. He is busy anyway and continues on his rounds.

When the door is closed, the nurse speaks again.

"Stay here. There are dozens of soldiers milling about checking IDs. If they come round say you're waiting for Dr

Reyes," and Lizama departs, leaving the president's secretary on her own.

The nurse hurries down the corridor and passes a stretcher with a wounded soldier. She notices the blank expression on his young face, a combination of morphine and shock. The man is bare-chested, a bloody dressing tied across his midriff with the words 'put other side to wound' stencilled across it.

Lizama does not think the man will survive and assumes that is why he has been left there, so the doctors can concentrate on saving those who still have a chance.

She carries on quickly down the passage and enters the reception area. The nurse takes the lift to the Traumatology Department on the third floor. The antiquated elevator surges slowly upwards and gives the sensation the floor is not rising, but sinking. A bell pings brightly and the doors open. Lizama steps out and sees who she is looking for.

Dr Alvaro Reyes is bandaging the arm of an old man. He chats away as he wraps the plaster around his patient's pale and wizened limb. The nurse waits for him to finish. It does not take long and the doctor hands the elderly man a prescription.

"And don't be playing football either," he adds with a smile, as he sends him on his way.

Reyes wipes his hands on a paper towel and notices his colleague.

"Hi Maria, what's up?" he says, dropping the towel into a bin.

Lizama hesitates. A group of nurses nearby are flirting with some carabineros. She leans forward and in a whisper tells the doctor about La Payita. He nods slowly, but says nothing. They take the lift to the ground floor and make their way to the side room, where the president's secretary is waiting.

Outside the Moneda the prisoners are lying face down on the ground. The cold tip of a gun barrel touches the nape of Carlos Jorquera's neck and a shiver, like a sharp-footed insect, runs down his spine.

"Wouldn't it be a crying shame," a voice mocks and the other soldiers laugh. But they are only playing games and to the press secretary's relief, the barrel is removed from his neck. He emits a low sigh and his heart beats dully like a funeral drum. He is in considerable pain. His shoulder has been dislocated by a blow from a gun butt and his face is covered in cuts from splinters.

A gleaming army boot appears beside Jorquera's cheek and he turns his head. An officer wearing a black beret and sunglasses towers above him, behind the sky is a grey and cloudy backdrop. The officer is distinguishable from the men because of his beret and uniform. On his hip a service revolver sits snug in a new leather holster and a shiny pair of handcuffs dangle from his belt. The well-polished official observes the dishevelled man at his feet.

"Well, if it isn't old Negro himself!" and he motions at the journalist to stand up.

The press secretary tries, but does not have the strength.

"Can't...my shoulder," he says.

"Give him a hand," the officer orders.

The soldiers obey and wincing with pain, Jorquera is brought to his feet. He stands and faces the officer. He is Colonel Rafael González and a member of the air force intelligence service SIFA, which explains his exotic uniform.

"This is Carlos Jorquera," the colonel tells the soldiers, "the Presidential Press Secretary. He shouldn't be here. I'm going to see what's going on."

González turns and walks away, leaving the prisoner guarded by soldiers who are noticeably more pleasant to him. They stand there with nothing to do except wait for the colonel to return. The air is cold and becomes colder as the afternoon draws on. Jorquera gives a sudden involuntary shudder and his glasses fall from his face onto the ground. Without his spectacles he cannot see clearly, but he does not dare stoop and pick them up. The soldiers do not notice and the press secretary is left gazing wistfully at his glasses, which lie in a blur at his feet. Firemen pass to and fro, carrying ladders and lengths of hose into the still burning Moneda. Water pours from the shattered entrance and floods into the plaza. One of them stops and recognises Jorquera.

"You Marxist sonofabitch!"

Then he sees the glasses lying on the ground.

"These yours?"

"Yes," replies the press secretary without thinking.

The fireman gives a small, twisted smile and pulverises the spectacles beneath his heavy boot. He walks away, leaving a broken mess. The act shocks Jorquera. Of all the insults and blows he has suffered since his arrest, this one hurt the most. He wonders what on earth could possess a man to wilfully destroy someone's glasses.

The partially sighted press secretary therefore fails to see the SIFA colonel approaching, until he is just a few feet away.

"OK, everyone follow me!" he orders and the prisoners all rise to their feet.

Jorquera and his companions are taken under escort across the Plaza de la Libertad and enter the MOD building on the opposite side. The group are taken below to the basement and led into a room. Inside are the three emissaries: Puccio, Vergara and Flores, who have been reunited after a brief interrogation.

Puccio looks across at the press secretary and makes a brief cutting motion with his hand. Jorquera understands. The president is dead.

As they wait in the basement, the atmosphere becomes more relaxed. The fact the emissaries are unharmed bolsters the others' spirits. Perhaps they will all soon be released. Amid the hubbub of conversation, González chats amiably to the press secretary.

"I often see you on TV. Whenever there's a story, you're always hovering in the background. There ain't no news without Negro Jorquera!" and the colonel chuckles at his own joke.

The press secretary does not know what to say. The situation is so absurd. Outside the Moneda he feared they were going to be put against a wall and shot. Now a senior officer wanted to make small talk. Perhaps this was what happened in a coup. First they chatted you up, then they killed you.

"Is there anything you need?"

"Actually, there is. I'm desperate for a piss."

González grins and escorts his prisoner to a bathroom, allowing him to go in alone. After relieving himself Jorquera stands at the basin and looks at his reflection in the mirror; not wearing spectacles he has to press his nose to the dimly lit glass and what he sees is far from reassuring. He looks desperate, like a man standing on a window ledge contemplating the traffic far below. The press secretary splashes some cold water on his face, then takes a drink from the tap. He dries his hands on his trousers and wanders out again, feeling more relieved than revived.

"Better?" asks the colonel.

"Yes...thanks," says Jorquera, who still does not know what to make of his obliging gaoler.

"Anything else I can do?"

The press secretary decides he might as well try and bum a cigarette. When he asks the officer looks disappointed. But it is only because he does not smoke.

"Don't worry!" he says. "I'm sure I can get one off my men."

The colonel departs and soon returns with two cigarettes, one of which he lights and hands to Jorquera.

"That's for later," he says and he slips the other into the top pocket of his prisoner's jacket.

The press secretary thanks the officer and draws deeply on his cigarette. Despite González's best efforts, small talk is proving difficult and after a few further exchanges, the conversation stops altogether. The pause lengthens and the silence threatens to become a void.

"Well, better be on my way," says the colonel finally, before they both succumb to embarrassment. "Nice talking to you and don't worry, I'll put in a good word."

González departs and Jorquera can only shake his head. He takes a last drag of his cigarette and stubs it out on the floor and goes over to join his companions.

"What was all that about?" asks Puccio.

"I think he loves me," says the press secretary.

*

At the Central Post of Public Assistance, Eladio is taken from the ambulance and wheeled into Accident and Emergency. The paramedics tell one of the doctors that he has a suspected ruptured appendix and do not mention they have just come from the Moneda, or that their patient was one of the prisoners. They take the GAP to a consulting room and lift him off the stretcher and put him onto a bed and leave. The doctor on duty examines Eladio who moans softly, his hands holding his belly. The medic has taken off his white coat, because the air conditioning is broken and the windowless room is stuffy.

He asks the GAP to pull up his shirt and gently presses his abdomen. Eladio cries out with pain when the doctor touches his lower intestine and the man tells him that he will have to be operated on. He goes off to inform the registrar and the GAP seizes his chance. He gets up, puts on the doctor's white coat and then sees a stethoscope lying on the table. He wraps it around his neck, opens the door and peers out. The place is full of nurses and medics running to and fro, as various casualties are brought in and friends and family follow desperately in their wake. Eladio steps out into the passage and casually walks towards the entrance. Soldiers hang about in various groups. No one stops him and no one asks him for ID. He looks just like any other a doctor.

The GAP crosses the hospital forecourt and approaches the main gates, smiling at the security guard who assumes he is on a call. He turns down the street and tries not to break into a run, but the urge is overwhelming. After a few short strides he takes off the stethoscope, drops it into a bin and increases his pace. Then he removes the white coat and throwing it aside, he crosses the road and begins to run. Eladio runs and runs and does not stop running until he is far away.

*

In the barracks of the Maturana Regiment in downtown Santa Rosa, young Osvaldo Puccio sits bound to a chair. The cords are tied so tightly, he can only move his head. With him are two plainclothes policemen from the Servicio de Inteligencia Militar, better known by its acronym SIM. The room is hot and they have taken off their jackets revealing leather shoulder holsters, both crammed with a pistol. The holsters make the SIM men sweat and their white standard issue shirts have damp patches around the armpits. There is a distinctive whiff of cheap cologne and body odour.

One of the policemen addresses the prisoner, while the other sits on a table and picks his nose. Beside him is a Uher tape recorder, the twin spools revolving slowly.

The SIM man doing the talking is short, about five feet six inches tall, with the distinctive build of a gymnast. He has rolled-up his sleeves and his biceps bulge pneumatically like balloons. Beneath his shirt the muscles are taut and defined. On his lip a military moustache bristles and his hair is as black and glossy as a crow's feathers. The SIM man observes Puccio as if he were some sort of invertebrate; interesting and slightly revolting at the same time. A pair of

Elvis-blue eyes, fringed with long dark lashes, stare coolly at him. They are ethereal, almost angelic in their beauty. The SIM man leans forward and speaks softly, fixing his prisoner with his Love-Me-Tender blue eyes.

"I want to know about your friends in MIR. I want all the information you have. Their names, their addresses, their occupations. Everything. Then, I want all the information that you don't have and I don't want to hear your excuses and your pleas because…(smile)…I've heard them all before."

The SIM man stands up and kisses his forefinger and thumb in a mocking act of devotion. He takes a step back and punches Puccio hard in the face, knocking both him and the chair to the ground. He picks the prisoner up and sets him down again. The SIM man leans close so that Puccio can feel his breath on his cheek, which smells of peppermints. He grabs the youth by the hair and proceeds to wrench out his moustache, stuffing it into his mouth.

"Names!" he shouts. "I want names!"

*

Alvaro Reyes and Maria Lizama enter the side room where the president's secretary is waiting. The doctor has met La Payita before. The previous Christmas he had been called to the Moneda and asked if he could attend to the president, who had sprained an ankle. The person who made the request was Arturo Jirón, then Minister of Health. Reyes duly went to the palace and inspected the president's swollen ankle. It was a bad sprain. He rubbed in some liniment and bandaged the foot, telling him to put no weight on it for three days. Afterwards, Reyes had lunch with the president's secretary and, like everyone else who had met her, found her charming.

Now they met again and introducing himself, the doctor reminds La Payita of their last encounter. His patient smiles and says she remembers it well. Reyes administers to her swollen knee and the graze, which he dabs with iodine. As he works she tells him how Olivares committed suicide and that the president was dead. The news does not surprise the doctor, although he is saddened by the loss. Reyes not only admired the president, he had also been a close friend of the television chief.

In the 1960s Jorquera, Tohá, Olivares and he used to meet in the café Sao Paulo in Huérfanos close by the Moneda, where they would drink coffee or have lunch. They would watch the pretty girls pass by in the street and talk politics. The air was filled with optimism and they hoped Popular Unity would win the next election. Those were good days. Now Olivares and the president were dead and the country in chaos.

After treating La Payita's knee, Reyes and Lizama put their patient in a wheelchair and take her up to the Traumatology Department for X-rays. There is nothing seriously wrong, the doctor is certain there is no fracture, but he wants to get the president's secretary away from the consulting room, in case someone discovers her. The X-rays are taken and Reyes pins the negatives to a light-board, but can find no evidence of a fracture. Nevertheless, he decides to put her leg in plaster so that no one will ask questions. It would also make it easier when the time came to spirit her away.

Reyes wheels La Payita out of the room to a surgery and proceeds to wrap her lower leg with strips of bandage. Lizama keeps watch by the door. The doctor finishes covering his patient's leg and washes his hands.

"I have to get back to work, in case I'm missed. You'll be OK here."

"What if someone comes? What do I say?"

"Don't worry, nobody will. The only person who uses this room is the duty registrar and that's me."

Reyes and Lizama say their goodbyes and depart, leaving

La Payita on her own. The nurse goes back to her ward and the doctor returns to his duties. There are wounded everywhere. The last time Reyes witnessed such scenes was in April 1957, during the fierce riots along the Alameda against the right-wing government of Carlos Ibáñez. At the time he was working as a junior in a hospital in Calle San Francisco. A female friend of his, a member of the Communist Youth, had been brought in with a bullet wound to the chest. There was nothing that could be done and the girl had died in his arms.

As the injured began to arrive that morning some young orderlies had asked Reyes, just as Edgardo Enríquez had been, what they should do to resist and like the minister he had told them not to sacrifice themselves. He sent the youths on their way and asked them to do their work as best as they could. At least they might save some lives.

*

A military jeep pulls up outside one of the tall, white apartment blocks in Remodelación San Borja and three doctors from the Moneda medical team get out. Patricio Arroyo, Danilo Bartulin and Oscar Soto stand and watch as the vehicle drives down the rain wet street, disappearing with a splash around the corner. They are alone on the empty pavement, the lilac flowers of the jacarandas nodding in the breeze. It is difficult for them to comprehend they have actually been released. They all breathe in deeply. The air smells of blossom and in their heightened state of awareness every tree and blade of grass seems vibrant and alive; the world made tremulous.

The doctors embrace each other and Arroyo and Soto wish Bartulin goodbye as he walks off to his apartment, which is in a separate high-rise. Soto accompanies his friend down the concrete path towards his own flat. Arroyo has invited his boss to stay, since he lived some distance away in La

Reina and would not be able to return before the curfew began at dusk. The doctors walk down the damp path, silhouettes against the apartment block which rises palely before them like a god. In the distance a shroud of freshly fallen snow covers the Andes.

*

At 4:00pm a group of soldiers enters the Ministry of Education. In his office Edgardo Enríquez waits and listens to the sounds of doors being kicked open, voices shouting and the tramp of heavy boots.

The noise increases and a steady crump-crump-crump comes down the corridor. The minister waits calmly, as though expecting an appointment. Outside, shouts and curses are directed at his staff. Suddenly, the door is flung open and an officer enters with a group of soldiers. Enríquez looks up from his papers.

"Yes...?"

"You! Outside! Now!"

The elderly man gets up and advances towards them.

"Move it!" barks the captain and Enríquez is propelled out of the room and into the corridor. The ministry's employees are sitting on the floor, with their hands behind their heads. They look terrified. The minister smiles, trying to reassure them.

"Sit down," says the officer.

Enríquez does not reply and remains standing. As a medical doctor and a former naval captain, he has no intention of obeying this upstart. The soldier's eyes narrow as the minister refuses to budge.

"I-said-sit," repeats the officer, clenching his teeth.

Enríquez observes the captain. The soldier is young and he estimates that he cannot be more than twenty-five or so. The adversaries face each other. The older man with his gravitas and his position, the younger with his uniform and his gun.

Neither is prepared to back down. A sergeant resolves the situation by bringing up a chair. He places it behind Enríquez and pushes him firmly into it.

"The captain said sit!"

For the next two hours the ministry employees are left in the corridor under an armed guard. They are forbidden to speak or even move. Time drags and their sense of fear and isolation increases. They can hardly breathe, they are so scared. Terror smothers them like bedclothes in a nightmare. The only sound is the ticking of the strip lights above their heads.

*

As evening approaches the sky above the city darkens and it begins to rain once more. In front of the palace two navy buses take the remaining Moneda prisoners into custody. The men are forced to walk through a tunnel of soldiers, who kick and beat them with the butts of their weapons. Such is the violence of the assault that one of the detectives has his sternum broken. Once inside the vehicles they are made to kneel on the seats facing backwards, their hands behind their heads. The buses then depart at great speed and several times the prisoners fall to the floor as they lose their balance, only to be kicked and beaten back onto the seats by their guards. Those who take their hands from their heads to grip the seat rails for support, have their knuckles smashed.

The buses arrive at the barracks of the Tacna Regiment. The prisoners are ordered from the vehicles and told to line up in the main courtyard with their legs apart, their hands once more behind their heads.

The commanding officer Lieutenant Colonel Luis Ramírez appears. He is a short, fastidious man in his mid-forties, with silver hair and a sour expression. The lieutenant in charge salutes him and informs his superior about the Moneda prisoners.

"So they're the bastards responsible for wounding General Palacios?"

"Yes sir!"

"Right. Form a firing squad."

The younger officer cannot actually believe what he has just heard and stands there frowning in astonishment.

"Sir?"

"You heard."

"But...what about their interrogation? They could have valuable information. Besides, they're prisoners of war."

"Precisely. Now shoot them."

"Is that an order?"

Ramírez's lip curls and he looks at his subordinate. It is the sort of look a schoolmaster reserves for a particularly dull pupil, or a peasant for his mule before he beats it.

The lieutenant is not so dim that he fails to understand and salutes his CO again. He turns and tells his men to bring up the machine guns. Detective Quintin Romero, who has heard the exchange, looks on as soldiers fix a pair of Bren guns onto tripods. Ammunition boxes are opened and a belt of bullets is fed into the breech. But the soldiers are conscripts and unused to handling heavy weapons and the process is laborious.

"Come on! Come on! Get on with it!" says Ramírez, impatiently stamping his foot.

When the guns are finally loaded and cocked, the prisoners are ordered to kneel. The soldiers roughly push them to the ground. Romero joins his companions and winces as the hard surface of the tarmac penetrates the material of his trousers.

"Clear the area!" orders the lieutenant.

He then notices there are people working in offices on the other side of the parade ground and tells his men to evacuate the building. The soldiers bring out the civilians and make them stand to one side. Although these people work for the military, they are shocked at what is happening and some of them go up and speak to Ramírez.

The colonel greets their enquiries with a look of contempt. He cannot understand what all the fuss is about. He tells them that these men are prisoners from the Moneda, who fought against the armed forces. Now they were under his authority. As the commanding officer it was up to him how he dealt with them and he has decided to shoot them. There was nothing more to be said and Ramírez dismisses the deposition with a surly wave.

Soldiers start to collect the prisoners' ID. When they get to the detectives, they also take their badges, which they put into a cardboard box. The brand 'Milko' and the words 'Good For Baby' are printed on the side.

The prisoners remain kneeling in front of the firing squad. Some look straight ahead and stare death in the face. Others close their eyes and pray silently. Ramírez raises an arm and is about to give the order to fire, when a soldier runs across the parade ground. There is a phone call for him. The colonel turns and walks away. No one else says a word and the prisoners can only await their fate. Romero's knees hurt and the small of his back aches. It surprises him that he is not actually scared. The detective feels ambivalent about dying. He just wishes the soldiers would hurry up and get it over with.

Romero looks about. Beyond the high walls of the barracks, a dark and sunless sky descends. The air is cold and damp. A gust of wind gets up and rain falls lightly across the square. After what seems like an age to the detective, although it is probably only a couple of minutes, the colonel returns. The prisoners are ordered to their feet and marched across to the stables on the other side, where they are again made to kneel. This time they face the parade ground, their backs to the walls. Romero realises that it is a better place to despatch them. There is less chance of ricochet. After a few minutes the prisoners are told to stand once more and taken into the stables.

A sharp smell pricks the detective's nostrils. The place reeks strongly of horse. But the odour also gives him hope. The Tacna were a cavalry regiment and having grown up on a farm, Romero knows how sensitive horses are to the smell of blood. If a bucket of offal were ever left in a stable, the horses in it went mad. Shooting them here would drench the place in gore. The soldiers would have to scrub away every speck of blood, if their mounts were ever to venture inside again.

The Moneda prisoners join scores of other captives. There are about three hundred in all. The new batch are assembled into files and told to take off their jackets and shoes, before being made to lie down on the flagstones with the others. In a corner a trio of soldiers sits behind a heavy machine gun. Another group is placed on the other side. Between them they could massacre all the prisoners within seconds.

*

In the Salon Independencia General Palacios tells his men to cover the president's corpse with a rug, which someone has brought from Osvaldo Puccio's office. It is made in the typical Bolivian Indian style, although it actually came from the industrial sector of La Legua, which the army were still attacking. A left-wing lawyer had sent the rug to Puccio as a gift and the Presidential Secretary was particularly fond of it. The soldiers drape it over Allende's corpse and place it on a stretcher. Then four of them take hold of each corner and carry the body out. But they have difficulty negotiating the marble staircase, the steps of which are wet and slippery and Palacios orders some firemen to lend a hand. At the bottom of the stairs the men haul the makeshift bier onto their shoulders and carry it outside to a waiting ambulance.

In front of the Moneda the press are gathered and the popping of flash bulbs briefly transfigures the faces of the pallbearers. The president's corpse is loaded into the back of the vehicle and the doors are slammed shut. The ambulance is driven off with a carabinero escort to the Military Hospital, its blue lights flashing in the rain.

VII
DARKNESS VISIBLE

Edgardo Enríquez is still seated in the same chair in the corridor of the Ministry of Education. Neither he, nor his colleagues, have moved in the past two hours. Nobody has uttered a word. The prisoners are guarded by conscripts; teenagers whose unaccustomed sense of power lends them a cruel arrogance. Bored, they lean against the walls, cradling their weapons. The rush of adrenalin they experienced storming the building with their safety catches off, has all but disappeared. They resent having to watch over a group of civilians, when there is still shooting going on outside. If they find one of the prisoners looking at them, they point their gun. Seeing that person's eyes widen in fear, gives them a fleeting feeling of satisfaction. The soldiers ache to pull the trigger. They hate them that much.

A scrape of hobnailed boots comes down the passage and the sergeant appears and addresses Enríquez.

"Come with me to the MOD."

The minister gets up stiffly and begins to thank his employees for their work that day. He is about to tell them how honoured he is, how proud they have made him, when the NCO interrupts.

"Come on! Let's go!" and he propels Enríquez along the corridor.

They descend the stairs, the sergeant hurrying the minister all the way down. At the entrance the soldier tells Enríquez to do exactly as he does and leaves the building at a run, weaving from side to side. The minister follows him as best he can, shots ringing out across the plaza. There are still some loyalist snipers in the surrounding buildings.

They make it safely to the Alameda and crossing the road, the pair dash up the steps of the MOD and enter the building. Inside a young naval officer greets Enríquez with a friendly smile. It is Daniel Guimpert, who is now a lieutenant. His father was a captain and a friend of the minister's from his time in the senior service. Enríquez knows the family well. He had once tended to the young Daniel, when he suffered from a bout of measles. The minister notices that he still has the same cheeky grin.

"This way...doctor!" says Guimpert.

Enríquez cannot help a smile. With people like Daniel around, things might not be too bad. He follows the young naval officer who takes him upstairs to the office of General Augusto Lutz, chief of the military intelligence service SIM.

"This is Edgardo Enríquez, the Minister of Education," announces Guimpert with a salute.

Lutz is standing at the window with his back to them. He does not turn round at the sound of the lieutenant's voice and continues to peer through the slats of the Venetian blinds.

"What should I do with him sir?"

"Take him to the basement," intones Lutz, as he gazes out of the window. "Make sure you leave him under an armed guard."

Almost as soon as he has entered the room, Enríquez is hustled out again and taken to the building's subterranean level, where the other Moneda prisoners are being held. But Guimpert does not know exactly where and mistakenly brings the minister to the wrong room. As they enter Enríquez is shocked to see about thirty men dressed only in their underpants and lying on the concrete floor, with their hands tied behind their backs. The room reeks of sweat and fear, like the lair of some cornered rodent. A trio of army officers sit on tables. The jackets of their uniforms are unbuttoned and each holds a bottle of beer in his hand. Ribbons of cigarette smoke hang in the glare of the lights above their heads. The soldiers observe the minister and his escort.

"What do you want?" asks one.

"This is Edgardo Enríquez. General Lutz told me to take

him to the basement."

"Yes, but not here. Can't you see we're busy," and the soldier indicates the prone captives with his bottle. "Take him elsewhere."

Enríquez observes the officers sitting on the tables. The one doing the talking has a foot on a chair and takes an occasional swig of beer. Next to him lies an open packet of cigarettes and an ashtray full of butts. Yet none of the officers are smoking. The minister can see the prisoners' bodies are scored with burns. One of the men looks up at him and makes an imploring gesture with his eyes. Enríquez understands, but there is nothing he can do.

"OK," says Guimpert and he escorts the minister out. As they walk down the passage, Enríquez remembers that he had promised to phone Raquel again. He has not spoken to her since that morning.

"Daniel, can I call my wife and let her know I'm OK. She'll be going frantic."

"No problem," says the lieutenant, still smiling the same smile.

He takes his charge to an empty office and picks up the phone.

"What's the number?"

Enríquez tells him and the lieutenant dials. As soon as he has done so, the call is answered. The minister is surprised since it was not within easy reach, but in the hall. He assumes his wife must have been sitting by the phone all day, waiting for him to call.

"Hello, is that *Señora* Enríquez? This is Lieutenant Daniel Guimpert…Yes, Daniel…That's right…Little Daniel with the measles ha, ha….Yup, fine thanks…nope, no more spots ha, ha…Look, your husband's here with me in the MOD…The minister's fine, don't worry….No, no problems at all. He'll be back home soon…"

As Guimpert continues chatting, Enríquez edges towards the phone.

"Hi darling it's me, I'm OK…"

At this the lieutenant slams the receiver down and turns round. He is furious.

"What the hell do you think you're doing?"

"I only wanted to say hello…"

"That was a serious breach of security! I didn't authorise you to speak!" and Guimpert glares angrily at the minister, who is both shaken and confused. How could a few spoken words to his wife be such a problem? There is a tense silence. The lieutenant then realises he has let his mask slip and softens his tone. "Look, you shouldn't have done that. I'll call your secretary in the ministry and she can pass on any message."

"I didn't know I wasn't allowed to speak."

"Never mind, it's done now. Come on."

They leave and Guimpert takes his charge to another office and places him under guard as Lutz had ordered. The lieutenant says goodbye and departs, still wearing the same boyish grin. In fact he had not called Enríquez's home, as the minister has been led to believe, but another number in the MOD and had merely spoken to a clerk.

In their apartment in Providencia, Enríquez's wife sits anxiously by the phone, waiting for her husband to call. She has heard nothing since she spoke to him that morning and he told her the ministry was under fire. Raquel is desperate to know if he is all right. She sits and waits, her only company is the steady ticking of a grandfather clock. The clock regularly strikes the hours, its chimes echoing down the corridor, but the phone does not ring.

*

Shortly after Enríquez is taken to the MOD, Arturo Jirón and Patricio Guijón arrive at the ministry escorted by some of Palacios' men. The doctors are then separated and Guijón is taken upstairs to an office, where he is debriefed by several senior military officials, including Admiral Carvajal. Guijón is the only known witness to the president's suicide. The military intend to ensure the doctor will go on the record, so that Allende will not be considered a martyr by his supporters. The point is academic. Those who wish to believe the president died in a firefight, will do so no matter what Guijón says. In any event, the violent death of a democratically elected president in office is martyrdom enough.

As the unfortunate doctor is being debriefed, Jirón is escorted downstairs to the basement. He passes the room where Enríquez was mistakenly taken to earlier. The door is open and Jirón glances inside as he passes and sees the same group of men lying bound and semi-naked on the floor. It is only a fleeting look, but it is all the former minister needs. One of the soldiers escorting him explains the men are loyalist fighters who have been captured from various government buildings.

"Glad I'm not in their shoes," he says.

Jirón is taken to a boiler room. It is full of prisoners facing the wall, their hands behind their heads. A lone soldier stands guard. He does not recognise anyone and assumes they are civilians from various ministries. He is ordered to line up next to them.

Time drags and gradually the former minister begins to weaken. He is exhausted and his body aches all over from blows dealt by the soldiers. The guard on duty notices and tells him he can put his hands down and relax. It is the first decent thing that has been said to him since he was taken prisoner. He has been beaten, spat upon and cursed. His stomach still hurt from a blow by a soldier's weapon and he fears he has internal bleeding. Jirón turns and leans with his back against the wall.

"You can sit down if you like," adds the young soldier. "But if I tell you to get up you'd better jump, or I'll be in trouble."

The former minister slumps gratefully to the floor. The youth reaches into a pocket in his battledress and offers him a cigarette, which Jirón accepts with a smile. His hands tremble as he smokes and he notices how filthy they are. Being a doctor he is used to them being scrupulously clean. But the state of his hands are the least of Jirón's concerns as he sits in the dusty confines of the boiler room, waiting and wondering about his fate.

An occasional scream floats down the corridor. The sound is terrifying, like a hog having its throat cut. The former minister presses his hands to his ears. It makes no difference, the cries penetrate straight through.

Later, an officer arrives and tells Jirón to follow him. He does not seem to mind that he has been sitting on the floor. The prisoner gets up wearily and is taken to the same room where Enríquez is being held. On seeing Jirón, the education minister goes to greet him. The two men are old friends and are glad to see each other. Enríquez appraises the new arrival. He can see his companion is suffering. His shirt is soaking wet and smeared with blood.

"What happened Arturo, are you wounded?"

"No. It's Perro Olivares' blood. The poor bastard shot himself."

The shirt is wet because Jirón was one of those forced to lie down in the streams of water that poured from the Moneda. Standing there blood-smeared and shivering, he looks a pitiful sight. Enríquez takes off his jacket and puts it around his friend's shoulders. With an arm draped over him, he leads his companion away from the soldiers who are gathered by the door. They sit down and Jirón informs his friend that Allende is dead.

Enríquez says nothing and nods. The news comes as no surprise. He did not imagine the president surrendering. The only way the military would ever have got him out of the Moneda was in a long wooden box. And so it was.

Some soldiers arrive and another prisoner is brought in. It

is Patricio Guijón. Jirón explains that he was part of the palace medical team.

"Ah! So we are all doctors here!" and the minister goes and greets the new arrival.

"Yes…" is all Guijón says.

The doctor from the medical unit smiles weakly, but he seems detached, his mind elsewhere. His eyes have a haunted look. It is as though he has witnessed some terrible event, which Enríquez can only guess at. The minister assumes it is because of the ordeal which he has been through. He does not know that Guijón actually saw the president commit suicide. But the doctor is suffering from more than just trauma. It is much worse. He feels cursed. He has become the Ancient Mariner, forced to stop and tell his tale to anyone who will listen. "The president shot himself. I saw him do it!" Already the memory hangs like an albatross around his neck.

*

At the Military Hospital in Providencia General Mario Bórquez arrives in an army vehicle. The Air Force Director of Health shows his pass to a soldier who checks it and salutes. The barrier is raised and he proceeds through the gates. The car draws up at the main entrance and the general alights. Earlier, Bórquez had been summoned to Admiral Carvajal's office in the MOD, where he was told he would be part of a team that would carry out the autopsy on Allende's corpse. The admiral explained the president had committed suicide with his own weapon.

In the Ear, Nose and Throat Department, Bórquez meets up with the other doctors of the autopsy team. All are members of the armed forces and all are in uniform. The medical chiefs make their way to the morgue, where the body lies and enter the room. Standing beside the president's shrouded corpse is another doctor, Tomás Tobar, from the

Institute of Medical Law. The doctors approach the body and Tobar draws back the white sheet covering it. The sight of the president's naked and disfigured corpse shocks them. As doctors they are all used to seeing and dealing with horrific injuries, but Allende's shattered head looks grim.

"My God," whispers Bórquez.

In spite of their political differences, he had enjoyed a close relationship with the president. Allende had personally invested him as a general, telling him during the ceremony that it was a historic day, since it was the first time that a doctor as head of state, had invested another doctor as a general in the armed forces. Surveying the mutilated corpse, the president's words echo in Bórquez's ears.

Once the initial shock has passed, the doctors sense of duty returns. Tobar works alone as the others watch. He extracts blood from the body's heart and fluid from the stomach, to see if there are any traces of alcohol. There are none. The heart is also in good condition for a man of sixty-five, refuting right-wing propaganda about the president's carousing and decadent lifestyle.

After Tobar has completed the autopsy, he stitches the corpse's head together. Seeing Allende's reassembled face, albeit minus his glasses, makes the doctors uneasy. It seems wrong for the President of Chile to be lying like a piece of meat on a cold mortuary slab. The sheet is quickly replaced and the doctors leave. In his report Tobar states that Allende's death was caused by 'encephalitic cranium trauma from a self-inflicted bullet wound.' The pathologist then fills out a form, which they all sign. The president's autopsy is now complete.

It is getting late and the doctors decide to eat in the hospital canteen. It is a relief for them to be out of the deathly confines of the morgue and in the world of the living again. The dining-room is full of military types, all discussing the day's events. There is a brittle atmosphere, as though people are talking and joking a little too loudly. The doctors try and discuss other matters, but it is difficult. The memory of the dead president will not go away. It is an image already etched into their psyche. The sight of Allende's mutilated and naked corpse, lying beneath the tungsten glare of the mortuary lights, will never leave them.

At a table nearby is General Palacios. He has come to see his sergeant who was wounded in the stomach during the final assault on the Moneda. The general was relieved to find the NCO in good spirits after his operation and would suffer no lasting damage. Palacios has also learnt that the young GAP he sent to the hospital had died in the ambulance. It seems strange, but he finds himself grieving for that youth just as much as he does for his own men. The kid from Colonia Boroa.

*

Dr Rodriguez Veliz is one of the hospital's senior medical officers. He has been on duty all day and now that his shift is almost over, he decides to visit the morgue to pay his respects to the dead president. Veliz had known Allende at medical school. They were not close friends and their paths seldom crossed after they graduated. Yet he had admired him as a man.

The doctor enters the Ear, Nose and Throat Department. It is empty and eerily quiet, like a crypt except brighter. He walks down the corridor, his footsteps echoing across the tiled floor. A single guard stands at the door of the mortuary which holds the president's body. The soldier looks at Veliz's pass and the doctor enters, closing the door behind him. The president lies under a white sheet on a table in the middle of the room. Veliz approaches and stands there looking at the body. Even though he is a doctor, he cannot bring himself to raise the sheet. He does not want to see his old university friend as a mutilated corpse. The lights hum gently and there is a faint smell of formaldehyde and dust.

Veliz then does something which he has not done in years. He clasps his hands in front of him and begins to pray. Alone, in the sterile sepulchre beside the body of his dead president, the doctor recites litanies he has not uttered in years.

Veliz leaves the department and goes outside for some fresh air. The sky is dark and the wind cold against his face. A fine drizzle forms a trembling halo around the street lights, their sodium glow reflected in the wet surface of the tarmac. A silence has descended over the city, punctuated by the occasional crack of gunfire. The doctor has heard that some fighters are still holding out at the State Technical University. As he stands there gazing up at the cloud-filled sky, Veliz tries to make sense of what has occurred. It is as if the whole of creation has been hurled into a void, leaving behind only darkness and chaos. The doctor feels an overwhelming sense of grief. He wants to know why this has happened, but cannot find an answer. He remains at the hospital entrance, a solitary figure in a white coat. Veliz clenches his fists and shakes them up and down in an impotent gesture of despair.

*

In the Ministry of Defence, General Nicanor Díaz is typing the draft of yet another junta proclamation. The lights in his office burn brightly as he works away at his desk. Amid the regular pounding of keys, a phone rings loudly. Díaz's secretary picks it up and informs his superior the Cuban ambassador Mario García Incháustegui wants to speak to him. Since that afternoon there has been a constant gun battle between those in the embassy and the soldiers surrounding it. The military cannot actually storm the building because of the Vienna Convention, which gives all foreign missions diplomatic immunity. But the soldiers have orders not let anyone either enter or leave the compound.

The place is effectively under siege.

Díaz stops typing and tells his secretary to transfer the call to his own line.

"Mr Ambassador what can I do for you?"

"General, your soldiers are shooting at the embassy. Need I remind you it is sovereign territory that you are violating?"

"Really? I didn't know Cuba had any sovereignty left to violate."

Incháustegui ignores the slight and continues.

"You also have an embassy and representatives in Havana…"

"Yes and every one of them's a damned Commie like you!"

"General, Chile has diplomatic missions around the world. If you mistreat other countries' stations, you'll jeopardise your own national interests."

"OK, OK I get your point. I'll tell the soldiers to stop."

"Also, several of us are wounded, including myself."

"Fine. I'll have a doctor from the Military Hospital sent round."

"I'd rather a civilian."

"A doctor's a doctor isn't he?"

"Not a military one."

"If you're so fussy, you can't be very badly wounded."

"That's not for you to decide…"

"And it's not for you to fuck about at a time like this!" and the general slams the receiver down. "Damn cheek," he mutters and turns to his secretary. "Get me the commander of the unit outside the Cuban embassy."

The subordinate goes to the two-way radio and makes the connection and the captain comes on the line.

"Yes sir?..."

"I've just had words with the Cuban ambassador. He says you're filling his front door full of holes. You must only shoot in self defence..."

"Sir, they're shooting at us all the time…"

"Then pull your men out of the firing line for God's sake! Just make sure no one goes in or out of the embassy..."

"Yes sir!..."

Díaz switches off the microphone with a sigh. He takes a cigarette from a packet on his desk and lights it and returns to the proclamation. The general types resolutely with either forefinger, stopping from time to time to draw on his cigarette. The steady clatter of typing fills the office, interrupted by the ping of the roll when it reaches the end. The lights above the general make his brilliantined hair shine like molasses as he sits hunched over the old manual, his broad frame stuck into a chair two sizes too small for him.

*

Several floors below General Díaz and his typewriter, three military doctors and an officer enter the basement room where Enríquez, Jirón and Guijón are under guard. One of the doctors is from the navy and looks as though he has only recently graduated from medical school. The other from the army is older. The third is Luis Veloso, the carabinero medical chief and one of the witnesses of the president's autopsy. The general looks at the three prisoners in front of him.

"Undress," he orders Enríquez.

"No," replies the minister.

"I said undress!"

"I am not going to take my clothes off!"

Veloso looks exasperated.

"How on earth can I conduct an examination if you're fully clothed?"

Hearing this Enríquez's irritation subsides. He thought the doctors had merely come to humiliate them. Even so, he is still not going to undress.

"If you want to know how I am, why don't you ask me?"

"OK. How do you feel?"

"Alright, I suppose. Considering. The country's at war, the president's dead, my wife has no idea where I am, or even if I'm still alive, we've been here for hours, we don't know why we're here, we're tired and hungry and I want to go to the lavatory."

"Sorry I asked," says Veloso and he turns to his colleagues. "Come on let's go," and the doctors and the other officer leave. When they have gone Enríquez asks the guards if he can relieve himself, but they refuse.

Later, the three prisoners are escorted from the basement to another office, where they are joined by Osvaldo Puccio. The two other emissaries Flores and Vergara, have been taken to the Military Academy. Puccio is frantic about his boy and the others do their best to reassure him. But they know that since the youth is a member of MIR, his prospects are not bright.

Some soldiers enter and the group are taken to the ministry's central hall. As they ascend the stairs Puccio feels a sharp pain, like a splinter of ice, in his chest.

"I need my pills," he gasps to one of the soldiers. "They were confiscated when I arrived. I had a heart attack recently. I need to take them now."

The soldier ignores him and the Presidential Secretary stumbles on, wheezing and clutching his chest.

The prisoners and their guards enter the hall, which is humming with activity. It is filled with people, both soldiers and civilians. The captives stand in lines, each leading to a separate table. At the table a suspect sits bound to a chair, while a group of soldiers interrogates them. The hubbub in the hall is punctuated with shouts and curses. An officer presides over each group, goading the interrogators and abusing the victim. The other prisoners can only stand and watch and wait for their turn.

The chief of military intelligence, General Lutz, strolls up to the group and introduces himself. He looks neither military nor intelligent merely cruel, like an inquisitor who has just come from a successful racking. He smiles and shakes the prisoners by the hand and addresses them all by their first names. Enríquez tells him about Puccio's medical condition and Lutz's face drops, as he makes a show of looking suitably appalled.

"I'll get the medication returned at once," he says and with a flourish, despatches an officer to fetch it.

Enríquez is disgusted by the whole charade. As a former naval officer he feels a deeper sense of grievance than the others. Not only has Lutz broken his oath of commission, he is a traitor and a disgrace to his uniform. The man's insincerity was breathtaking. All around them people were being beaten and abused and yet the general affected concern over their colleague's medical condition.

The interrogation of the other captives in the hall continues. After the officers have obtained whatever information they can from their victim, they tell the soldiers to take them either to "the Chile Stadium", or to "the Tacna Regiment". The prisoners then leave under a hail of blows. Some stumble and fall. The soldiers curse and shout at them to get to their feet. If they fail to rise they are dragged out by their heels, leaving long smears of blood upon the tiled floor.

Observing all this, Lutz becomes agitated. It is difficult for him to sustain his carefully contrived bonhomie amid such scenes and he ushers the men into a side room. He closes the door, but the cries of the victims and the shouts and curses of the torturers penetrate the thin walls. In an attempt to drown out the noise, the general talks loudly and tries to make conversation. Even so, there is little to be said and none of the prisoners feels like talking, at least not to Lutz. The general then remembers Puccio's medication and orders one of the guards to go and find the lieutenant he sent on the errand. The officer soon arrives and the general asks him what has happened.

"Sir, Mr Puccio's medicine is in the magazine."

"What...?"

"I don't know why…"

"Well, bring it here."

"Sir, you have the keys."

Lutz mutters darkly and fishes out a bunch of keys from a pocket and hands them to the officer who leaves. A few minutes later a young soldier appears solemnly bearing a cushion, on top of which is a small brown bottle. Next to him is the lieutenant.

"What on earth…?" asks the chief of SIM.

"The tablets sir. Extremely dangerous. Made from nitro-glycerine…," announces the officer.

Despite their predicament the prisoners try hard not to laugh. The Presidential Secretary has been prescribed Trinitrina, a heart drug that contained one part in a thousand of nitro-glycerine. It was a common medication for those suffering from angina and helped widen the arteries.

Puccio calmly takes the bottle and opens it. He pops two pills into his mouth and swallows.

"Watch out," says Jirón, looking gravely at Lutz. "He might explode…"

The prisoners are taken outside. The night is cold and smells of rain. They all inhale deeply, filling their lungs. The cool, damp air is refreshing after the suffocating confines of the MOD. The men are put on a bus and told they are being taken to the Military Academy. Although the vehicle has a seating capacity of sixty, they are kept separate and forbidden to talk. As the bus is about to leave, an officer steps on board.

"Anyone moves," he tells the guards, "and you shoot the lot."

The soldier gets off and the doors close with a hiss. The driver guns the engine and the bus speeds down the wet and empty streets towards the academy. Inside the prisoners sit with their hands clasped behind their heads. Each has the uneasy feeling that his ordeal is only just beginning.

On arrival at the Military Academy, the men are split up

and put into separate rooms. They are bare except for a wrought iron bed and a mattress. The door to each is then locked. Alone in his new cell, Enríquez lies down on the bed. It creaks under his weight and the horsehair mattress is lumpy and hard, but he is grateful of the chance to rest. As the minister lies there he feels a stab of hunger and realises he has had no sustenance since coffee and biscuits that morning. The need for food torments him more than fatigue. He lies there with his hands folded across his stomach and stares up at the ceiling.

A group of cadets chat in the corridor outside. Eighteen-year-old boys who are being groomed to become officers and leaders of men. Enríquez tries to make out what they are saying, hoping their conversation might yield some information. He is tired and the voices are faint and interrupt each other. Eventually, the minister succumbs to exhaustion and he shuts his eyes and begins to doze.

Enríquez has barely fallen asleep, when he is woken by a bright light shining in his face.

"Get up!" orders a cadet with a torch.

The minister obeys and rises to his feet.

"What's your name?'

Enríquez tells him and the cadet then leaves. The minister yawns and settles back on the bed. Outside, the group make obscene comments about the president and his wife. Their obscenities are punctuated by gales of laughter. In spite of all the noise, the minister falls asleep again. But each time he does so, the same thing happens. The torch in his face, the order to get to his feet and tell them his name.

*

The prisoners at the Tacna regiment are lying on the stable floor. They are cold and stiff and have not moved in hours. The lieutenant on duty asks them if they want to do some exercise. All murmur their assent and the officer tells them to stand up. At his instruction they do some PT for a while, before being told to lie down again. The prisoners get back on the floor, their chests heaving after the brief, if strenuous exertion.

Every two hours the officer on duty is changed and each replacement is handed a list, which he reads out and takes a roll call. When one of the officers comes to the batch from the Moneda, he cannot resist mocking them.

"So you're the sonsofbitches who thought they could defy the glorious Chilean army! What a fucking rabble! They might as well have given you popguns for all the difference you made…"

This proves to be too much for one of the GAP who swears vehemently at the officer, questioning both his sexuality and his parentage. Hearing this the other prisoners freeze. How could the man be so stupid? The lieutenant is furious and demands to know who the culprit was. He curses and shouts, but no one will own up. Soldiers begin to march along the lines of the prisoners, swearing and kicking at them.

"Which mother's cunt was it?" they demand.

No one speaks and so they pick on one man and beat him senseless. The commotion brings other soldiers into the stables. Colonel Ramírez is among them. He seems even angrier than before, if that is possible.

"You Commie bastards!" he shouts. "We're going to shoot the lot of you…!"

One of the detectives in the stables is Carlos Espinoza. He is lying next to Coco Paredes. Since the GAP's outburst the guards have been lashing out indiscriminately at the Moneda prisoners and the former Director of Investigations seems to get the worst of it. A group of soldiers stand over him and order him to lift his head. He does so and one of them delivers a sharp blow with his gun butt. Espinoza hears the crack as Paredes' skull strikes the flagstone floor.

"Sonofabitch!" they shout.

Shortly afterwards Espinoza, Paredes and some GAP are taken outside and lined up against a wall. The former minister is still groggy and can barely stand and has to be supported by his companions; his head lolling, his chin resting on his chest. Espinoza holds one of his arms and looks ahead. A group of soldiers load their weapons, an officer with a pistol standing by. As they line up the detective hopes these teenagers have taken their basic training seriously and can shoot straight. He does not relish being finished off by the lieutenant.

The officer gives an order and the firing squad all raise their rifles. Espinoza does not close his eyes. Instead he looks straight down the barrel of a soldier's gun. The hole seems to get wider and wider until he thinks he might fall into it, or else it will swallow him up. The detective stares into the void and waits for the command.

The officer yells "fire!" and there is the crash of a fusillade.

Espinoza instinctively shuts his eyes at the rifles' crack, expecting a bullet to tear into his chest. But nothing happens. He opens them and sees the soldiers laughing. The detective realises the men have only fired blanks and still giggling, they lead them back to the stables.

Later, a prisoner asks if he can go to the toilet. Permission is denied and he is told to go where he lies. The man refuses and the guards kick and shout at him, until he finally soaks himself. They leave the prisoner groaning in his own puddle of urine. No one else asks to relieve themselves that night.

Enrique Paris is also singled out for abuse. It takes a while before the soldiers discover which one of the Moneda prisoners he is. When they do the guards take great delight in mocking the psychiatrist.

"If you're the president's shrink," one of them jeers, "I reckon you must be as cuckoo as him!"

In the middle of the night some soldiers bring Paris to his feet.

"Come with us," they tell him. "You're going to be assessed."

They take their prisoner to a room, where a group of officers are waiting. Standing next to them is a man dressed in black, a white clerical collar around his throat.

"This is the chaplain of the Second Division," Paris is told. "If you want to go to confession you can have more time."

The psychiatrist looks at the young priest, whose dark eyes are filled with compassion. Briefly he forgets his own predicament. He pities the man whose fate it is to bear witness to the condemned's final moments. Paris is not religious, but seeing the officers beside the priest, he is reminded of the Roman soldiers surrounding Christ.

"I'm not a believer," he says.

"If there's anything I can do…" ventures the chaplain.

"It's OK Father. It's not your fault," the psychiatrist replies with a smile. "Perhaps you can forgive them for me."

"Come on," says a captain. "The CO is waiting."

And with that the soldiers lead Paris away.

*

Orlando Letelier is also incarcerated at the Tacna Regiment. He was brought there from the MOD that morning, but has been isolated from the other prisoners. His room looks out onto a courtyard and all day he has heard the sound of rifle volleys. The defence minister has been unable to see the actual firing squad which was around the corner, but has witnessed soldiers dragging corpses away. Some of them he recognised were from the Ministry of the Interior. He does not know what has happened to either the president, or his erstwhile colleagues and fears they might all be dead.

Letelier has spent the day pacing his room and fretting. Not only do his teeth hurt, he also is suffering from nicotine withdrawal. He normally got through two or three packets a day and has not had a cigarette since his arrest. But his craving for a smoke pales into insignificance compared to his fears about his family. How would Isabel and the boys cope without him? Would he ever see them again? He curses the day he ever met Pinochet. Of all the military high command, the army chief's treachery was the worst. His ingratiating attitude had soon palled with the minister. He recalled recently telling Isabel: "Pinochet gives me the creeps. He's flattering and servile like the man in the barber's shop who follows you out into the street, constantly brushing your collar and lapels, until you give him a tip. He's always calling me 'sir' and helping me put on my coat, or trying to carry my briefcase." Now he knew why. It also explained how a man who finished in the bottom third at Military School had managed to become a general.

The minister shivers and looks out of his window at the dark and starless sky and remembers the dream he had the previous night. He was at a party and had been performing *la Cueca*, Chile's traditional folk dance. He moved and turned gracefully, but was alone on the dance floor. Around the room the military high command watched. Pinochet smiled from his chair as Letelier looked at him. Then he turned his back and as he did so, they all started whispering.

In the hour before dawn Letelier hears a voice say: "bring out the minister now. It's the minister's turn."

He listens as footsteps echo down the passage and his door is opened with a rattle of keys.

"It's your turn," says a soldier.

"Come on, move it!" says the officer beside him.

The minister follows them. He sees one of the soldiers is carrying a dark cloth, which he assumes will be his blindfold. Letelier is calm. He does not know why. It feels strange for him to be witnessing his final moments. It is almost as if he is having an out of body experience and all this is happening to someone else. In a minute or so he will be dead. His life ended, snuffed out like a candle.

As they continue along the passage, the minister wants to

make sure he carries himself with dignity in his last moments. He does not want his legs to buckle, or worse, faint. He wants to face his killers with equanimity. Letelier wonders if he will accept the blindfold. He thinks not. No, he will look the bastards in the eye. What if they offer him a cigarette? Sure, why the hell not? He will have a final puff.

At the end of the passage are some concrete stairs, which descend into the courtyard and the place of execution. The minister is marched down and when they get to the bottom, the sergeant shouts "halt!". Letelier has one foot on a step and the other on the ground. It feels odd standing like this. He wants to shift and get his feet on the level.

"Don't move," hisses a guard, who jabs him in the ribs with his gun.

Outside in the courtyard two officers are having an altercation. Plainly it is about him. In a deathly pantomime first one man points at the prisoner and then the other does the same, as they continue to argue. Letelier stands there patiently awaiting his fate. After a couple of minutes one of the officers shouts across the square.

"Take him upstairs!"

The guard who poked him with his weapon whispers in his ear.

"It's your lucky day asshole. They're not going to whack you!"

Letelier is marched back to his room and the door is locked behind him. He knows he should feel relieved, but he does not feel anything at all. It is simply that his time has not yet come.

VIII
WEAK WITH THE DAWN

Day breaks over the stables of the Tacna Regiment. Inside the prisoners remain prostrate on the flagstones, as they have been all night. Above their heads sunlight pours through the tall, dusty windows and forms geometric patterns on the opposite wall. At this early hour the light does not descend as far as the floor and hangs tantalisingly above the prisoners, like a cluster of golden fruit.

The morning sun reveals droplets of condensation and Carlos Espinoza tries to quench his thirst by licking them up. The flagstones are cool against his tongue, but he gathers more dust than moisture and decides it is not worth the effort. Resigned to dying of thirst, the detective swallows and lays his face down on the floor again.

As dawn broadens into morning, the prisoners are ordered to their feet and told to go outside, where they will be given breakfast. The men all rise and are led out of the stables into the brightening day. The overcast skies have been cleared by the night's rain and in the east a new sun shines. Its light strikes the roofs and buildings and makes the stone gleam. The prisoners stand there gazing up at the sky and are filled with hope. The promise of spring is everywhere. A soft wind shakes the silver leaves of the poplars and along the telephone wires songbirds sing.

A voice calls out across the parade ground.

"Strength comrades! Strength!"

The man continues to shout encouragement at the prisoners, his fist raised as some guards escort him back to his cell. It is the Socialist deputy Vicente Sotta. He is also under arrest, but like Letelier he has been kept apart from the others. Sotta recognises some of those from the Moneda, including Paredes and Jorge Klein.

The prisoners are lined up next to a field kitchen. A large

aluminium cooking pot steams above a gas stove, blue flames roaring at its base. Behind the pot a pair of fat cooks in striped aprons ladle a portion of beans into a mess tin and hand it to the prisoners as they file past. Each person is also given a cup of black coffee. For the hungry and exhausted captives, food has never tasted so good. In a short time the beans are wolfed down and the tins wiped clean.

After they have finished their meal, the prisoners stand about sipping their coffee and warming their hands on the tin mugs, as they talk in low voices to one another. They hazard at what might happen, but no one really knows. The optimists think that they will simply be questioned and released.

Others are less confident. Everyone is concerned about Colonel Ramírez, who plainly wants them all dead. But for the moment it seems the decision is out of his hands.

Espinoza is listening to one of these conversations. He is worried about the GAP. At least he is a detective, with a badge and ID to prove it. He wore the uniform, he just happened to be on the wrong side. He had acted as a loyal government servant, obeying his commander-in-chief who was the president. The GAP on the other hand were irregulars and little different from other left-wing paramilitaries. The carabineros in particular loathed them, as they believed it was their constitutional right to protect the president. As far as they were concerned these men had usurped their duties and now they were going to pay for it. It might seem like a contradiction, but the detective was not going to argue about it. Not with the military anyway.

Espinoza sees one of the GAP walking, or rather lumbering towards him. He has a black eye and a badly broken nose. The bodyguard walks with a tilt like a Hollywood cowboy, arms trailing by his sides. His hands are like hams and look as if they could straighten horseshoes. It is Jano.

"How's it going comrade?" he says in a voice that seems

to come from the bottom of a well.

"Not so bad. How about you?"

The GAP snorts with disdain, the air wheezing from his smashed nostrils. He shakes his head in disgust.

"What a fucking mess…"

The detective nods as his companion continues to curse.

"Fucking *pacos*. They were meant to be on our side. Assholes! Even the palace guard were fucking chicken!"

Jano squares his shoulders and looks around, as if he has just entered the ring and is sizing up an opponent. He spits on the ground and faces the detective.

"Don't worry you guys will be OK."

"You think so?"

"Sure. You're uniform. They take care of their own."

Espinoza says nothing. He does not want to admit the man's suspicions coincide with his own.

"I'll tell you something else comrade…"

But Jano does not finish his sentence. It is as if he has decided not to reveal what he knows, or else suspects his companion already understands. The detective has no idea what he is thinking about.

"Tell me."

"We waited too long."

"Too long…for what?"

The GAP observes Espinoza and smiles sardonically, as though he is being deliberately obtuse.

"The revolution comrade. The doctor was a fool to ever believe in democratic socialism…everyone knows you can't have both…now he's dead."

"Maybe you're right."

"You know I'm right. And I'll tell you something else…We're all going to die too," and Jano turns and points a thumb and forefinger at his fellow prisoners. "Bang!"

"What makes you so sure?"

"Because, if it were me comrade, I'd do the same fucking thing."

One of the soldiers nearby sees them talking and tells Jano to move away. But he does not budge. The soldier advances and stands between them.

"Move it!" he orders.

The GAP refuses to obey and stays rooted to the spot. He bunches his hand into a fist and raises it to the guard's face. The soldier pales and involuntarily takes a step back. For a moment it looks as though Jano is going to punch him. Instead he glowers at the conscript.

"*Fuerza!*" he says, his fist clenched.

The GAP walks away, slowly and deliberately like only tough guys can. Espinoza stands there watching, the cup of coffee cooling in his hands.

*

Later that morning the detectives are separated from the other Moneda prisoners and taken to an office, where they are debriefed by an inspector and another detective from Investigations. Jano is correct in his assumption. The military does not condemn them. The officials seem content to confirm what they already know: that the men were in the Moneda as part of the presidential protection unit and defended the palace out of loyalty to their commander-in-chief. They had acted as faithful public servants and should be treated as such. The detectives are told to remove their shirts and are given a cursory medical examination by a doctor. Afterwards, they are ushered onto a bus and taken to the Investigations Building, where they are met by General Baeza and the Prefect of Santiago General Julio Rada. Allende's military attaché Commander Sergio Badiola is also present.

Baeza remains seated at his desk, as he addresses the detectives.

"Gentlemen, you are no longer under arrest. What happened, happened. You were in the wrong place, at the wrong time. It would be churlish to condemn your loyalty and given the circumstances, it could be argued that you had little choice in the matter. You are required to turn up for work tomorrow at eight o'clock as usual. That is all."

The detectives are then dismissed and various police vehicles take them back to their houses.

Espinoza's car drives down the city boulevardes, shaded by palms and plane trees. The streets are full of people going about their daily lives and the detective finds it hard to believe that only the day before, the place was filled with tanks and soldiers and the sound of battle. There are still military forces about, but far less than he imagined. He wonders if the coup itself was just a dream. Perhaps he would wake up and find that it had never happened.

The police car drops Espinoza at his house and drives away. He opens his front door, which faces directly onto the street and goes inside. The detective surveys his modest living-room. Everything is exactly as his left it. The potted geranium on the glass coffee table, the shelves lined with cheap paperbacks, knick-knacks and photographs. Above the mantelpiece is a cuckoo clock, which he had bought on a skiing holiday in Bariloche. The mechanism has stopped and silence invades the room. The detective feels as though he has died and his ghost has come back to haunt the place.

Espinoza goes into the kitchen to make himself a cup of coffee and returns and sits down on a foam-filled armchair. He is illuminated by the wan light filtering through the net curtains. The detective takes out his badge and lays it down on the table. One thing is certain. He will not be reporting for duty the following morning. Or the morning after that. Or the one after that. Or ever.

*

Shortly after 7:00am the president's air force attaché Colonel Roberto Sanchez leaves his vehicle and enters the

Ministry of Defence. The night before General Baeza had called and told him that he was to accompany the Allende family, as they buried the president in the family plot at Viña del Mar. Baeza had added that Admiral Carvajal would give him further instructions the following morning at the MOD.

Sanchez ascends the stairs to the fifth floor and Carvajal's office. He knocks and a voice tells him to enter. The colonel opens the door and sees the navy chief at his desk having breakfast.

"Morning, morning," says the admiral, wiping some crumbs from his mouth with a paper napkin. "Fancy a pastry?" and he points to the plate on his desk.

"No thanks, sir."

"Suit yourself, they're jolly good. Take a seat."

Sanchez removes his cap and sits down.

"Coffee?"

"Yes, please."

The admiral pours his subordinate a cup and hands it to him.

"The president's body is in the Military Hospital. You're to collect it and then proceed to Los Cerrillos, where a DC-3 is waiting. The family will also be there. You'll accompany them to Quintero air base and an escort will take you to the Santa Inés cemetery. A burial party is on standby."

"Anything else?"

"No. Should be pretty straightforward. The president must be buried as soon as possible. Don't want any public demonstrations."

"What about his family?"

Carvajal takes a sip from his cup and scowls.

"What about them?"

"Well, what's going to happen?"

"Hell, I don't know. The junta will have to decide. Exile most probably."

"I see sir. Is that all?"

Carvajal nods and Sanchez gets up, replaces his cap and

salutes his superior and leaves. He descends the stairs, walks through the main hall and past the sandbagged entrance to his vehicle.

"Where to colonel?" asks the driver.

"The Military Hospital," he says and the corporal turns the jeep round and speeds off towards Providencia.

A few minutes later they arrive at the hospital gates and Sanchez explains to the guard that they have come for the president's body. He is asked to wait and the soldier makes a phone call. Presently a doctor emerges and approaches the vehicle.

"Colonel, the president's body has already been collected. A squadron of tanks arrived a short time ago."

"Where did they go?"

"Towards the city centre."

It is where the attaché has just come from and he tells the corporal to return as fast as possible. The vehicle sets off and races down the street again. As they head towards Plaza Italia, Sanchez sees a squadron of tanks. He flags down the commander and enquires about the president's coffin. The man looks blankly at him.

"No idea sir. We're just a patrol."

Sanchez swears loudly in exasperation and tells his driver to head towards Diez de Julio, to try and intercept the escort. In spite of the speed at which they travel, they see no other tanks and arrive at the airfield of Los Cerrillos. A DC-3 is parked near the control tower. Next to the plane are a group of civilians, whom the attaché assumes to be the family. There is no sign of any tank.

The jeep pulls up beside the plane's wing and Sanchez gets out and greets the small gathering. He recognises the president's sister Laura and his nephew Patricio Grove. The colonel asks if the coffin has arrived and they all answer negatively. There is nothing to do except wait and so they stand around, no one saying very much. After half an hour, the tank containing Allende's coffin appears. At the same time Hortensia also arrives, together with Eduardo Grove and his seventeen-year-old son Jaime, who is a godson of the president. Allende's widow is barely recognisable. She is wearing a wig and a scarf and her eyes are hidden by dark glasses.

After Hortensia escaped from Tomás Moro with the presidential chauffeur, she took refuge at the house of Inés and Felipe Herrera. The Herreras decided to keep the news of Allende's death from her until that evening when Eduardo Grove phoned, informing them of the preparations for the funeral. It was only then that they told Hortensia what had happened, knowing that at least she would be allowed to lay her husband to rest.

Grove had been called by Admiral Carvajal, who told him the president had committed suicide in the Moneda and that he was to be buried in the family plot at Viña. Allende's nephew demanded the president be buried in Santiago, but Carvajal dismissed the idea saying that it was impossible "for security reasons". At midnight two senior officers, one naval and one military, appeared at Grove's front door and handed him the necessary travel documents before departing again.

Hortensia had a restless night. Despite the sedatives given to her by a doctor, she barely slept and cried out constantly for her husband. At 1:00am she appeared at the Herreras' bedroom door in her nightdress, looking like a waif.

"We must go to the Military Hospital," she said. "Salvador is wounded, I must see him."

Without a word Inés got up, put her arm around the president's widow and gently took her back to bed.

Earlier a family friend had phoned and offered his condolences over the president's death. Hortensia went pale with disbelief and shock.

"Is Salvador really dead?" she had asked.

When Grove arrived the next morning, he greeted his aunt and told her that he was taking her to the Military Hospital.

"How is my dear Salvador?" was the immediate response.

"Tencha," replied her nephew. "Salvador is dead."

It was only then Hortensia finally realised that her husband had died in the Moneda.

Allende's widow sees Sanchez and approaches him. She tells the attaché that she wants to speak to him alone. The colonel nods and leads her to an office in one of the nearby buildings, letting her enter first. He closes the door.

"Yes, Madam President?"

"Colonel Sanchez, I want to speak to my daughters Beatriz and Isabel. Where are they?"

"They're at the Cuban Embassy," he says and writes down the number.

Hortensia goes to the phone on the desk and dials the number and speaks to Tati.

"I'm at Los Cerrillos with the Groves. Papa is to be buried in the family plot at Viña. I want you and your sister to attend the funeral."

"But Mama," says her eldest daughter, "we don't have any guarantees of safe conduct from the military. If we try and leave, the soldiers will arrest us."

She then explains how her husband and the ambassador had been inveigled to leave the embassy the day before in order to negotiate, only to be met with a fusillade of bullets. Fortunately, the soldiers opened fire prematurely and the two men had been able to take cover behind some cars in the compound. Still under fire they crawled back to the embassy, with the ambassador badly wounded in the hand. After this incident Incháustegui told them that if either Beatriz or her sister tried to leave the embassy, they would mostly likely be killed.

"OK, I understand," answers Hortensia, ending the conversation with a kiss. She is distraught. As if her husband's death were not enough, now even her own daughters were unable to attend their father's funeral. The president's widow turns away and Sanchez leads her outside into the bright spring sunshine.

They rejoin the rest of the family and the group boards the DC-3. The president's coffin has been placed in the middle of the aircraft and is covered by a grey army blanket. On one side Patricio Grove sits next to Hortensia and beside her are Laura and Colonel Sanchez. On the other side are Jaime, Eduardo and an air force sergeant. As the plane taxis down the runway, the sergeant leans forward and amid the din of the aircraft engines, says to Allende's widow that it is unforgivable the last journey of a Chilean president should be done so shamefully and in such secrecy.

The flight to Quintero airport takes only a few minutes and the plane soon touches down. On the runway a naval hearse and two vehicles are waiting. The DC-3 draws up and deposits its passengers on the apron near the terminal. The coffin is unloaded by a group of marines and put into the back of the hearse. The naval party, headed by a Commander Contreras, salutes the family as they approach. Hortensia nods stiffly, but Laura ignores them.

The group gets into the cars and travel the short distance to Santa Inés cemetery. When they arrive the place is deserted and ringed by soldiers. The family alight from the vehicles and follow the hearse through the cemetery gates as it drives at walking pace to the plot, which has already been prepared. At the graveside Hortensia informs Contreras the military authorities have told her that she would be able to see her husband for the last time at the cemetery. This is untrue and Contreras knows the junta would never have given their permission.

"Madam President," he says. "I am sorry. I am not authorised to do so. Besides, the casket is completely sealed."

The situation would have remained there, but being made of lead the coffin is extremely heavy. As the burial party attempts to move the casket, its lid shifts and it is plain that it has not been sealed as the commander claimed. Hortensia shoots him a dark look, which he is able to perceive even behind her sunglasses.

"Madam President," he says, shuffling his feet uneasily. "It seems I am mistaken."

Contreras orders his men to raise the lid, but all that can be seen beneath the pane of glass is a pale mound swathed in bandages. Inwardly the commander breathes a sigh of relief. The president's widow is undeterred and asks for the entire coffin to be opened. This time Contreras is adamant.

"Madam President, I cannot permit it."

Hortensia gives up, knowing that she is never going to be allowed to see her husband one last time and lets the lid be replaced. Six workers in overalls using heavy ropes, lower the casket into the vault. From their expressions the president's widow realises they have no idea whom they are burying. A wave of anger surges through Hortensia, swamping the feelings of grief, which have ebbed and flowed like a sad tide within her since that morning. She steps forward and begins to speak.

"Here lies comrade Allende. The people will not forget him," and she plucks a wild flower and drops it onto the coffin. "It is an absolute disgrace that the elected President of Chile should be buried like a dog!"

The president's widow stands there dignified in black, the sea breeze tugging at her scarf. Laura also plucks a flower and throws it into the open grave. The yellow bloom misses the coffin and a grave digger climbs down and places it on the lid, together with the other. As he clambers back up, she sees his eyes are filled with tears.

Colonel Sanchez stands behind the family, slightly to one side. He realises now that he should have remained with the president in the Moneda. Only two months before Allende had asked him to stay on as his attaché and he had accepted. Sanchez knows it was his duty to be with the president to the end, but he had failed. The colonel stands at the graveside and realises that perhaps just once a man is called upon to make such a decision. Sanchez knows that he made the wrong one. He had saved his own life. But at what cost?

The family proceeds to throw handfuls of earth into the grave and together, Contreras and Sanchez do the same. The president's widow and his sister then turn and walk away, each supporting the other. The Grove cousins go after them and the rest of the military follow at a discreet distance. The group slowly makes its way towards the hearses, the sounds of the grave diggers' spades behind them. Dark clouds gather overhead and obscure the sun. A long shadow falls across the cemetery and from the sea, a wind gets up and blows through the tall cypresses.

IX
A CAGE OPENS

Unlike the other detectives who have been released, their chief Juan Seoane remains in custody at the Tacna Regiment. One of his colleagues has given him a jersey, which the inspector now wears as the day has turned cold and grey. The soldiers take Seoane to another stable and keep him there on his own. A single guard is placed on the door.

The afternoon passes slowly for the inspector. He is glad his men have been freed and tries to remain hopeful. If the others have been released, surely it will only be a matter of time before the same happens to him? Then he can go home and reclaim whatever there is that remains of his life.

The stable block is bare and Seoane paces up and down, peering occasionally out of a window, until the guard catches him and warns the detective to keep inside. Later, the inspector is joined by four youths who were caught breaking the curfew. They have been badly beaten, their faces bearing the signs of their ill-treatment. The youths are frightened, but they are reassured when Seoane tells them he is an inspector from Investigations.

"Why are you here?" asks one.

"I was in the Moneda with the president."

The others congratulate the older man on his loyalty and a bond is instantly formed.

As darkness approaches, the temperature drops. Seoane sees an old tarpaulin lying in a corner and suggests they all get under it. They huddle together beneath the stiff and musty canopy and try and generate some body warmth. The hours pass and the group chat to pass the time. The youths ask Seoane about the assault on the palace and the inspector tells them what he witnessed. They are impressed by the defenders' resolve and believe the president should have called upon the people to defend the building. The youths are certain the military would not have opened fire on civilians. But the inspector disagrees.

"No, Allende was right," says Seoane. "If people had marched on the Moneda, the soldiers would have shot them. There would have been a bloodbath."

There is silence and after a while one of the youths speaks.

"Comrade, I know we can trust you. The thing is…well, we need your advice."

"OK. Ask away."

There is a brief murmuring among the group, before the youth speaks again.

"We're from MIR. That's why we were breaking the curfew. We were trying to reach some comrades in La Legua. What should we do?"

The news does not surprise the inspector, he had suspected as much.

"Work on your cover stories. You were going to visit friends, play football. You didn't know there was a curfew. You're just four dumb kids et cetera. Unless someone has given the military your names, or you're on a list, they won't know. And even if they do have your name, or you are on a list, tell them they're mistaken. Yours is a common name. Lots of people are called 'José This' or 'Jaime That'. Deny everything. As soon as you admit you're MIR, you're dead."

The youths are silent. Although they did not incriminate themselves during their initial interrogation, none of them know how long they can keep it up. The military were brutal and relentless. One of them, surely, would break.

Night falls and the prisoners drift off into an uneasy sleep. Seoane wakes with a start in the early hours. It takes him a while to work out where he is and he turns and looks at the youths snoring beside him and he remembers. The inspector shivers and his breath condenses in front of his face. It is cold, but he is glad there are no guards shouting at them or beating them. After a few moments Seoane closes his eyes and goes back to sleep.

At dawn a squad of soldiers arrive and kick the prisoners awake. The tarpaulin is dragged away and they are ordered to their feet. Each is handed a bucket, a rag and a bottle of detergent and told to clean the latrines. The men are escorted outside and set to work, while the soldiers stand over them and mock. It is a filthy task, the sole purpose of which is to humiliate them. In spite of the foul nature of the work, Seoane polishes the ceramic bowls until they gleam. He does not want to give the soldiers an excuse to hit him.

Later that morning a man in a grey three-piece suit appears and tells the inspector to stop working. He has an orange cravat, similar to the ones worn by the Infantry School soldiers who assaulted the Moneda. Seoane assumes he must be a member of the armed forces, possibly SIM. The man in the three-piece suit takes him outside and the inspector is united with the Moneda prisoners, who have spent another night in the stable. They seem a dispirited and dishevelled bunch and Seoane realises that he must look as bad.

The soldiers guarding the prisoners are in an ugly mood and whip them into line, using lengths of electric flex. As he joins his comrades, the inspector cannot help wishing that he was back cleaning latrines.

At the head of the queue is Paredes, who stands facing a small table. An officer sits behind it, rapping out questions while a subordinate takes notes.

"Name!"

"Eduardo Paredes."

The officer raises his eyes and looks at the former Director of Investigations.

"Don't they call you Coco Paredes?"

"Coco Paredes then."

"No! You're Eduardo Paredes!"

"As you wish."

"Shut up! Just answer the questions!"

And so on as each man is asked his name, title and

occupation. When all the Moneda prisoners have given their details, their hands are bound and they are told to lie on the ground. Seoane is among them. He is worried. There are senior government figures present and yet they are being treated worse than criminals. The four youths who were with him that night also join them. They try and catch his eye, but the inspector turns away. It must not seem as though they have struck up a rapport.

On the other side of the parade ground comes a sound of engines and two army lorries approach. The vehicles draw up alongside the prisoners and they are bundled into them. The inspector is one of the last to be put aboard. In the back of the lorry, he hears the voice of Enrique Huerta protesting about the crush of bodies on top of him. But there is nothing anyone can do. The Palace Intendant continues to shout, until a soldier pokes his head inside and tells him that unless he keeps quiet, he will shut him up for good.

As Seoane sits in the back of the lorry, an officer with a bandaged neck appears. He recognises the man. The captain had been at the Moneda and the inspector assumes he was involved in the assault.

"You Juan Seoane?"

"Yes."

"You're going to be interrogated. You going to be good?"

The inspector looks at the soldier.

"When have I ever been bad?"

The officer with the bandaged neck smiles and helps him down from the vehicle. Some soldiers then escort their prisoner across the parade ground. Behind him the inspector hears the lorries being driven away, but he does not look back.

Seoane is taken to an office. In front of him a trio in civilian clothes are sitting behind a table, including the man in the three-piece suit. The inspector realises they must be from Investigations or SIM. He is shown an empty chair and sits down opposite his inquisitors. The detective is struck by the irony of the situation. He has questioned suspects like this numerous times. Now it is his turn.

"Sleep well inspector?" asks the man in the three-piece.

"Better than the first night, thanks."

"We want to ask you some questions…"

"Well, I didn't think you wanted to talk football."

Seoane smiles, but the other man's expression does not change. The inspector realises this interrogation will not be an informal one.

"Were there arms in the Moneda?"

"Sure there were."

The man in the three-piece frowns. He is surprised by the inspector's frankness.

"Why didn't you report it? You knew about the Arms Control Law."

Now it is Seoane's turn to look perplexed.

"General Sepulveda had an office in the Moneda. He was head of the carabineros. He would have known all about the arms. Besides, there's also the president. What was Sepulveda meant to do? Inform Allende of his own armoury? They weren't the only weapons either. I was never on duty at Tomás Moro, although some of my men were. There were arms there as well. The president's attachés often visited him at home. They would have seen the GAP and their weapons. Why are you asking me? Ask Sepulveda. Ask Badiola, Sanchez or Grez."

The panel exchange looks, but say nothing. The man in the three-piece then asks Seoane what he knows about Plan Zeta. The inspector is baffled.

"I've never heard of it."

"Bullshit!" snaps the interrogator on his left.

"I swear I have no idea what you're talking about."

"It was the Communist plan to take over the country by armed rebellion," explains three-piece.

"Well, why don't you ask them?"

"Don't get cute you sonofabitch!" shouts the other man on

the inspector's right.

Seoane realises he has overstepped the mark and while he might be a senior detective, he must be careful. These men are not playing games. Plan Zeta may well be a right-wing fantasy, but the military believe it. The trouble is that there has been so much hysteria in the previous weeks about Communist plots and a left-wing insurrection, that even Seoane had wondered whether some of them were true.

"I apologise sir," says the inspector, facing the man who made the outburst. "The truth is I don't know anything about Plan Zeta. There may be have been a Communist plot, but I wasn't party to it. I'm not a Communist and never have been. I'm a public servant and a member of the armed forces like you. I was given my orders by Alfredo Joignant, the Director of Investigations, and they were to remain with the president in the Moneda. I did my duty. If I stand accused of this, then I accept whatever punishment you wish to give me. But I assure you I have never heard of any Plan Zeta."

There is silence. Seoane is unsure whether the interrogators believe him. They change tack and three-piece opens a large manila folder and asks the inspector to identify some mugshots of the GAP. He recognises one in particular, it is Wagner Salinas, the heavyweight boxing champion. But most people would have known this. He is told that Salinas and a companion have been picked up in Curicó and are now in custody. There are others and the inspector recognises several faces, but does not know their names, only their *noms de guerre*. People like Jano.

"They never used their real names, they went by nicknames."

"Like what?" asks three-piece.

The inspector does not want to say, in case he compromises his erstwhile colleagues. So he makes some up.

"You know, the usual: 'Chico', 'Gordo', 'Pepe'. Those sort of names. Besides, the GAP weren't under my command."

This information at least seems to satisfy the men from SIM and the photos are put back into the folder.

The interrogation continues, always returning to Plan Zeta. The circular motion of the talk wears Seoane down and he finds it difficult to concentrate. Sometimes the inspector feels as if he is not really present and that he is listening to all of this in another room. He can hear himself talking and voices questioning him, but there is a disconnect. The interrogators' faces drift in and out of focus. Seoane is so tired. He has barely slept in forty-eight hours. If only they would give him a break. Slowly, the room begins to spin.

"Inspector!" says a voice.

Seoane's head jerks upright, as if tugged by a wire.

The questions have stopped and the interrogators are conversing together in low voices. The inspector wonders what time it is and guesses it must be mid afternoon.

The man in the three-piece suit calls out and a soldier enters and Seoane feels the cords on his wrists being cut. He is offered a coffee and a cigarette and accepts both gratefully, although he can barely hold either because his hands are so numb.

"The interrogation is over, for the time being," says the senior SIM officer, his voice neither friendly nor unfriendly. "You're to remain in custody, until we work out what to do with you."

The inspector is dismissed and gets up off the chair, which he has been sitting on for the last three hours and is escorted outside. The guards take him to another stable. It is in much better condition than the one where he spent the previous night and was used as accommodation for troops. There are wooden bunks with blankets and mattresses and some tables and chairs. Sitting on a bunk is another prisoner. It is the Socialist deputy Vicente Sotta.

"Hello comrade, how are you?" he asks with a smile.

Seoane, glad to see a friendly face and hear some kind

words for once, is overcome with emotion. He goes to the deputy and unable to stop himself, breaks down in tears. Sotta puts his arm around the weeping detective and comforts him.

"You have suffered comrade, you have suffered."

The soldiers who escorted the prisoner stand in the doorway watching and Sotta admonishes them.

"Why don't you go and get him something to eat instead of just gawping?"

The men exchange looks and leave, returning later with some bread and cheese. When they have gone Seoane wipes his face with his shirtsleeve. He looks exhausted. He is unshaven and his eyes are bloodshot from crying and lack of sleep.

"Eat," says the deputy, indicating the food. "You'll feel better for it."

The inspector does so and after he has finished, Sotta lays him down on a bed.

"Sleep," he tells him. "I'll watch over you."

Seoane closes his eyes, grateful for the chance to rest. He dozes for an hour, before being woken by a soldier. It is the same officer with the bandaged neck. He looks down at the dishevelled prisoner lying on the wooden bunk.

"You're going to be released," says the captain. "Why don't you go and spruce yourself up a little? You look a sight."

The inspector gets up feeling dazed and goes to the washroom. Inside are a row of basins. He fumbles with one of the taps, picks up a bar of soap and washes his hands and face. The sensation of cleanliness feels strange after the filth and degradation of his detention and he watches as the suds gurgle down the plughole. Seoane finishes his ablutions and looks about for a towel. There are none and so he returns to the dormitory, his hands and face dripping, but feeling refreshed.

An escort arrives and the inspector embraces Sotta and

tells him that he will pass on a message to his family, so they will know of his whereabouts. He is escorted outside and taken to the same building, where the other detectives were brought the previous day and like them, he too is given a brief medical examination.

"Inspector Seoane your position is still under review," says an officer from Investigations. "There will be a hearing at a later date, otherwise you're free to go."

The detective asks for permission to call his wife and this is granted.

A military vehicle takes him to his home in Recoleta, which he last saw two days before. But it might as well have been a hundred years ago for the inspector, so much has changed. His wife is standing on the doorstep. The vehicle has barely come to a halt before she is running towards it, tears streaming down her face.

X
DAWSON ISLAND

In the Military Academy the prisoners from the MOD are joined by other senior officials, whose liberty is considered a threat to the new regime. They have been singled out in two junta proclamations stating that: 'the following must present themselves at the Military Academy, by either Wednesday or Thursday.' Failure to do so would mean that they had, 'put themselves beyond the bounds of military jurisdiction, entailing consequences that are easy to imagine.' Since the proclamations various names on the list have been arriving at the academy, either singly or in small groups and bringing only a travel bag with a few personal belongings. The prominenti are a disparate band ranging from ministers and government officials, to well known left-wingers and academics. In all there are around forty of them. By Thursday afternoon most of the people featured on the two lists have arrived and form themselves into small groups, swapping tales about the coup. The 'heroes' are those who were with Allende in the Moneda. But they are too modest to accept such an accolade and besides, the president is dead.

At midday on Friday, the prisoners receive a visit from General Gonzalo Prieto, the junta's new Minister of Justice. He is accompanied by his deputy Colonel Max Silva. The justice chief is polite and refers to them all as *señores ministros*. He also offers them his condolences over the death of the president.

"I understand how keenly you must feel such a loss," he adds.

The comment raises a few eyebrows, but the prisoners say nothing and Prieto continues.

"The situation, of course, is extremely grave and you are being kept at the academy for your own safety. Naturally, this cannot continue for ever and this is why the junta is considering exiling you all..."

At this the whole group erupts in protest. They want to know just what they have done to deserve such a punishment and demand to know on whose authority the decision has been made. Carlos Briones speaks for all.

"General Prieto, we are servants of a democratically elected government, which has been violently overthrown by the military. This action in itself is illegal and anathema to Chile's constitution. Furthermore, we wish to see what charges have been formulated against us and we will duly contest any such charges in court. We have been denied our liberty and the most basic human rights. Three days ago we were members of the government and you, like us, were loyal to the president. Now Allende is dead and the country at war."

The justice minister is taken aback by Briones' words and begins to bluster.

"I...er...*señores ministros*, look I understand you're upset and I don't particularly want to get into semantics about the legality of the coup..."

"Semantics?" says Jose Tohá. "Unbelievable!"

Prieto ignores the interruption and carries on.

"... You are fortunate to be alive. There are some in the junta who wanted you all dead. Exile is preferable to a firing squad surely?"

The justice minister, hoping he was being candid, has only made a bad situation worse.

"It is disgraceful!" and Osvaldo Puccio gets to his feet. "We are not guilty of any crime!"

"That, minister, is a matter of debate," answers Prieto, an edge creeping into his voice. "If you wish, you can formalise your arguments in writing and I'll present them to the junta. The decision about your future will be theirs and theirs alone. I shall be here at the same time tomorrow. Otherwise, I wish you all a good day."

With that the justice minister and his subordinate, who has

not uttered a word during the entire meeting, leave. The brief silence which follows their departure, is soon replaced by an agitated hubbub. Prieto's words are discussed ardently. Did the junta really want to have them all killed? It was possible. Hundreds of people were under arrest and many have been murdered. If they were to be exiled, what would happen to their families? Would they be allowed to join them? Where would they be sent? Perhaps only Comintern countries would accept them, even though only a few of them were actually Communists. No one much fancied going to the Soviet Union or the Eastern Block, although Cuba was an acceptable destination for some. The atmosphere in the room is gloomy. In spite of all this Briones, Tohá and Puccio immediately set about drafting their defence.

*

The following day the Military Academy prisoners are waiting in the dining hall, clutching their mess tins as they queue for yet another meal of beans. The justice minister has not returned and consequently their neatly written statement of several pages remains in Briones' pocket, undelivered and unread. Before the cooks can fill their bowls, an officer approaches and orders the prominenti back to their rooms, telling them to collect their bags as they will be leaving in ten minutes.

"Everyone should assemble in the main square," says the officer. "A roll call will be taken."

"Where are we going?" someone asks.

The officer does not reply and walks away.

The prisoners do as they are told and go back to their rooms and collect their belongings. They gather in the academy's square as they wait for further instructions. The afternoon is dull and grey and the cold air reeks faintly of sulphur. The few trees scattered around the barracks struggle into leaf, but spring remains a foreign country. In the distance the snow-shrouded Andes rise steeply out of the city smog. The drab enclosure and the grandeur of the horizon, only heightens the prisoners' sense of isolation. A few sparrows scratch about the dirt and then depart in a flurry, as if too they cannot wait to leave.

The prominenti are told to form a line. As they shuffle themselves into place, a jeep passes through the main gates and draws up opposite and a civilian gets out. He is young, short and has blond hair. It is the Presidential Secretary's son Osvaldo. His father cannot believe his eyes. The son he thought he would never see again, has returned like Lazarus from the dead. The younger Puccio recognises his father among the crowd and walks towards him. The minister is overjoyed to see his boy, but his first question is typically practical.

"Have you eaten?"

"No Dad."

The youth has spent the last couple of days in the Chile Stadium. His face still bears the scars of the beating he received from the SIM men at the barracks of the Maturana Regiment. His moustache has been plucked out, his top lip is badly swollen and he has a black eye and a bruised jaw. He looks as if he has not slept in days. Hidden from his father's gaze beneath his shirt are scores of welts and bruises. He is lucky to be alive.

Earlier that morning General Baeza had ordered that the young Puccio should join the prominenti at the Military Academy. Undoubtedly, the Presidential Secretary's position had saved his son's life.

Father and son stand together for the roll call. When the name "Puccio, Osvaldo" is called, both reply "present."

The officer taking the roll call has not been told about the new arrival and looks up with a scowl and down at his list again.

"What the hell," he mutters, adding another name. "We'll take both of you."

After the muster the prisoners are ordered into buses and told to lie on the floor. A group of officer cadets toting machine guns, grenades dangling from their webbing, are their escort. They tell them that if anyone moves or talks, they will be shot. The buses drive off at great speed and the prominenti have to grasp the steel seat supports, to stop themselves sliding across the floor as the vehicles careen around the corners.

The buses arrive at Los Cerrillos air base and the prisoners are ordered out. Nearby a DC-6 is waiting. The men are led towards it, shoved and insulted by the soldiers as they walk. At the aircraft steps they are told to put down what they are carrying and a group of conscripts rummage through their belongings. When they have finished they are ordered to pick up their bags and told to board the plane.

In the aircraft the men are arrayed along each side. At either end stands a soldier with a machine gun. No one dares speak. They have not forgotten the justice minister's chilling admission, that there were those in the junta who wanted them dead. They wonder if this is about to happen and they are being taken to some remote spot many miles away, in order to be despatched. With this thought in the prisoners' minds, the aircraft engines splutter into life and the DC-6 taxis down the runway, carrying its human cargo towards an unknown fate.

The journey in the propeller driven aircraft is arduous. The plane is constantly buffeted by the winds and air currents that pour across the mountains and the DC-6 does not touch down until 10:30pm. The prisoners know only that they have flown south, since the cordillera was on the port side of the aircraft during the flight. The men are ordered from the plane and one by one, they leave the fuselage and step out into bleak mid winter. The blast of freezing air shocks them and they all catch their breath. They are only wearing city clothes suitable for a temperate climate, which give no protection against the Antarctic chill. The sky is awash with stars and snow lies thickly on the ground. As they line up on the runway the prisoners see the words 'Punta Arenas' emblazoned on the terminal building. They have arrived at Chile's most southerly airport, which lies at a latitude of 53 degrees south and is only a few miles from Tierra del Fuego.

The prominenti stand on the icy tarmac in their thin-soled shoes and blow on their fingers for warmth. They look around and shiver as a cruel wind knifes across the dark sound of the Magellan Straits. Halogen lamps illuminate the runway in a bright and wintry glare. At the edge of this halo of light, soldiers lurk in the shadows. It is the last thing they see before each man is hooded and pushed into the back of an armoured personnel carrier. The prisoners are squeezed into two APCs and the heavy metal doors are bolted shut. The engines start with a diesel roar and the captives feel themselves moving, the hoods smothering them as they jolt from side to side. Again they cannot help wondering if this is to be their final journey, before the inevitable bullet in the back of the head.

After an hour the vehicles come to a halt and the doors open. The prisoners are told to get out and their hoods are removed. They are at a quayside. A line of trawlers lie moored along a jetty and waves lap gently against snow-covered piles. The chill air smells of oil and brine. Next to the fishing boats a cargo ship is berthed, the yellow light from the portholes illuminating its cast iron sides. The men are taken on board the hulk and led down a steep ladder into the hold.

In the iron belly of the ship they are told to neither move, nor talk and that sleeping is prohibited. Everyone is exhausted by the journey and the cumulative effects of a lack of sleep, so the last order seems unnecessarily vindictive. They all try to stay awake, fearful of the consequences if they do not. But the day has been long and finally one of them succumbs. It is the Socialist senator Aniceto Rodriguez. He lies slumped, his head resting on a table, snoring softly.

A guard pokes the senator sharply in the ribs with the barrel of his machine gun.

"You! No sleeping!"

Rodriguez jolts upright, looking dazed and he rubs his eyes and yawns. Orlando Letelier is sitting beside the senator. After his incarceration at the Tacna Regiment, he had been taken to the Military Academy the following afternoon, along with Enrique Kirberg who was rector of the State Technical University, which had been one of the main pockets of resistance during the coup. It was only then the defence minister learnt about the Moneda's bombing and that the president was dead. He makes a head count and realises someone is missing. It is Daniel Vergara, the Under Secretary for the Interior and one of the emissaries. Letelier wonders what has become of him and cannot help fearing the worst.

To the minister's relief Vergara finally arrives, his hand swathed in a bandage. A soldier had accidentally dropped his weapon in the APC, making it discharge. The bullet had struck the roof and ricocheted into the emissary's hand. He had not heard the shot because of the din of the engines, nor felt the bullet because of the cold. It was only when blood began to pour down his fingers, that he realised he had been hurt. Vergara informed the soldier next to him about his wound, but was told that he would have to wait until they reached their destination.

And so the emissary had sat there blindfolded, with a badly injured hand for the entire journey. On arrival at the quayside an official was told that Vergara was wounded and he was taken to the ship's mess room. A group of officers, none of whom were medics, examined the prisoner's hand. They probed the wound without anaesthetic and informed him the bullet was too deep and he would have to wait until the following day, before anything could be done. They bandaged his hand with a dressing from a first aid box, then told the emissary to pick up his bag and took him below to join the others in the hold.

At midnight the ship's boilers rumble into life. The heavy ropes securing the vessel are released and the hulk turns slowly and heads for the deeper waters of the sound. The prisoners sit silently in the hold as they listen to the throb of the engines, each man alone with his thoughts. The lights in the ceiling burn brightly and hurt their eyes, but no one dares sleep.

At 5:00am the following morning the steamer docks and the subterranean rumble from the engine room dies. Soldiers faces appear at the hatch and the prominenti are ordered out from the hold. One by one they climb the iron ladder and step out onto the deck. It is not yet dawn and stars illuminate the dark Antarctic sky. They stand on the frosted boards and wait in turn to descend the gangplank to the quayside. The narrow bridge is covered in ice and each man picks his way carefully down it, a holdall in his hand. Some are elderly and some, like Osvaldo Puccio, have serious medical conditions. One such man is Julio Palestro, the former Head of Welfare. Over sixty he has a damaged spine and renal problems because of diabetes. Suddenly, the elderly politician trips and plunges with his suitcase into the icy harbour.

The splash is followed by shouts and the sound of people running. Some marines appear with a boat hook and lower it over the side and catch the coat of the flailing man. They grab his collar and haul the gasping former welfare chief out of the water. The other prisoners watch aghast as their companion is lain choking and shivering on the snow-covered ground.

As the soldiers stand there the two doctors among them, Arturo Jirón and Patricio Guijón, go and tend to their companion. Palestro's lips are blue and his teeth chatter uncontrollably. He tries to speak, but can only jabber. Guijón massages his chest and Jirón takes his pulse and tells one of soldiers to get some sugar and biscuits.

"Quickly," he says, "or he'll die."

The soldier runs off and soon returns with some food and Jirón feeds it to his half-frozen patient. After a few minutes Palestro recovers enough to be able to stand and is helped into a nearby lorry.

The rest of the prisoners assemble on the quayside. In silent awe they survey their new surroundings. Snow smothers everything. Even the telephone wires have been transformed into long, thick cables of frost. In the black waters of the harbour, icebergs drift mute and ghostly.

An officer tells the prominenti to put their bags into the back of the lorry while others, including the elder Puccio, are told to get in. The remainder are formed into three lines and marched away, an escort of marines on either side. They leave the dockyard and ascend a steep hill, before turning into the open road. They walk slipping and sliding in their city shoes, their feet already numb from the cold. In the stillness of the grey and freezing dawn there is no sound, except the wind and the uneven creak of footsteps upon the snowy road.

After a kilometre the road begins to descend. At the bottom of the hill in a small valley, lies a military camp. It is surrounded by a high barbed-wire fence. The prisoners are marched through the wooden gates and taken inside one of the huts, where they are given a cup of coffee. It is the first sustenance they have had since breakfast the previous day. The prominenti warm their hands on the tin mugs and stamp their frostbitten feet. In a corner a cast iron stove heats the low-beamed room. The air is thick and smells of melting snow and damp clothes. Pools of water soak the wooden floor. There is a line of bunk beds, the bare mattresses covered with army blankets.

A short, fat man enters the hut accompanied by two NCOs and the marines guarding the group snap to attention. It is the commandant of the base Jorge Fellay.

"Welcome to Dawson Island," he announces. "You are

prisoners of war."

XI
BRAND NEW DAY

It is high summer in Santiago and Patricio Aylwin has been elected as Chile's first democratic president since the coup. After the long, grey years of the Pinochet era, the city appears transformed. It is not just the happy crowds thronging the Plaza de la Libertad outside the Moneda, cheering and waving all manner of flags: from the red, white and blue of the Republic to the hammer and sickle of the Communist Party. The place feels different. It feels free.

I am here on my first foreign assignment as part of a post-graduate degree in journalism at the London College of Printing. For our second term we have to make a half hour radio documentary. My topic is Chile's transition to democracy. I have already voiced several reports for Independent Radio News, known by its acronym IRN, and for the first time I feel like a real journalist. There are scores of correspondents from around the world and quite a few from Britain. At twenty-four I am at least a decade younger, but they have taken me under their wing, as they are a friendly bunch and perhaps also because I speak Spanish and know the lie of the land. I first arrived in Santiago in 1984 to teach English and then spent another year there after I graduated from university and witnessed the Concertación's 1988 'No' campaign against Pinochet's rule, taking part in demonstrations and going native. At times like this I think that I am more Chilean than the Chileans; apparently it is a common affliction among gringos.

The crowds in the plaza push and shove and shout. People sing and dance and let off fireworks. The air is filled with smoke and the screech and bang of explosions, although this time they are festive. They see my microphone and torrents of words gush into it.

"*Viva Chile!*" "*Viva democracia!*" and "*Pinochet mierda!*"

are the most common refrains.

When I have enough 'vox pops' and what journalists like to call 'wild track', which is background noise, I return to the offices of Radio Co-Operativa and file another report for IRN. The radio station was one of the few independent broadcasters during the 'No' campaign and was regularly taken off air. The newsroom is happy, every face is wreathed in smiles. When the station's manager introduces me to his other colleagues, I am referred to as *'Justin del BBC'*. At first I think it is simply because he wants to impress, but soon realise that it is South American shorthand for 'Brit journo, works in broadcast.' Everyone has heard of the BBC.

The reason I am able to use Radio Co-Operativa's facilities is because one of its owners is Carlos Figueroa, a leading Christian Democrat politician who ran the 'No' campaign and is Aylwin's fixer. Figueroa is now a senior member of the party, having held junior ministerial positions during President Eduardo Frei's government in the 1960s. When Pinochet seized power he returned to his legal practice, but had always worked behind the scenes in pressuring the military to return to democracy. In addition I am also a family friend, since I know his children well. It is for this reason that Figueroa, in spite of his hectic schedule, has granted me an interview which will take place at his home the following Sunday.

A couple of days later I press the buzzer on the iron gate of a Spanish-style residence in the upper class suburb of Las Condes. In the distance Manquehue mountain rises green and massive. The Andean sun will soon sear the spring grass from its lower flanks, so that only thorn scrub and cacti remain. Across the road a uniformed carabinero stands beside a wooden guardhouse, shaded by a pale flowering acacia. It seems an anomaly now democracy has been restored, but there are radicals on the far right and the far left who wish my host harm. For this reason Figueroa is permitted to keep a six-shot revolver at home.

A dog barks savagely and gives me a fright. I need not worry, it is only a neighbour's Alsatian. Almost every house in the vicinity has some sort of land shark, which patrols the front yard. A maid in a pale blue pinafore opens the gate and I am ushered inside. The dog next door whines and whimpers and sticks its damp nose under the fence, trying to get a sniff.

I am greeted by Figueroa's youngest daughter Maria Luisa, who is dark-eyed and pretty in that distinctive Latin American way, which speaks of fire and earth.

"*Hola Justicia*," she says using her nickname for me as she rises on her toes, kisses my cheek and gives me a squeeze. Maria Luisa looks tanned and lovely, her olive skin burnished by the summer sun. I feel white and sickly in comparison. "*Papi,*" she calls out. "*Justin ha llegado*." She turns and smiles. "He'll be here shortly. He's been going non-stop for days. Driving us all nuts. What do you want to drink? Coke?"

I tell her Coke is fine and Maria Luisa shows me into the living-room, which is pleasantly cool after the heat outside. The walls are whitewashed and hung with family portraits and traditional Altiplano tapestries made by native Indians, while the floor is laid with polished terra cotta tiles the colour of burnt sienna. The furniture is a mix of old European and traditional Chilean, the surfaces of which are strewn with framed photographs: some of them are of the family and others from Figueroa's political days. There is a signed black and white photo of the Christian Democrat President Eduardo Frei in a morning coat and wearing his sash of office. Its simple inscription reads: 'to Carlos Figueroa, friend and colleague, affectionately Eduardo'.

The maid returns with a glass of Coke and ice and a bowl of peanuts on a tray and puts it down on the low table in the middle of the room. Maria Luisa and myself sit and chat, her hand resting on my knee. This does not mean that she is in love with me, all Chilean women do this with their friends.

After a few minutes, a voice booms from the hall.

"*Hola Justin! Hace mucho tiempo. Cómo estás?*"

It is Carlos Figueroa. He is stocky and balding, the hair on the sides of his head silver and black, so that he looks like a badger. And like the burrowing omnivore he is broad-shouldered and muscular, his arms strong and hairy. I get to my feet and my host grins and wraps me in a bear hug.

"Come, come, let us sit. Tell me what you've been doing," he says gruffly with a thick accent. Although Figueroa can read the language, his spoken English is rudimentary and we have agreed to conduct the interview in Spanish. Maria Luisa will act as a translator if needed.

My host listens as I tell him about my work for IRN and the reports I have made at Radio Co-Operativa. He makes approving noises and is glad there has been so much foreign press coverage of Aylwin's inauguration. Chileans are proud they have returned to democracy under their own volition and peacefully, with no intervention from foreign governments, including the United States. It still rankles with many people that the former US president Richard Nixon and his Secretary of State Henry Kissinger, aided and abetted the coup. Undoubtedly the uprising would have happened without their involvement, but it was not a purely Chilean affair*. The Christian Democrats also bore some responsibility, since they urged the military to intervene. And this really is the point of my interview. Why did the Christian Democrats ask the generals to overthrow Allende's government?

We start with recent events in Chile and slowly work our way back to 1973. The interview is jovial and occasionally congratulatory, as is to be expected when friends converse

---

* *US interest in what the State Department refers to as 'the South American cone' has always been high on the political agenda. The CIA spent over a million US dollars in 1970 in their attempt to stop Allende gaining power.*

over a shared history. Gradually, the tone becomes more sombre, as we talk about the coup and the days and weeks which preceded it. After the Tancazo, Allende felt obliged to include the armed forces in his cabinet, but the move did little to dampen the febrile atmosphere. Nothing it seemed could surmount the political impasse. The president refused to hold a plebiscite that he was sure to lose and elections were not due until November 1976.

After skirting around the subject, I finally ask the question that has to be asked.

"So, why did the Christian Democrats support military intervention in 1973?"

Figueroa looks at me and grins. He is annoyed, but hides his irritation like a boxer who smiles when he has been hurt by a punch.

"The Christian Democrats were not responsible for the coup. We were not in government. The people responsible for the coup were Popular Unity and their leader was Allende. He had ample opportunity to step down. He knew the situation was impossible. He was in power, but he had no power."

"Yet there was democracy..."

"Democracy is a double-edged sword. It can be abused just as easily as it is used. Look at what happened in Weimar Germany. The Nazi party won a narrow majority and Hitler became Chancellor. That was the end of democracy. The same happened, more or less, with Allende who could not control his left wing once he was in government. In 1970 he won just 36 per cent of the popular vote. He only became president because Radomiro Tomic handed him the Christian Democrat bloc, when Congress had to ratify the vote. Chile suffered greatly as a result of Tomic's vanity. I say this as a friend and former colleague."

I pause and watch the cassette spooling in the recorder and glance at the recording levels. Maria Luisa coughs politely. It is a warning, but I ignore her.

"Is it not strange for a centre-left party to encourage the military to oust a democratically elected president?"

Figueroa huffs and sits back on the sofa, his arms crossed. I move the microphone a little closer in his direction, its black flex coiled snakelike around my fist.

"Look, you can have good governments and you can have bad governments. You can have right-wing governments and you can have left-wing governments. What you cannot have is chaos," and the politician thumps a cushion to emphasise his point, sending the needle of the recording level into the red. "At that time Chile was in chaos (thump). The economy was in chaos (thump), the entire country was in complete and utter chaos (thump, thump). What you cannot live through is chaos! (big thump)."

Figueroa's hazel eyes blaze fiercely under bushy brows. His anger is genuine.

"Nobody imagined the coup would be so brutal, or that the dictatorship would last so long. The military promised to hold elections within a year. One year! We had to wait seventeen."

My host is well and truly put out. He looks like a bank manager who has handed over the keys to a trusted aide and is surprised to discover the vaults have been robbed. No one speaks and birdsong streams through the open window.

A timely voice calls from the hall. It is the maid telling us that lunch is ready. Figueroa leaps up from the sofa and gives me a slap on the shoulder. The interview is over.

"*Vamos gringo!*"

He leads the way and we enter a large room with a wooden ceiling. In the centre a table is spread with a white linen cloth and laid out with polished silver candelabra and cutlery. Figueroa takes his place at the head as *pater familias,* his elegant wife Sara at his side. The rest of the family, which include several grandchildren, sit in no particular order further down. I am placed at the opposite end with Maria Luisa.

Grace is said by the youngest child and lunch is then served by the maid. The main course is a tender fillet of beef, with sautéed potatoes, rice and green beans. Figueroa holds court as head of the family and makes a variety of pronouncements on politics, people and just about everything under the sun. He is a veritable force of nature. The old boy is a generous host, the wine is plentiful and there is much laughter. Between mouthfuls of roast beef and slugs of red wine, Figueroa makes a joke about gringos coming to Latin America to "steal our women" and gives me a wink. I am forgiven.

After pudding is cleared, coffee is served and the women light cigarettes. It is 5:00pm before I get up and thank my host. I am embraced by the family who all rise from their chairs, except Figueroa who remains seated and grins.

"Say hello to Maggie for me," he says.

Chileans hold the British prime minister in high esteem as a result of the Falklands War. During the 1982 conflict the country gave covert help to Britain, since they shared a common enemy in Argentina. The two Latin American nations almost came to blows over the disputed Magellan straits in 1978. Chileans also consider themselves to be an island nation: to the north is the Atacama, to the east are the Andes, to the west is the Pacific and to the south lies Antarctica.

Maria Luisa walks me to the gate. Next door's Alsatian pads restlessly back and forth behind the fence, but does not bark.

"*Ay Justicia*, I thought my Dad was going to hit you."

"Me too."

We laugh and she gives me a kiss.

"See you soon and don't ask any more difficult questions."

"Would I do such a thing? Please thank your father again for me."

Maria Luisa gives me a hug and waves goodbye as I walk down the street. I reach the main road and take a taxi to my hotel in Providencia. The tape recorder sits on my lap and I rewind the cassette and press play. Figueroa's voice booms out. The audio levels are fine and you can actually hear the blows as he thumps the cushion.

At the hotel reception I collect my room key from the small, moustachioed concierge and take the lift to the fifth floor. I enter the bedroom and hang the 'do not disturb sign' on the handle and close the door. The place is airless and I go to open the windows. A rush of street sounds greet me from below, a tide of heat rising with them. I watch the traffic squeeze by and look at the park beyond with its water sprinklers and bright green lawns and decide to take a shower. When I have finished I return to the room, my bare feet leaving damp prints on the carpet. I sit down on the bed and flip open the tape recorder and put the cassette in a box, marking it with a dateline and the name of the interviewee and place it next to the others on the side table. There are four C90 cassettes. My documentary is coming along nicely. I have two more interviews to do before I return to London.

I have a free evening and want to visit Bellavista. It is Santiago's bohemian quarter and full of restaurants, bars and nightclubs. In the daytime the place is something of a tourist trap, situated as it is in the lee of San Cristóbal Hill and opposite the Municipal Zoo. At night the freaks come out and you can score anything from heroin to transsexuals. Neither is my particular medicine, but it is nice to know the opportunity is there should the need arise.

It is too early to go out and I lie down on the bed to rest. The walls of the room are cream and the plaster scraped in small undulating waves like a petrified sea. The curtains are nylon and orange coloured and the MDF furniture has a uniform mahogany veneer. Above my head is a gaudy oil of Easter Island, the Moai gazing impassively out to sea. Opposite the bed the television's dark mirror reflects the shape of a human being, who could be alive or dead.

Hotel rooms in foreign countries seem strange. They are

familiar and yet alien. A haven in many ways, but also a prison. Perhaps purgatory is more apt: a captive place for lost souls. It always feels as though the room is haunted by the ghost of a previous occupant and that you are trespassing. I close my eyes and sleep and dream of nothing.

I wake to the repeated sounds of a car horn. I turn my head and see the sun has gone from the window. The curtains glow faintly in the evening light and the walls are washed with shadow. My watch reads 8:30pm. I get up and take a clean shirt from the cupboard and dress. In the bathroom I comb my hair and splash on some aftershave. I take a last look in the mirror and make what I think is a movie star face and leave.

It is dark when I cross the Pio Nono Bridge. The moon is full and bright and shines like a silver dollar on the waters of the Mapocho. Clouds of moths flutter palely against the gas lamps, as they burn their wings in impassioned but unrequited love. I leave the moths to their amorous adventures and approach Bellavista.

The streets are thronged with people making the most of the extended weekend. Monday has been declared a holiday in celebration of the recent elections and the atmosphere is like a carnival. A lorry full of soldiers in combat gear approaches. Howls and whistles of derision are hurled at the men, who stand silently holding onto the canopy frame. As they roar past one of the soldiers at the back grins and raises a middle finger in salute.

I enter a bar playing live music. The band perform songs from Chile's most famous folk groups, including Quilapayún and Inti Illimani, both of whom were exiled by the Pinochet regime. The musicians are native Indians with red skin, high cheekbones and dark, straight hair. I order a *pisco sour* and stand with my back to the counter, enjoying the music. After a while I fall in with a bunch of students, who are out having fun. Amid the din and people shouting to be heard, we become friendly as more *pisco* appears. I find myself sitting next to a beautiful girl with almond green eyes and long, dark lashes. She looks like a cat and with her hand resting on my thigh, promises to be just as slinky. She is gorgeous and way out of my league. I would never be able to pull a girl like her at home. But here I am a gringo and therefore exotic and the rules are different.

Her name is Magdalena and she is studying law at the University of Chile, the campus of which is near by. I tell her it must be fascinating and that she must be very intelligent. This trick usually works. We talk a bit, although not much and listen as others hold forth. Suddenly, she turns and kisses me full on the mouth. The cat has caught the canary. She breaks away and spits out a load of feathers. Then Magdalena raises a hand and yawns, flashing an impressive set of pearly whites and fixes me with her feline eyes.

"*Vamos*," she says.

"*Si, vamos.*"

It is a short trip back to the hotel. We enter the lobby and walk past the yucca plants and potted palms and I ask for my room key at reception. The concierge with the moustache gives me a sly look, but says nothing. Once in the lift we start kissing and fumbling with each other. Her breath is hot in my ear and on my cheek. She kisses deep and longingly. I open the door of my room and we go inside. The door closes. No time even for the 'do not disturb' sign...

The next morning the girl is gone. The room is filled with sunshine since I failed to close the curtains when I returned. Nothing remains of her presence, except the dent in the pillow where she laid her head. I get up and shower, then go downstairs for breakfast. Most of it has been cleared away and I settle for fresh coffee and croissants and jam.

The day promises to be fine and I decide to climb San Cristóbal Hill, which has a spectacular view over the city. At the top is a statue of the Virgin, where the faithful pray and push votive notes through the grille at her feet. I take the same route back to Bellavista and after crossing the Pio Nono Bridge, I turn right up the street towards San Cristóbal. I pass the University of Chile campus, where the previous night's encounter studies her law. There is a funicular railway, but I need some exercise and take the path which leads up the hill. Hardly anyone is about. The day is hot and I remove my cotton jacket and begin to sweat. Every so often I pause and look back. The city streets stretch out before me and the Mapocho flashes silver in the sun. In the centre of Santiago I can make out the rectangle of the Moneda and the twin plazas on either side. I carry on up the path, stopping occasionally to rest. After half an hour I reach the top and walk across the domain towards the marble statue of the Virgin, which stands pale and serene in the sunshine. It is the same one that General Alberto Bachelet saw from his office window on the day of the coup, when he was under arrest at the Ministry of Defence.

An old lady kneels at the little chapel, fingering her rosary and crossing herself as she prays. On a park bench two lovers are entwined and I sit down on another in the shade. In the long grass crickets make their shrill music and the summer air reverberates to their song. When I have got my breath back I go to the kiosk and buy a ticket for the railway. I pay and enter through the turnstile. Apart from a solitary tourist, the place is empty. I sit in a gondola and shut the steel door and with a mechanical whirr, the car begins to descend. After my slog up the hill, the journey is unexpectedly pleasant. The motion brings a light breeze and the city expands telescopically as we approach. It only takes a few minutes and the antiquated carriage slows and shudders to a halt as it reaches the bottom. I get out and make my way towards Bellavista. Most of the bars are closed and the place is a ghost town, compared to the previous night. I have a cold beer and an *empanada* at a café, then return to the hotel to escape the soaring temperature. The sky is a molten furnace and heat shimmers in waves above the road.

Although it is a national holiday, not everyone has taken time off. One such person is Dr Patricio Guijón, the member of the Moneda medical team who witnessed Allende's suicide and was later exiled to Dawson Island. He is now a general surgeon and works in a practice not far from the presidential palace. I have tracked him down through a contact. Our meeting is scheduled for 7:00pm, after he has finished his day's work.

I arrive at the clinic in good time and sit in the waiting-room. Apart from the practice nurse, I am the only person there. The doctor appears shortly before the appointed hour and greets me warmly. His handshake is firm yet gentle, as a surgeon's should be. He is white-haired, although it is thinning and swept back from his forehead and his eyes are tawny. Guijón sends the nurse home then shows me to his consulting room, which has the usual medical charts on the wall and a raised bed for examinations, its curtain drawn aside. Only this time it will be me doing the examining. He closes the door and sits down behind his desk on which a pile of manila envelopes are stacked, presumably his patients' medical records. The doctor looks as if he has had a long day and gives a tired smile.

"Thank you very much for your time."

"Not at all. Delighted," he says. Guijón means it, although he wishes he had been able to take the day off. But that would have meant cancelling appointments, which he would never do. He fiddles distractedly with his stethoscope as we make small talk and I adjust the levels of the tape recorder.

I ask him how he came to be part of the palace medical team and he tells me that he knew its head Oscar Soto. The opportunity of a position came up and he took it. He also admired Allende.

"Don't forget he was a qualified doctor. That is impressive in a president."

Guijón puts the stethoscope down and folds his hands in

his lap.

"So what happened when you got to the Moneda that morning?"

"Everyone from the medical team gathered in the dispensary on the ground floor. There were eight of us in all and Oscar was in charge. We didn't have anything to do because we were doctors and not involved in the defence of the palace. Allende appeared and told us that we were going to be busy. He meant that he expected fighting and therefore plenty of wounded. He was wearing a tin helmet and holding an AK47. It was very strange to see him dressed like that."

"Were you armed?"

"No. As I said we were doctors. Our job was not to fight, but to save lives."

"Did you think the military would assault the Moneda?"

"We didn't really know what would happen. It was all so incredible. Such a thing had never occurred before in Chile's history. Not like this. As the morning progressed the situation deteriorated and shooting started. Then the junta made the announcement that they would bomb the Moneda. Shortly afterwards the president appeared again. In spite of all this, he was in good spirits. While we were chatting the phone rang. A GAP picked it up and said Admiral Carvajal, one of the members of the junta, was on the line. Allende took the call. We couldn't hear what the admiral was saying, but later we learnt that he was offering the president the chance to flee in an aeroplane. We all heard his answer, which was 'stick it up your ass!'" and Guijón smiles. "Then he left."

The doctor relates what happened next, with the president calling a meeting in the Toesca Salon, asking the civilians to leave before the bombardment. The palace medical team decided unanimously that it was their duty to remain. Guijón and Soto took cover in an office next to the dispensary, while others sat out the bombing in a corridor on the first floor. Fortunately none of them were injured.

"We felt the bombs. There were seventeen explosions in all. Some apparently didn't go off. They weren't as loud as I expected, because they were incendiaries. Even so it was terrifying. You didn't know if the next one was going to land on your head. When it was all over we returned to the dispensary and helped tend those who had been wounded. Some of the detectives, I believe, were killed. Part of the building was on fire and teams were organised to douse the flames. We expected the soldiers to assault the palace at any moment.

"But Allende and his entourage continued fighting?"

"Yes...they did. It was going on upstairs, mostly from the presidential offices. Anyway we were not involved, we were on the ground floor. Not long afterwards we heard hysterical shouts: 'Perro's killed himself! Perro's killed himself!' I didn't know who called out, although I discovered later that it was Carlos Jorquera, the press secretary and one of Perro Olivares' best friends. For some reason he shot himself. I don't know why. He was an emotional man...They found him in the staff dining-room. We went to see what we could do. Arturo Jirón, the former health minister and Oscar Soto were already there. Blood was pouring from a head wound. There was nothing anyone could do. Jirón held him in his arms until he died..."

I keep eye contact with Guijón and nod slowly, not wishing to interrupt.

"Jirón went to find Allende and well...it was very sad. He came to see for himself and looked shocked. Jorquera burst into tears and the president comforted him. He said 'poor Negro' several times and embraced him tenderly like a child. We had a moment's silence and then Allende left. I think he realised then that the situation was hopeless."

"What did you do after that?"

"We went up to the passage on the first floor, as it seemed safer. Later, the president and some others joined us. Shortly before 2:00pm, after a discussion with his advisers, Allende declared that we were to surrender and ordered everyone downstairs. I took off my white coat and hung it from a window, to show that we were giving up. We walked past the president who stood at the top of the stairs and shook all of us by the hand, thanking us for our support. As we descended someone, a sniper or a soldier, shot at the window and narrowly missed Oscar.

"When I was at the entrance on 80 Morandé, I realised that I had nothing to show what I had been through. I have three sons and I thought they might want a memento. It was the first time that I had been in a war... and, fortunately, the only time. There were some gas masks in the upstairs passage and I thought I'd take one of those."

"You didn't think it was dangerous to go back there?"

The doctor shakes his head,

"Not at the time. I'm sure I wasn't thinking logically. You don't in that situation. You're traumatised and also your body is full of adrenaline...I went upstairs and looked about in the corridor, but I couldn't find any, the GAP must have taken them. Then I remembered I had seen some in the Salon Independencia. So I opened the door and saw Allende sitting on the sofa, with a gun between his legs. At that moment he pulled the trigger...bang, bang...two shots just like that, which blew off the top off his head."

Guijón pauses as if he still cannot believe that he saw his president commit suicide.

"What did you do?"

The doctor smiles wanly.

"Well, I went straight to Allende and took hold of his wrist and checked his pulse. Completely pointless. He died instantly of course. As I sat beside him some GAP appeared. Coco Paredes was with them and one or two others, including Enrique Huerta. Arturo Jirón and Oscar Soto also turned up. It was hard to believe the president was actually dead, that he had committed suicide. There was a moment's silence, then the others left. I stayed."

"Why?"

"You know, I don't know. But I did. Maybe I thought it was safer to be where I was. Anyway, a few minutes later some soldiers arrived. I thought they were going to shoot me. I was very frightened and told them I was a doctor. They didn't believe me until they saw my ID. Then one of them went to get General Palacios."

"What was he like?"

"He was very calm, unlike some of the soldiers. One of the lenses of his glasses was shattered and his uniform was covered in dust. He also had a bandage on his right hand. He really looked like he had been in a battle. I was then escorted outside into Morandé and that's when I saw my colleagues lying down in the road. I asked Palacios if they could join me as they were doctors and non-combatants like myself and he agreed. After about an hour the other doctors were released, but myself and Jirón were taken to the MOD for questioning."

"Why did they not release you as well?"

"Because I saw Allende commit suicide. They wanted to know if it was true. Some of the military thought he may have been killed by one of the GAP, unable to do the final act himself, or because he was badly wounded."

For years Guijón was the only person who publicly stated that Allende had died by his own hand and furthermore that he had witnessed it. No-one else would corroborate his version of events. For this reason the rumour persisted that the president had been killed in a firefight and Guijón's evidence was treated by many with contempt.

"Why do you think people believed that Allende was killed by soldiers and had not taken his own life?"

"Well…people believe what they want to believe. But the military did not allow independent observation of the autopsy and they buried the president quickly the next day. And for understandable reasons a lot of people did not trust the military's version."

"But you witnessed Allende's death and went on the record to say that he had committed suicide. Why didn't Arturo Jirón or Oscar Soto support you?"

"I guess you'd have to ask them..." and Guijón's voice tails off. Being regarded as the military's stooge is an unenviable burden to carry. "The truth will be known one day. Soon I hope."

We talk about his confinement in the MOD and at the Military Academy. The doctor then describes the journey south to Dawson Island, where he and Jirón saved the life of Julio Palestro, the social welfare chief who fell off the ship's gangplank into the icy waters of the harbour. After nine months Guijón was released and allowed to return to medical practice in Santiago.

"Did you think about emigrating?"

"No. Chile is my home. I was glad to be able to stay."

Guijón has given me an hour of his time and I do not want make his day any longer than it has been already. I thank him and he courteously shows to me to the door. As I am about to leave he makes one last comment.

"Some years ago the BBC interviewed me about Allende's death and I thought then that I would be believed. Perhaps this time I will be."

*

Armando Uribe is sitting at a table on his own. He is at Tavelli's, a well known café in Providencia, which is famous for its ice creams and coffees. It is also patronised by Santiago's chic women, who like to gossip over their double mochas and vanilla milkshakes. I assume the man reading La Epoca is Uribe, because he is the right age and looks dapper in a grey suit and dark blue tie. He was formerly Allende's ambassador to China and after the coup endured many years of exile, firstly in the United States and latterly in France, where he was professor of philosophy and law at the

Sorbonne. Apart from being a distinguished diplomat and scholar, Uribe is also a poet.

I approach the table and introduce myself. He looks up with languid brown eyes and greets me with an avuncular smile.

"Well spotted. My disguise cannot be very convincing," he says in a voice as rich and dark as treacle. Uribe is about sixty and bald, with a large Iberian nose and fleshy ears. The skin on his head and hands is mottled by age and the southern sun. His eyes are hooded and melancholy. I take a seat and see that he has already ordered himself a fresh orange juice.

"What would you like? The juice here is excellent. They squeeze it by hand," he adds, indicating his own drink.

As he says this a street kid sidles up to the table, making sure the waiters do not see him.

"*Da me moneda,*" he pleads, holding out a grubby hand.

"*No tengo moneda chico. Pero puede tomar mi bebida si quiere.*"

The boy grins and grabs Uribe's drink and downs it in one, wiping his mouth with the back of his hand, just like they do in cartoons. A waiter comes and the kid scarpers. I order an orange juice and Uribe does the same.

"I've drunk mine already. I'm very greedy," he says.

The waiter goes off to get our order and we talk. Uribe has only just returned to Chile from Paris and says he is still trying to acclimatise himself.

"Everything looks the same, but everything has changed."

"For better or for worse?"

"Both. Pinochet has gone, but there's no Allende either."

Uribe is a self-confessed acolyte of the former president and dismisses any criticism of the Popular Unity government as either 'Yankee propaganda', or 'reactionary nonsense'.

"Listen," he says, his smoky voice redolent of a late night talk show host. "Allende was trying to do what no-one, but no-one, had ever tried before. Socialism through democratic means. It had not been done in Russia, or China, or Cuba, or anywhere else. They all had revolutions yes, but one dictatorship was replaced by another. Allende was born a democrat and died a democrat..."

The waiter reappears carrying a tray with our orange juice, a plate of wafer biscuits and two glasses of sparkling water. He sets them down on the table and departs, as Uribe continues.

"Nixon and Kissinger were determined that Allende's socialist experiment would fail. And they did so not only because they despised his politics, conveniently labelling him a Marxist as if he were just another Castro, but also because they wanted to set an example to Latin America and the rest of the world, that this sort of government would not be tolerated. Ever. Both France and Italy were moving in that direction. And the coup stopped leftist politics in Europe dead. That is why you had anarchists like the Baader Meinhof gang and the Red Army Faction. They weren't simply anti-capitalist, they were against everything that capitalism stood for, including western-style democracy. What is the point of having democracy, they would argue, if a foreign power can simply remove a government it doesn't like and replace it with one that is more amenable? Both those terrorist groups are a direct result of American interference in sovereign states. From the Bay of Pigs to Vietnam to Chile, US foreign policy in the late twentieth century has been a disaster. I don't suppose this will ever change."

A fractured light falls through the jacarandas which shade the terrace and shadows dance in the breeze. Sparrows flit among the tables, searching for crumbs on leftover plates. A waiter moves about flicking a linen napkin at the birds, as though performing a curious dance. We take up our drinks and sip them. Uribe is not wrong about the orange juice, it tastes as if it has come straight from the tree.

"There is an argument that Allende held on for too long

and had he stepped down after the Tancazo, there would have been no coup…"

Uribe opens his eyes wide, as though what I have just said is not only wrong, but also preposterous.

"Why should he step down? He increased his majority in the mid-term elections in March. He had another three years of his mandate. Popular Unity's work had barely begun, even so we had already made great progress on a range of social issues: workers' rights, unemployment benefit, labour laws."

"But the writing was on the wall. Everyone knew the coup was inevitable…"

"Inevitable only because the military made it so and to do it they broke their constitutional oaths! When you become an officer in Chile, you swear allegiance to the flag and dedicate yourself to the Republic and its constitution. Every soldier who rebelled broke their oath of commission, including and especially Pinochet."

Whether you agree with his rhetoric or not, Uribe is to be admired both for his conviction and that he has stayed true to his principles down the years. The man is not for turning.

"Was Allende right not to call on the people's support during the coup?"

My companion nods and smiles professorially.

"That's a good question since it involves ethics, which is essential to the human condition. I would say 'unfortunately, yes'. Unfortunate, because by not doing so Allende lost power, but in doing so he also saved many lives. As he said himself in his last address to the nation: 'other men will survive this bitter and grey moment in which treason is trying to gain the upper hand. Just remember, sooner than you think avenues shall again be opened, down which free men shall march towards a better society.' And here we are in Tavelli's drinking fresh orange juice."

Uribe pauses and takes another sip of his drink. I check the cassette in the recorder and see there are only a couple of minutes left on the reel. It is a good time to stop and turn it over. I rewind the other side, then continue with my questions.

"Are you confident that this time democracy will last?"

Uribe reflects before answering. A sparrow alights on the back of a chair beside us and cocks its head, as though waiting for an answer.

"Well, there are two points to be addressed. Firstly, what do you mean by democracy? No country in the world is truly democratic. They are run by political elites, which represent vested interests and these people are very powerful. But they can do nothing without the support of those who finance them. All politicians essentially are in the pockets of big business, or lobbyists. They can all be bought. There are almost no exceptions. Those who don't take bribes and kickbacks get favours. In so-called democratic nations there are all sorts of constraints, which means 'democracy' is qualified. Will it last in Chile? Yes, I think so, because the world is a much safer place than it used to be. The Cold War is over. Much of the conflict in the world was a result of friction between the super powers. I include China of course. Now, with what is surely the end of the Soviet Union, this has changed. But for how long? Well, that is another question."

"You seem pessimistic."

Uribe gives a sad smile. The smile of someone who has known too many disappointments in life to pretend otherwise.

"An unfortunate condition of philosophy professors."

"Is Chile not as democratic a nation as it is possible to be?"

The former diplomat shakes his head forlornly, as the sparrow continues to listen to its tutorial.

"No. For reasons I just explained. This is what Allende wanted to change. He wanted to let the people decide their own future and not submit to political blocs, who only seek power for its own sake. That is true democracy. You remember the kid who was begging earlier? OK. There are plenty like him in Chile and throughout Latin America and indeed the world. Poverty is everywhere. But it doesn't have to be. It's just the way society is and nobody seems to want to change it. Or not enough. That kid should be at school, but he's not because his father, or his mother, has told him to beg. I understand why they do it, maybe the father's in prison, or can't work, or can't find a job, whatever reason. The point is they're poor and they need every *peso* they can get. So they send their children out onto the streets. The result is that boy isn't going to school, so he'll never learn anything. He probably can't even spell his name, let alone write it. What sort of job will he get if he's illiterate? Manual labour at best. Then what if he has an accident and can't work again? There are no benefits here. None worth speaking of. He'll have to beg or turn to crime. He may not even have a home. He might have run away, because his father's a drunk and beats him. Living on the streets is tough for an adult, imagine what it's like for a child? Think of the prostitution. It's not just girls, but boys too. He can make a day's money in five minutes if he wants. Just suck some old guy off..."

I look across the street. As we sit in Tavelli's drinking orange juice and the chic ladies in cashmere laugh and flick their glorious manes like thoroughbreds, a few metres away there are children in rags parking expensive cars.

"So you think nothing will really change?"

Uribe raises his hands as though weighing the question and all its possibilities.

"We shall see. President Aylwin has established a truth and reconciliation commission. That's a start. It's an important historical act; those who committed crimes during and after the coup must be named and indeed shamed. Whether they get punished or not, is another matter. I hope so. Justice should be seen to be done. But I don't suppose the real criminals like Pinochet will ever go to court. They're too powerful. It will just be small fry."

"Pinochet has made himself a senator for life, so he can't be prosecuted."

"I know. The irony is bitter. He destroyed the constitution, then protects himself with the state's legislature."

"What can you do?"

"What can anyone do? There is a word that has given me great comfort over the years, especially when I was in exile and at times despaired. I heard a voice, I'm not talking about a physical voice, but my own inner voice and the word I heard was *esperanza*..."

"Hope..."

"Yes. There is always hope...hope...hope..."

I listen to these words again as I replay the interview back at my hotel. Uribe's sombre voice echoes like an omen from the underworld. They will be the last words of my radio documentary. I get up and open the windows and feel the cool air upon my face. The sun has disappeared behind the mountains and the sky is rose-coloured. The great peaks of the Andes darken slowly in the twilight and a crescent moon climbs the heavenly steps of the constellations. My suitcase is packed and my passport and airline ticket are on the table. In less than twenty-four hours I will be back in London.

XII
TEA WITH PINOCHET

Autumn winds have begun to tear off the leaves of the plane trees, which line the streets and parks of London. The sky is filled with clouds and the evening sun is opaque; its nacreous light washed out, like a corpse that has been drained of blood. The wind whips the grit on the pavements and people wrap themselves up against the cold, as they make their way home after a day's work. They flow in a relentless tide towards the tube stations, disappearing into their cavernous maw. Night encroaches and the streets empty. Double-decker buses and black cabs swish up and down the damp roads, their lights casting amber trails along the tarmac.

As midnight approaches two thickset men in an unmarked car drive quickly up Harley Street, one of the capital's most prestigious addresses and where the wealthy take their cures. In a pocket is an international arrest warrant issued by the Spanish judge Baltasar Garzón. The men are detectives from Special Branch and are in a hurry because the person they have come to apprehend is recuperating from a back operation and is due to return home shortly. He is none other than General Augusto Pinochet, formerly President of Chile.

The general is an Anglophile and regularly visits London. He enjoys shopping in Jermyn Street in the West End, where he buys shirts and silk ties. He stays at the Dorchester in Park Lane, with its grand reception rooms and uninterrupted views of Hyde Park. In the evenings Pinochet often goes to the theatre. Since his English is limited, he prefers musicals and ballet. He also likes the art galleries and museums, particularly the National Army, which is next to the Royal Hospital in Chelsea. He admires the veterans as they totter down the road in their tricorne hats, scarlet coats decked with an array of medals. "*Realmente son héroes*," he says as they pass by.

Unfortunately for the general the law on crimes against humanity has changed, especially concerning victims of kidnap and torture. More than three thousand people died, or disappeared, during the coup and its aftermath and although the great majority were Chilean, by no means all of them were. Some in fact are Spanish. It is these victims who will prove to be Pinochet's nemesis. While the general has been taking the airs of his favourite foreign city, Garzón has been busy collating evidence in his offices in Madrid. Pinochet has a misplaced sense of security, because he is a former head of state and therefore believes he is immune from prosecution for any crimes that occurred during his time as president.

The reality is rather different. In 1984 the United Nations issued its Convention Against Torture and most states voluntarily signed up to it, including Britain and Spain. It was a noble principle, but no one ever imagined the decree would be acted upon. Garzón has been able to issue the arrest warrant through the legal principle of 'universal jurisdiction', which permits a national court to try a person suspected of a serious international crime, even if neither the suspect nor the victim are nationals of the country where the court is located and the crime took place outside that country.

The detectives drive through the main gates of the London Clinic, an anonymous red brick 1930s building. Behind them is a van with armed police. The men from Special Branch enter the hospital and flash their badges at the duty registrar, whose glasses almost fall from her face in shock. They tell her their business and she composes herself and answers that the person they want is on the eighth floor. The detectives take the lift and when they emerge into the corridor, they see a swarthy, olive-skinned man standing outside a door. Apart from his darker complexion he looks like them and carries himself just as they do, which is not surprising since he is also a policeman. The difference is that he is not British, but Chilean.

The man looks at the pair from Special Branch as they approach and can tell they are officials from somewhere and so he smiles.

"Is this General Pinochet's room?" one of them asks.

"Yes," answers the bodyguard softly.

"We have a warrant for his arrest," says the other detective, producing it from his pocket.

The Chilean looks at it. His English is good enough to understand the words and the official seal also seems genuine. He nods and knocks twice, then opens the door.

Inside the room an elderly grey-haired man with a moustache is asleep on a metal-framed bed, his body propped up by pillows. His face is vaguely familiar, like a faded film star whose years of glory are now no more than a celluloid dream. It is of course Pinochet. There is another older bodyguard, who is standing at the end of the bed.

He approaches the men from Special Branch, a look of curiosity rather than concern on his face. He is about fifty and plainly the senior of the pair.

"Yes please?" he says.

"Sir, we're from Special Branch," and the detective shows the man his badge. "We have a warrant for the arrest of General Augusto Pinochet, charged with crimes against humanity," and he hands him the document.

The silver-haired bodyguard looks at the warrant and reads it slowly. As soon as he holds it he knows the document is genuine and when he has finished reading it, he also knows that his principal is in trouble. He returns the warrant to the detective, who gives him a copy. There is a flurry of whispered Spanish from the bodyguards, as they decide what to do. They are sure that Pinochet has diplomatic protection and is therefore immune from arrest, but they realise that in the short term they must obey. The situation can be resolved by the embassy in the morning.

"OK," says the senior officer. "I will tell the general."

The bodyguard goes to rouse the patient, gently patting his shoulder. In his morphine-induced sleep, Pinochet hears voices and gradually regains consciousness. He is groggy and when he opens his eyes, he sees a blurred array of faces. He fixes on one and realises that it is his senior bodyguard. The man looks worried and the general gives him a reassuring smile.

Whatever sanguinity Pinochet feels upon waking, it is soon dispelled by his chief protection officer who translates as the detectives from Scotland Yard tell him that he is wanted on charges of crimes against humanity, including kidnap and torture. Heavily sedated and barely able to think, the general feels as helpless and hopeless as a baby. As he lies there trying to take in what is happening, the detectives disarm the bodyguard and disconnect the phone. They also remove the television and after exchanging embarrassed pleasantries, they leave.

With the warrant safely delivered, Pinochet is now a suspect and Scotland Yard moves swiftly. The armed police enter the London Clinic and take up positions outside his room. They also stand guard at the entrance. No one else enters or leaves the building that night.

*

News of Pinochet's arrest hits the wires and airwaves in the early hours. It is too late for the newspapers whose editions have already gone to press, but television and radio talk of little else. Although it is Saturday, by mid morning a small crowd of protesters ignore the October chill and gather outside the gates of the hospital, waving banners and placards while a middle-aged Latin American with a goatee shouts through a loud hailer. There are about twenty of them, but they more than make up for their lack of numbers with their enthusiasm. Most are Chilean and former exiles, some victims of the man who lies in a room eight floors above them.

The Chilean Ambassador Mario Artaza is quoted as saying that the general has diplomatic immunity and no one is sure what will happen next. The following week questions are asked in the House of Commons and it soon becomes clear the majority of the House believe that Pinochet should be extradited to Spain to answer the charges. Although there is a Labour government, there is cross-party support from both benches. The argument that other countries' affairs are their own is a tough one to swallow, when the suspect is accused of crimes against humanity. But there are some on the right who are adamant in their condemnation and consider the arrest of a former head of state as anathema, whatever the charge. It is partisan, narrow-minded and no way to conduct foreign affairs. None is more vocal than the former premier Margaret Thatcher, who is now a member of the House of Lords. Largely retired from politics, the grand dame rouses herself for one last battle. She has not forgotten the general's help during the Falklands War, when Britain's special forces used Chile's Patagonian territory as a base to monitor Argentina and even conducted a raid against its most southerly airfield at Rio Grande, destroying several planes. In return a grateful Thatcher gave Pinochet a squadron of Hawker Hunters and three Canberras, aircraft capable of flying at high altitude beyond the range of conventional defences and useful for monitoring the borders of a mountainous country.

The baroness also considers Pinochet a personal friend. He and his wife Lucia Hiriart have often visited her and Denis for tea at their house in Chester Square in Belgravia. They are intimate affairs, the only other person present is an official from the Chilean Embassy, who translates for them. For his part the general is charming and solicitous. He always remembers Thatcher's birthday and sends her chocolates and flowers. The admiration is mutual and even flirtatious, the baroness is well known for her love of handsome men, even when they are former dictators.

In her drawing-room at Chester Square, Thatcher sits down at her desk and writes a letter to the Times. The room is elegantly furnished and decorated with pale colours, the damasked curtains are yellow and the wooden shutters painted magnolia. In one corner stands a grand piano. She is a competent musician and plays well, far better than she will ever admit. The piano gives an understated elegance to the room, as though the place still echoed to the sounds of Mahler or Debussy, the dying notes lingering in the air like some celestial dust. A gilt Empire mirror hangs above the marble fireplace and the walls are hung with nineteenth century watercolours and prints: some political cartoons by Rowlandson and Gillray, others rural and city scenes. There are several framed photographs of the famous, as you would expect from someone who has spent many years in public life. In pride of place is a quartet of Thatcher and Denis and her great political love Ronald Reagan and his wife Nancy. The Big Gipper grins broadly and his spouse does the same, but she looks half-starved, her jewelled hands like claws. Next to them in a silver frame are President Gorbachev and his wife Raisa, their arms linked, smiling and content. Behind them stands a suited Pinochet wearing Chile's presidential sash, very much in the second division as far as world politics go, but favoured nonetheless.

The cold fury the baroness felt when she heard of the general's arrest has abated and she is composed as she pens her letter. When she has finished she corrects her draft and after making several emendations, hands it to her secretary to type and then send as an email. The Times publishes the former prime minister's missive the following day at the top of its letters' page.

Sir, I have better cause than most to remember that Chile, led at that time by General Pinochet, was a good friend to this country during the Falklands War. By his actions the war was shortened and many British lives were saved. There were indeed abuses of human rights in Chile and acts of violence on both sides of the political divide. However, the people of Chile, through successively elected democratic Governments, have determined how they should come to terms with their past. An essential part of that process has been the settlement of the status of General Pinochet and it is not for Spain, Britain or any other country to interfere in what is an internal matter for Chile. Delicate balances have had to be struck in Chile's transition to democracy, balances with which we interfere at our peril. General Pinochet must be allowed to return to his own country forthwith. Next week, Britain will welcome the democratically elected leader of a country which illegally invaded British territory, causing the loss of more than 250 British lives. It would be disgraceful to preach reconciliation with one, while maintaining under arrest someone who, during that same conflict, did so much to save so many British lives. I remain convinced that the national interests of both Chile and Britain would be best served by releasing him, which the Home Secretary has it in his power to do.

The baroness has a point. The visitor to Britain that she is referring to is none other than Carlos Menem, himself a former political prisoner and now Argentina's president. It is an irony not lost on anyone in South America that his country only returned to democracy, after it was defeated in the Falklands. Arrayed against her are Britain's Prime Minister Tony Blair and his front bench, which includes Jack Straw who once visited Chile as an idealistic youth in the 1960s. As Home Secretary the decision to extradite or release Pinochet, ultimately lies with him.

The phone lines between Santiago and London burn hotly, while the general is moved from the London Clinic and taken to Grovelands Priory hospital, situated in the endless suburbs of north London. He is followed by the protesters who pursue him like a bad dream and keep up their noisy demonstrations outside the gates. Soon this proves too much for the hospital, which tells its patient that he is well enough to leave. And that is the heart of the matter. The likelihood of Pinochet being extradited to Spain and answer Garzón's charges, hinges on his state of health.

The 'pro' and 'anti' battle lines have been drawn, but both sides have to wait until the legal process has been exhausted and that, as everyone knows, will take a long time. The most urgent matter for the general's entourage is where their principal should stay. The first option of a house in Belgravia not far from the Thatchers is rejected by the police as posing too great a security risk, as well as making it hard to manage the protesters. Another idea of an isolated refuge in the green, hog-backed hills of the West Country, is also dismissed as being too far away for court appearances. The issue is resolved when Pinochet's supporters select a house in Wentworth, an exclusive private estate in Surrey and just over an hour's journey from central London.

The general arrives at his new home in early December. The place is called 'Everglades' and is situated in a cul de sac next to the famous golf course of Sunningdale. It is secluded and partly obscured by a thick row of leylandii, which fill the wintry air with their murderous scent. But it is also close to the A30 and the protesters take up their pitch on the opposite verge and make their presence felt every weekend. Amid the occasional hum of traffic and thwack of golf balls, Pinochet can hear the sound of drums, horns and constant chanting.

"Chi-chi-chi, le-le-le! Asesino Pinochet!"

Inside the modest four-bedroomed house, the general and his wife are guarded by armed police night and day. Initially he is not permitted outdoors, but this is relaxed after a few weeks and he is able to take the air on a small patio behind the house. Wrapped up against the winter chill and leaning heavily on a walking stick, Pinochet looks out onto the garden with its neat lawns and rose bushes, emperor of all he surveys.

The following year on 24th March, the Law Lords decide the general can only be prosecuted for crimes committed after 1988, the date when Britain implemented legislation for the United Nations Convention Against Torture in its Criminal Justice Act. Any charges prior to this date are dismissed by the judges, although some still remain. If the decision is a victory for Pinochet and his supporters, it is a hollow one, since it means he still cannot leave Britain. It also makes no difference to Baltasar Garzón, who promptly adds another thirty charges to the original indictment.

As far as Thatcher is concerned, it is time she visited her old friend as he languishes in the stockbroker fastness of Wentworth. They will take tea together and talk about the old days. The next morning she has her hair done. After a light lunch she changes and puts on an emerald green dress, adorned with her favourite diamante broach, given to her by Denis as a wedding anniversary present. With an eye on history, the baroness also agrees the press can record the meeting. Then just before 3:00pm she leaves her house in Chester Square and makes the journey to Everglades, an ITN crew trailing her armoured Jaguar.

When Thatcher arrives at the Surrey estate, the Pinochets are standing at the front door waiting to greet her. The general is wearing a dark blue suit, a striped shirt and a spotted silk tie, with its ubiquitous pearl pin. It is a look he has cultivated ever since 1988's plebiscite, when he tried unsuccessfully to shed his military image and make himself look more democratic. His silver hair is slicked back and he looks like an ageing gigolo, as he grins from ear to ear and grips his wooden walking stick. Lucia appears dowdy in comparison, wearing a brown silk dress and clumpy shoes.

Thatcher emerges from the limousine into the pale spring sunshine, clutching her handbag and begins to hold court.

The camera is rolling and the pictures of the meeting are beamed live across the country. The Iron Lady's rhetoric rises to the occasion and, if you listen carefully, you can hear the sound of three thousand people turning slowly in their graves.

"General, I am here to thank you on behalf of the British nation for all the help your country gave us during the Falklands. The information you gave us ... communications ... and also the refuge you gave to any of our armed forces who were able, if they were shipwrecked, to make their way to Chile.

"I'm very much aware that it is you who brought democracy to Chile, you set up a constitution suitable for democracy. You put it into effect, elections were held and then, in accordance with the result, you stepped down."

Pinochet listens to all this and nods thoughtfully, as though he is merely hearing something which he already knows to be true, but is happy to be reminded. In return the general makes self-deprecating noises.

After issuing her brief statement, the baroness is shown indoors by Pinochet, who moves awkwardly using his stick. They enter the living-room which is rectangular, with white walls and a cream coloured carpet. The company take their places on the chairs and sofas, which are also white and placed opposite each other. A translator sits down next to the general. The room is spartan and cold and almost monastic in its asceticism. On the mantelpiece above the fireplace is a crucifix. In spite of the charmless atmosphere and the click and whirr of cameras, the group attempts small talk. The conversation continues in the same brittle vein for the next few minutes, until Thatcher's advisers tell the press that it is time to leave. The journalists put away their gear and depart. The baroness waits until they have gone and when she has been assured they are alone, she lets rip.

"Augusto, I am so sorry that we have to meet like this. It is an absolute disgrace that my government can treat a friend and former ally in this way. I am almost ashamed to call myself British."

The translator has to talk rapidly in the general's ear as Thatcher rattles on, barely able to contain her righteous indignation.

"I am trying to ensure that you are able to leave as soon as possible and I hope this will be the case. You shouldn't have to stay in this godforsaken place a moment longer."

The baroness is not boasting. She has put her considerable political skills to good use and has been lobbying Tony Blair. She has had several phone conversations with the Prime Minister, both at Downing Street and the country residence of Chequers. Thatcher will not give up and Blair is wise enough to listen to her counsel. In spite of being a Labour premier, he is very much on the right of the party. It is Blair who coined the term 'New Labour', so as to distance his party from the shibboleths of its socialist past. Pinochet's detention is a headache he could do without, particularly with the usual gamut of domestic and foreign problems, with which a prime minister must always deal. The peace process in Northern Ireland is precarious. British troops are stationed not only in the province, but also in Kosovo. Furthermore Sierra Leone is in crisis and it looks as though he will have to commit forces there as well, in order to avoid a repeat of the Rwandan genocide. Privately Blair agrees with the former prime minister that Pinochet should be on the next plane home, although he does not actually say this. Instead he makes reassuring noises and often repeats the phrase "I know". Nevertheless, he offers the baroness an olive branch and tells her that he is putting pressure on the Home Secretary to get the issue resolved quickly, but he is hampered by the legal process etc etc.

Having ventilated her anger, Thatcher calms down and the tea becomes a convivial affair. A butler fusses back and forth, filling porcelain cups with Earl Grey and offering cucumber and Marmite sandwiches and chocolate biscuits.

The Pinochets also drink tea, although being Chilean they would prefer coffee or *mate*. They reminisce about the past and the general insists that when he is released (hands clasped in prayer, eye roll heavenward), the Thatchers must come and stay with them in Santiago. The baroness has never been to Chile and has always wanted to visit. She agrees and says they will come in the New Year, so long as Denis' health is up to it. The former prime minister's husband is frail, otherwise he would have joined her. Pinochet has promised to take him to Santiago's Club de Golf in Las Condes. It has been a long-standing joke between them that whoever loses at golf, buys the lunch.

The afternoon grows dark and it is early evening, when Thatcher finally pats the general's knee and announces it is time for her to leave. The company all rise and Pinochet is helped to his feet by the butler and an aide.

"Augusto it has been a pleasure to be with you, and you too Lucia. I hope that when we next meet, the circumstances will be altogether different."

The baroness offers her hand to Pinochet, who clasps it reverentially and then raises it to his lips to kiss. He is genuinely touched by her visit and for the first time since his arrest, he is close to tears. His guest senses this and smiles kindly.

"Please don't worry Augusto. I am sure you'll soon be back in Chile and all this unpleasantness can be forgotten. In fact I am certain of it," she adds in a familiar voice, which brooks no dissent.

The Pinochets accompany her to the door and watch as their old friend gets into her limousine. Then, with a final wave and a crunch of tyres on gravel, the baroness departs.

*

Thatcher's political instincts serve her well and she is right in having assured Pinochet that he will not be extradited. As the year draws on and spring turns to summer and then to autumn and winter, the general's health begins to decline. The following January a medical team, led by two gerontologists and a neurologist assess Pinochet's condition and conclude that he has deteriorated since his house arrest. How much is a moot point, but it is enough for the Home Secretary to declare a few days later that he is 'minded' the general will not face charges on the grounds of ill health. His release is only a matter of time.

Shortly after 8:00am on 2nd March 2000, Jack Straw appears on the steps of the Home Office. He looks tired, his nose and cheeks pink in the chill, as he stands there blinking behind his lawyerly glasses. The earnest student of politics and admirer of Allende, now holds one of the highest offices in the land. He, more than anyone, knows the compromises a politician must make once they attain government. Even so, it is cold comfort. The Home Secretary observes the phalanx of media before him and their battery of equipment, the lenses pointed like daggers at his heart. He clears his throat and makes his dry as dust statement; the words taste like ashes in his mouth.

"I have today decided that I will not order the extradition of Senator Pinochet to Spain. I made this decision under section 12 of the Extradition Act 1989. I have referred the case to the Director of Public Prosecutions for consideration of a domestic prosecution, in accordance with Article 7 of the United Nations Convention against Torture and Other, Cruel, Inhuman or Degrading Treatment or Punishment..."

When Straw finishes he refuses to take any questions and goes back inside. He returns to his office and slumps down exhausted at his desk. He asks to be left alone. Although the Home Secretary is an agnostic, the words of St Mark echo in his heart like a chill wind blowing through ruined choirs: 'for what does it profit a man if he gains the whole world, yet loses his soul?'

It is a result that everyone expected, including the former

exiles who have protested so vociferously and for so long. Their victory at least is a moral one. Pinochet's arrest and incarceration have been enough. A spotlight has been shone on his regime and like bacilli under a microscope, there has been nowhere to hide. Life will never be the same for Chile's erstwhile dictator.

The news is received rather differently in Wentworth. At Everglades the atmosphere is euphoric as the Pinochets celebrate with their entourage and the national anthem is sung. Someone puts a CD of Latin American folk music on the Hi-Fi and the general even performs a wobbly jig with his wife. He looks ten years younger. The months of anguish and frustration sloughing off his body like a serpent's skin.

Pinochet and his retinue are packed and ready to depart. At 9:45am his convoy leave Wentworth with a police escort and make their way northwards. An ITN camera crew try to follow, but they are intercepted. The motorcade heads for the A1 and the RAF base at Waddington in Lincolnshire. A Chilean Air Force Boeing 707 has been waiting for them since dawn. Shortly before 1:00pm the general's convoy eases through the gates and drives out across the runway. A ramp is lowered and Pinochet is the first to go aboard, followed by his wife and the rest of the group. As he settles into the comfortable leather seats, he is offered a glass of champagne. Perhaps it is the VIP treatment or the joy of the moment, but whatever it is the general's sense of pride and entitlement have been restored. He cajoles his staff to get a move on, as the ground crew stow the luggage and demands to be airborne as soon as possible. Pinochet does not want to spend a moment longer on British soil. Lucia smiles uxoriously and tells him not to worry.

Just as the plane is about to depart, there is a delay and the aircraft door slides open. A car races across the tarmac and a man gets out, bearing a small parcel. 'What now?' the general thinks. Surely there has not been a last minute appeal? There is no need to worry. The man is not delivering another warrant, but a gift from Lady Thatcher. It is a solid silver replica of a salver cast in 1588 to commemorate Sir Francis Drake's defeat of the Spanish Armada. It is also inscribed with a dedication and the baroness's signature.

There are no more delays. The aircraft door is shut and the plane taxis down the runway and takes off and disappears into the rain-filled skies above England. After refuelling at the British military base on Ascension Island, the aircraft continues its journey. Shortly before the plane is due to enter Argentine airspace, permission to overfly is refused by air traffic controllers. Argentina apparently having not forgotten Pinochet's covert aid to Britain during the Falklands War. The aircraft is forced to divert over Brazil, Paraguay and Bolivia, adding another hour to the journey. At 9:27am the following day, Boeing 707 finally touches down at Pudahuel airport in Santiago. It is late summer and the sun shines brightly above the Andes, whose peaks are denuded of snow. Around two thousand people have gathered to greet the former dictator. Most are from the military who have come with their families, the others are right-wingers and assorted hangers-on. There is no one from the Chilean government. Pinochet leaves the aircraft in a wheelchair, but he is not seated for long. Amid shouts and cheering the general rises to his feet and greets the faithful like a conquering hero.

EPILOGUE

Conditions for the prisoners at Dawson Island were harsh. A former naval camp, it was used only during the summer months and was not designed for the rigours of the Antarctic winter.

The men were forced to do hard labour, building roads and digging ditches. They had to cut wood for fuel and draw their own water from a well and there was no electricity in the huts. Their letters were censored, both in what they wrote and in what they received and they were only allowed to correspond with their immediate family. In their free time they played chess with a home made set, sang folk songs, or carved pieces of wood and stone. Anything to keep themselves busy. Some wrote diaries, but always hid the notebooks from the soldiers who periodically searched their quarters. Their discovery would have entailed solitary confinement and possibly worse.

Nevertheless, the prominenti were not forgotten. There was an international outcry about their detention and eventually the junta allowed a visit by the Red Cross on 29th September. That afternoon a football was produced and the prisoners were ordered to play a match for the visiting officials. They were only too happy to oblige and played for more than three hours. When the Red Cross left, the ball was taken away and the men were put back to work.

One person in particular was unable to endure the privations of Dawson Island. He was José Tohá, the former defence minister. His spirit was crushed by the coup. He constantly blamed himself for the military uprising, because as a minister he had been responsible for the appointment of some of the high ranking officers who subsequently rebelled.

Tohá was convinced that this misplaced trust had directly resulted in the coup and the death of his friend Allende.

At Dawson Island the former minister's guilt made him silent and withdrawn. It was not long before he became too sick to do the hard labour of the other prisoners. He lost weight and languished pathetically in his bunk. His companions complained to the authorities that he needed proper medical care and eventually he was taken to the military hospital in Punta Arenas and then to its equivalent in Santiago. In spite of Tohá's frail condition, he was kept in custody and repeatedly interrogated and brutalised by the military. He lost his eyesight and as a near skeleton, he was taken to the Military Academy. On 15th March 1974 he was found dead, hanging from a strap tied to the bars of his window. Although at this stage Tohá had been too weak to stand, the military coroner recorded a verdict of suicide. The Catholic Church denounced the verdict and in Santiago, the Cardinal Archbishop Raul Silva held a requiem Mass for the former minister. Something the Church would not have done for a suicide.

The prisoners at Dawson Island considered themselves lucky that José Tohá was the only victim of their confinement. After a year they were dispersed and the majority were, as General Prieto had predicted, sent into exile by the junta. It was only then the prominenti realised how fortunate they were, after hearing about the fate of the other Moneda prisoners, including the GAP.

*

The last that was seen of Allende's entourage and his bodyguard, was at the barracks of the Tacna Regiment. Eduardo 'Coco' Paredes, Jorge Klein and Enrique Huerta among others, all disappeared. They were taken from the barracks to the military base at Peldehue, on the outskirts of Santiago. Here they were made to kneel in front of a hastily dug pit and dispatched with a bullet to the back of the head. Grenades were then tossed in after them and their corpses covered with earth.

The president's physician and personal friend Enrique Paris also disappeared, although he shared an even worse fate than his companions. After Paris was taken away that night at the barracks, he was interrogated and brutally tortured. A few days later a victim so badly burned that he was unrecognisable, was brought to the José Aguirre Hospital in Santiago. The man's injuries were horrific, the flesh was scorched and hanging off his bones. It looked as if he had been burned in a car crash. There was little the medical staff could do, the victim was dying.

The terrible injuries Paris received had been administered with a blowtorch. He died later that day and the military came to take away his body. Such was the climate of fear at the time that not one member of the medical staff sought to contact Paris' family, saying either that they had seen him or that he was dead, even though some had known the psychiatrist when he had previously worked as a consultant at the hospital. The family remained unaware of his fate until 1991. In that year excavations began on Section 29 of the General Cemetery in Santiago, where many of the victims of the coup were believed to have been buried. After weeks of forensic work 126 victims of the Pinochet regime were recovered and 98 of them identified. Among the dead was Enrique Paris. His bones were removed and having lain for eighteen years in an unmarked grave, Allende's close friend and confidante was finally given a proper burial.

*

After imprisonment on Dawson Island Dr Edgardo Enríquez was released, although he and his wife Raquel remained under house arrest in Santiago. In 1975 they were exiled and went to Britain, where they lived in Oxford.

Orlando Letelier and his family also joined them for a time in the old university city, before emigrating to the United States. In 1978 Edgardo and Raquel moved to Mexico, where they were happy to be in South America again. They remained there even after democracy was restored in Chile, unwilling to trust the country's fragile political climate. But their fears were unfounded and they returned to Santiago in 1991. Edgardo Enríquez died in 1996.

*

In July 1974 the Central Committee of MIR decided that Miguel Enríquez should leave the country and raise funds abroad. Allende's nephew Andres Pascal, who had been at the Indumet shootout with Miguel, would take over his duties. MIR's leader was reluctant to leave Chile and asked to be given until the end of the year to think about it. But he never had to make the decision. On 5th October the army surrounded his house in the working class San Miguel district of Santiago, after a tip off from an informant. In the subsequent firefight Miguel was killed and his girlfriend Carmen Castillo was wounded by a bullet in her right arm.

Castillo was taken to the Military Hospital and then to the infamous DINA* detention centre at 1470 Calle Borgoño where, despite being pregnant, she was raped and tortured. Later she was released and exiled. As a result of her ill treatment Castillo gave birth prematurely to a son, but the baby died a month later.

On Miguel's death his brother Edgardo assumed the leadership of MIR. He agreed to leave for Europe to raise funds and later returned to South America, intending to enter Chile. In April 1976 he was picked up by agents in Uruguay and taken back to Chile as part of Operation Condor, an

---

**Dirección de Inteligencia Nacional - Chilean secret police in the Pinochet era, reformed as CNI in 1977.*

agreement between the Pinochet regime and neighbouring nations to pursue and assassinate leftists in Latin America and beyond. Delivered into the hands of DINA, Edgardo was tortured and executed. His body has never been found.

*

At Dawson Island Orlando Letelier kept his fellow prisoners' spirits up by singing folk songs on a guitar, which he had obtained after bartering with one of the guards. He was so popular that the military liked to listen as well and often put in requests. Letelier's musical abilities did more for the prisoners' welfare than any Red Cross parcel or visit.

Despite the rapport with his gaolers, the defence minister was shocked by the transformation of the Chilean military after the coup. It was like Jekyll and Hyde. Overnight they had turned Latin America's most respected military force, into a machine of brutal state repression.

Shortly after their arrival at Dawson Island, the prominenti were visited by a military delegation. As the group entered the camp, Letelier recognised one of the officers as a former classmate from the Military School. They had been good friends and had shared a bunk bed. His erstwhile companion had done well and was now a full colonel. Letelier inveigled his way into the group and greeted his old army friend, hoping the senior officer would put in a good word for them. There was a brief exchange, before the defence minister returned to his companions looking pale and shaken.

"What is it Orlando? What did he say?" they asked.

"He told me that if he'd had his way, he would have had us all shot. When I asked him why, he said: 'because if you ever get out of this place, your children will come after me'. And to think he used to be my friend."

After a year at Dawson Island and another camp, Letelier was exiled with his family and eventually settled in the United States. As a former ambassador in Washington he had good contacts and was active in his opposition to the Pinochet regime. He lobbied both the US Congress and European governments, as well as writing numerous articles and speaking publicly. His endeavours were notably successful and prevented several international loans being granted to the military government. On 10th September 1976 the junta deprived Letelier of his citizenship, but the move only made Allende's defence minister even more vocal in his condemnation.

That the same day Letelier addressed a pop concert in New York's Madison Square Gardens, which had been organised by Chile's pro-democracy supporters.

"Today Pinochet has signed a decree in which it is said that I am deprived of my nationality. This is an important day for me. A dramatic day in my life in which the action of the fascist generals against me, makes me more Chilean than ever…I was born a Chilean, I am a Chilean and I will die a Chilean. They were born traitors, they live as traitors and they will be remembered for ever as fascist traitors!"

Letelier's words were more prophetic than he could ever have imagined. On 21st September he was killed by a car bomb in Washington's Sheridan Circle, just 200 yards from the Chilean embassy. The force of the explosion blew off the car floor and with it Letelier's legs. His American assistant Ronni Moffitt who had been sitting in the front passenger seat, staggered from the car and collapsed on the grass, where a passing nurse administered first aid. Her husband Michael, who had been in the back and was virtually unscathed, tried to pull Letelier clear from the wreckage, but was unable as his friend was trapped beneath the steering column.

Michael then ran around hysterically yelling: "DINA did it! DINA did it! Fascist assassins!" The emergency services arrived and Letelier and Ronni were taken to the George Washington Hospital, where he was pronounced dead. Meanwhile surgeons worked desperately to save his assistant. But their efforts were in vain. Ronni's carotid artery had been punctured by a piece of shrapnel. She drowned as blood rushed through her severed windpipe into her lungs.

Michael Moffitt was correct about DINA's involvement in Letelier's assassination. An FBI investigation found the Chilean secret service was responsible and had used Cuban exiles and a DINA agent Michael Townley, who had dual citizenship, to carry out the atrocity. Townley and his team had acted under direct orders from DINA's head General Manuel Contreras and his aide Colonel Pedro Espinoza. In a plea bargain Townley admitted guilt as an accessory to the killings. He had built and placed the bomb, but had not activated it. He was the prosecution's chief witness in the subsequent trial and served only a token prison sentence, before disappearing into the US witness protection programme.

In 1990 Contreras and Espinoza were tried in Chile and found guilty of murder and served brief prison terms in military, rather than in civilian custody. At his trial Contreras went on the record to say: "my orders only ever came from Pinochet." After his release Contreras was rearrested in 2002 and convicted of further crimes against humanity and given a life sentence in 2005.

*

Osvaldo Puccio and his son remained on Dawson Island for eight months. They were transferred to two more prison camps and held for a further four months. The Presidential Secretary was then imprisoned in Santiago, while his son went into exile in Romania. After a year he was reunited with his family in the former German Democratic Republic. In 1984 the Puccios were permitted to return to Chile, where Osvaldo senior died in 1989. His son joined the diplomatic service and became Chile's ambassador to Austria. The author interviewed him at the Chilean embassy in Vienna in 1995.

In Ambassador Puccio's office there was a large black and white photograph of his father as Presidential Secretary, behind him on the wall hung a portrait of Allende. The interview was cordial and informative, with the ambassador answering every question to the best that knowledge and memory would allow. Nothing was off limits, including his own period of detention and interrogation. He described his torture "as unsophisticated as it was brutal."

Surprisingly, the grey-haired ambassador held no animosity for the men who abused him. "They did what they did," he said. "That is their problem, not mine." We discussed other Moneda prisoners who had died, including Enrique Paris. Why had the military treated some, such as Allende's friend and personal physician, so terribly? For the only time in the interview, Puccio was lost for words. "I really don't know," he said, finally. "There was a lot of hate in those days. But what they did to poor Paris was unconscionable."

Would the ambassador have done the same again as he did that day in the Moneda, when he defended the palace with a machine gun? "Yes," he said. "I would. But I must be frank with you. My marksmanship was very ineffectual."

*

Dr Oscar Soto was sent into exile and settled in Madrid, where he continued to practice medicine before retiring. In 1996 he published an account of his time at the Moneda and the coup. In his memoir 'El Ultimo Día De Salvador Allende', he confirmed Dr Patricio Guijón's version of Allende's death by suicide as being correct.

*

Luis Gonzalez or 'Eladio', the GAP who faked appendicitis and fled from the Central Post Hospital, was one of the few members of Allende's bodyguard to survive. He made his way to the Mexican embassy and later turned up in Havana.

Another GAP who survived was Pablo Manuel Zepeda or 'Ignacio', who was among the group which saw Allende's body in the Salon Independencia. Zepeda was taken to the Tacna Regiment barracks along with the Moneda prisoners, but was mistakenly separated and placed in a different group. This action saved his life, as he did not join those who were taken to Peldehue and executed. Even so Zepeda's ordeal was far from over. Despite severe torture, he continued to deny ever being involved in paramilitary activity. He was taken to the National Stadium and subjected to further torment. This time his fingernails were removed with pliers, but he maintained his story: he was not a paramilitary, just a civilian worker who had been wrongly arrested. Unable to break Zepeda, the military released him in December. He went into exile, first to Spain and then to Mexico. On his eventual return to Chile, Zepeda gave testimony to the Rettig Commission on national reconciliation.

The majority of the GAP did not survive. 'Jano,' whose real name was Daniel Gutiérrez, was among those slain at Peldehue. Most of Allende's bodyguard were murdered either on 11th September, or shortly afterwards.

*

On 18th September 1973 Deputy Inspector Juan Seoane was formally dismissed from the Investigations Service and denied a pension. Later he was exiled and went to live in Cuba, before finally returning to Chile. Quintin Romero was also dismissed and became a chemist, owning a pharmacy in Maipú on the outskirts of Santiago. Carlos Espinoza's decision to hand in his badge was academic, since he too was sacked.

After the restoration of democracy in 1989, all the Moneda detectives were given an honourable discharge and their pensions were restored.

*

René Largo Farías was arrested along with others closely associated with the Popular Unity government and exiled. He lived in Mexico with his wife Maria Cristina and their daughter. His wife then died unexpectedly a few months later. Largo Farías was allowed to return with his daughter to Chile in 1985, but was unable to work as a journalist and made a living as a taxi driver. One summer night in 1992 he was lured to a bar in downtown Santiago, either by right-wing paramilitaries or plainclothes police, on the pretext of listening to a folk group. He was well known as a music critic and in the 1960s had had his own radio show. The following day the former OIR chief was discovered bleeding and unconscious in a side street. He had been severely beaten and died three days later in hospital.

*

Ariel Ulloa, the Socialist paramilitary who fought his way out of the Indumet complex, successfully went to ground. He slipped out of the country, seeking sanctuary first in Cuba and then Algeria. He returned to Chile in 1989 and was the Socialist mayor of Concepción for several years.

*

Miria Contreras or 'La Payita' found sanctuary in the Swedish embassy and later lived in exile in Cuba. Despite the best efforts of Domingo Blanco or 'Bruno', her eighteen-year-old son Enrique was killed alongside the GAP and their leader in the grounds of the Intendancy. A bronze memorial plaque outside records their names. Her other son Max survived. La Payita died in Santiago in 2002.

Dr Alvaro Reyes, who treated the president's secretary, was betrayed by an informant and taken to the National Stadium and tortured. He was then moved from the stadium and put in jail, where his family could visit. After concerted legal pressure Reyes was released and allowed to return to medicine.

Maria Lizama hid La Payita for several days in her house at great personal risk, before helping her escape. The military never discovered what the nurse had done, although she always lived in fear of a knock on the door in the middle of the night.

*

General Alberto Bachelet suffered grievously for his loyalty to Allende. The senior air force officer was imprisoned after the coup and tortured. He was released and then rearrested again. As a result of persistent ill-treatment, Bachelet died of a heart attack while still in custody. His wife and their only child Michelle went into exile and later his daughter became a doctor. She then went into politics and joined the Socialist Party. Michelle Bachelet was president of Chile from 2006-2011 and was re-elected for another term in December 2013.

*

General Javier Palacios was the only senior rebel officer whose actions during the coup can be considered honourable, or at least not cowardly or cruel. He had no knowledge of the fate of the Moneda prisoners and said that it was General Brady's decision to have them all killed.

Palacios deplored the brutality of the coup's aftermath, considering it anathema to the military code. He later went on the record to say that Allende's conduct during that day had been "valiant" and that the president was "a fighting cock". He repeatedly clashed with Pinochet and resigned from the army in 1977, taking up a lucrative position with CORFO, a government agency. Palacios died in 2006.

*

Joan Garcés was forced to leave Chile and went to France, where he worked for UNESCO and became a professor of law. He also wrote a number of books and articles about Allende and the Popular Unity government, namely 'Democracy and Counter-Revolution' (1975) and 'Allende and the Chilean Experience' (1976). In 1996 Garcés filed a criminal complaint in Madrid against Pinochet and the junta for 'crimes against humanity'. It was this complaint which formed the basis of Judge Baltasar Garzón's own indictment of Chile's former president. Garcés also travelled to the US several times after Pinochet was arrested in 1998, requesting President Bill Clinton declassify State Department documents relating to Chile during the Pinochet era. In 1999 President Clinton acceded to the request and a declassification of documents began.

*

Hortensia Allende sought exile in Cuba and then lived in Mexico. The president's widow often spoke out against the regime that had overthrown her husband. Hortensia campaigned around the world and even stood as a candidate for the rector of Glasgow University in 1977, to highlight the injustices of the Pinochet regime. In 1983 she lectured in the US, despite the Reagan administration initially denying her a visa. She returned to Santiago in 1988 as the Concertación began its successful 'No' campaign against Pinochet's rule. Hortensia died peacefully in 2009. Thousands attended her funeral, including the then president Michelle Bachelet and former presidents Ricardo Lagos and Eduardo Frei.

Hortensia's daughters Carmen Paz and Isabel, now a Socialist deputy, survive her.

Beatriz or 'Tati' Allende went into exile in Cuba with her diplomat husband Luis Fernández de Oña, where she gave birth prematurely to a son. Emotional by nature, her life was made worse by Fernández de Oña admitting that not only was he a member of the Cuban secret service, but that Fidel Castro had ordered him to marry Tati, so that he could spy on her father. He also confessed to having another family in Cuba and subsequently left her and returned to them. Alone and isolated, Beatriz Allende shot herself in 1977.

The president's sister Laura was diagnosed as having inoperable bone cancer in 1975. She was allowed to remain in Santiago because of her condition, although at one point the junta denied her medical treatment in order to encourage her son, Andres Pascal, to give himself up. But there was a national outcry and the military relented. After her niece's suicide, she left Chile to help care for Tati's two children.

In 1981 and close to death Laura asked for permission to return to her country, but this was refused. On a bright May morning she jumped to her death from a balcony at the Havana Riviera Hotel.

*

After his return to Chile General Pinochet retired to a house by the sea, not far from Neruda's own residence at Isla Negra. Unlike the poet he could find no peace, as lawyers argued back and forth about his fitness to stand trial. In the end it all came to nothing, as the general died in December 2006. Yet there was justice of a sort. Following his arrest and detention in Britain, Pinochet's reputation was in tatters.

Senior army officers condemned his refusal to admit any responsibility for crimes that occurred during his regime, while others such as General Contreras were vilified and imprisoned. The generalissimo's last fig leaf of decency was removed following a US investigation into international money laundering after the attacks of 9/11. The investigation revealed the Pinochet family had $28 million salted away, in over 100 separate accounts in nine American banks. Many of them under the name of 'Daniel Lopez'. At the time Allende's daughter Isabel commented: "Pinochet is like Al Capone. We always knew he was a murderer, now we know he's a thief."

ACKNOWLEDGEMENTS

I first visited Chile as an eighteen year old in 1984 and was there for six months. I did so again after I graduated from university in 1987 and this time stayed for more than a year. I witnessed the Pinochet regime at first hand, albeit as a foreigner who had little knowledge of the country, its people or its language. Fortunately this has improved over the years.

There are many people who have made this book possible and whom I wish to thank. It would, however, be irksome to the reader if I were to list them and several, although by no means all, feature in the narrative already. The reason I visited Chile in the first place was because of José Manuel Eguiguren, a man of remarkable vision and the founding headmaster of three schools in Santiago. His foresight and wisdom were essential touchstones in my early encounters with his country and his compatriots. Apart from José Manuel and his family, I would like to thank Minister Carlos Figueroa and especially his daughter Maria Luisa, whose introductions and insights have helped in so many ways. I would also like to thank the late Dr Henry Hudson FRACS and his family, who once took me under their wing and gave encouragement to a callow author. It was through them that I met their relation Cardinal Raul Silva.

I could not have written this book without the contributions of the following interviewees: Dr Patricio Guijón, Dr Miguel Lawner, Ambassador Osvaldo Puccio and Professor Armando Uribe. Their reflections of their experiences during the coup and afterwards proved invaluable. In addition the diplomat and author Esteban Tomic and former MIR activist Adriana Borquez, also provided valuable information.

For students of Chile and the 1973 coup there are a variety of sources, which I found useful in writing this novel and I list some of them here. Unfortunately several are available only in Spanish. For those that are available in both Spanish and English, I have used the latter's title.

BIBLIOGRAPHY

Andy Beckett - *Pinochet In Piccadilly*. Faber 2002.
Sergio Bitar - *Isla 10*. Pehuén 1987.
Sheila Cassidy - *Audacity To Believe*. Harper Collins 1980.
Carmen Castillo - *Un Día De Octubre En Santiago*. LOM Ediciones 1999.
Marc Cooper - *Pinochet And Me*. Verso Books 2000.
David Cordingly - *Cochrane The Dauntless: The Life And Adventures Of Admiral Thomas Cochrane 1775-1860*. Bloomsbury 2008.
John Dinges and Saul Landau - *Assassination On Embassy Row*. Pantheon Books 1980.
Edgardo Enríquez - *Testimonio De Un Destierro*. Mosquito 1992.
Oscar Guardiola-Rivera - *Story Of A Death Foretold*. Bloomsbury 2013.
Ignacio González Camus - *El Día En Que Murió Allende*. Santiago 1988, Editorial Catalonia 2013.
Alistair Horne - *Small Earthquake In Chile*. Penguin 1990 edition.
Joan Jara - *Victor, An Unfinished Song*. Bloomsbury 1983, reprinted 1990.
Carlos Jorquera - *El Chiche Allende*. Ediciones BAT 1990.
Orlando Letelier - *Testimonio y Vinculación*. Siglo Xxi De España Editores, SA 1995.
Gabriel García Márquez - *Clandestine In Chile*. NYRB Classics, reprint 2010.
Pablo Neruda - *Memoirs*. Souvenir Press Ltd 2004.
Osvaldo Puccio - *Un Cuarto Siglo Con Allende*. Editorial Emision 1985.

Oscar Soto - *El Ultimo Día De Salvador Allende.* Aguilar 1999.

Patricia Verdugo - *Chile, Pinochet And The Caravan Of Death.* Lynne Rienner Publishers Inc 2001.

Justin Kerr- Smiley was born in 1965 and brought up in Scotland. He was educated at Ampleforth and Newcastle University. Awarded a BBC bursary for post-graduate studies in journalism, he worked as a radio reporter in Sydney and London. He then spent 15 years with Associated Press Television News and reported from Northern Ireland, the Balkans and South America. His first novel *Under The Sun* is published by Arcadia. In 2011 he received a travel scholarship from the Society of Authors in order to research *Goodbye To The President*.

Printed in Great Britain
by Amazon.co.uk, Ltd.,
Marston Gate.